Where The Rivers Flow

PATRICK MCWHORTER

Where the Rivers Flow
Cover design by Patrick McWhorter. Author photo on cover by Elliot McWhorter

Published by

6148 Jones Road, Flowery Branch, GA 30542

ISBN-13: 978-0-9827486-6-4

Printed in the United States of America

2016 - First Edition

PROLOGUE

"To the place where the rivers flow, there they flow again."

Ecclesiastes 1:7 (World English Bible)

1933

Sudden rain created a startling clatter on the metal roof of the tiny, haphazard shed attached to the backside of Potter Riley's barn. Under the light of an oil lantern hanging from a bent nail in the rafters, four men sat around a rough-hewn table, each gripping a tight fan of playing cards. In silent concern for the rain, three of the men – two in their fifties, grim, and one in his twenties, sneering – lifted their dull eyes briefly to the ceiling before resettling their stares at the fourth man, Bondurant Woods, called Bonder. In the middle of the table, piled around a half empty bottle of whiskey, like firewood around a doomed saint, lay sixty-one dollars in crumpled bills. It was up to Bonder to throw down seven dollars or five cards.

The stub of a cigarette hung from his lower lip and smoke drifted over the cards he studied too long. The empty glass before him was the reason for taking his time; he was not comprehending the cards. They looked good. But how many had he drawn? How many had the others drawn? His awareness had fled with most of his money.

"Play or fold," said one of the older men, his voice a dog's growl.

Bonder squinted at the cards and then at the few bills on

his side of the table. Ten or twelve dollars maybe. Not enough to buy groceries for more than a couple of weeks, so why worry about it? Nevertheless, Charlotte's voice warned his mind, "Don't you take the baby's food money and go gambling again!" He shook the sound away. Enough money sat in the middle to buy plenty of groceries, maybe even pay down on an acre or two of land. All he had to do was lay the money down.

He fumbled for seven dollars and pushed the bills to the middle.

"Let's see 'em," he said.

The two older men lay their cards out. Three fives for one, pair of queens for the other.

The sneering young fellow, son of the barn owner, grinned at the paltry showing and laid down. "Ha," he said at Bonder. "Three tens. Let's see yours."

Bonder frowned at the young man's cards. Three tens. He looked at his own again: kings. Weren't there three of them? Yes, a third responded to his shifting them. He smiled and spread his cards on the table.

"Kings," he said and reached for the pile of bills and the bottle, which they had already agreed would go to the winner of this hand.

The young man's mouth dropped. He stared at the kings a moment before looking angrily at Bonder and slamming his hand on the table.

"You're drunk!"

Bonder looked up with a flinch. The two older men cut their eyes at each other. One of them cautioned, "Flynn!" The boy had played poker with them when Potter was home, when Potter sat in, and Potter never let him drink. However, Potter was not home tonight.

The young man did not acknowledge his elder, but glared at Bonder's lidded eyes. "You're drunk," he said again and leaned toward him.

Bonder hesitated a moment as though considering the charge. "Yeah," he said. He cupped his hands around the money and pulled it with the bottle toward himself.

Flynn Riley stood quickly. He grabbed the bottle and thrust it to his mouth. He turned it up and drank as the others watched.

"Flynn," the older man said louder. Still the young man paid no attention. He lowered the bottle and set it on his side of the table, his mouth playing at a dare. Suddenly he laughed, spraying a mouthful of whiskey over Bonder and the table. With an arc of his hand he swept the cards off the table as Bonder reeled backward.

"You didn't have but two kings, you drunk!"

The older man on the right stood and moved toward the door of the shed. The rain was a roar on the roof now. The other man eased out of his chair and joined the first, looking back cautiously.

Bonder stood and frowned, whiskey running down his face, dripping from his jaw. He looked for the cards on the wet table. When he saw nothing he leaned to the side and saw them scattered on the dirt floor.

"No. Three kings!" he said, pointing at the floor with a wavering arm and looking at the others for confirmation.

Flynn reached for the money, grabbed a handful and began stuffing bills into his jeans pockets. "You're blind drunk! Can't even see what you played!" The two older men hurried out the door into the storm.

Bonder watched Flynn, his eyes growing large with realization at what the man was doing. He snatched up what money was left before it all disappeared. As the young man stuffed a few remaining bills into his shirt pocket, Bonder lunged at Flynn, knocking the lantern into a wild orbit that threatened to send it off the nail. His hand shot to Flynn's pocket and ripped it as he took hold of the wad inside it.

Flynn reacted by knocking Bonder's hand away. Bills fluttered before their faces. Bonder's fist caught Flynn solidly on the mouth and sent him backward into an old Poplar limb used for roof support. The support snapped and Flynn fell backward to the dirt. He no sooner hit the ground with a thud than a broken joist, part of the shed's roof, dropped onto his chest. Flynn exhaled, loud, as the air was forced out of him, his extremities rising reflexively and dropping flat.

Bonder stepped closer and leaned under the fallen roof section. A hanging sheet of tin wavered to the right of Flynn's head, channeling a stream of water to the ground. Rain poured through the opening in the shed's roof, spattering onto Flynn's motionless face. A narrow length of rough timber extended from the roof to a depression in the young man's midsection. Blood seeped into the depression around the timber.

Dazed, Bonder pushed at the joists of the low roof. Flynn's torso moved slightly with the timber, but the roof section was too heavy to dislodge.

"Hey!" he shouted as he turned to push open the door. He searched the blackness a moment before he caught sight of shapes under a nearby tree, flashing with light reflected from the swinging lantern. "Hey! The boy's hurt. Help me get this off him!"

The shapes hurried toward him and the faces of the men came into view. They followed him inside and leaned, dripping, underneath the sagging roof.

"Oh, man!"

"He's dead."

"Help me get this..." Bonder put his shoulder to the timber and strained.

"He's dead all right," the other man said.

"Push here," Bonder motioned toward the beam as he continued to shove, his feet slipping against the forming mud.

"God help us when Potter gets back."

The door slammed shut behind the elders and Bonder was alone. He turned and called after the men. "Come back!"

"I'm gettin' the law, Woods."

Bonder opened the shed door to call after the men but the dark had them already. Their footfalls were barely audible over the drum of the downpour.

The law. That meant certain jail time. He had done a year before, for public drunkenness and resisting arrest, and it was hell. He looked back at Flynn. The blood had stopped and rain pooled in the boy's eye sockets and open mouth. He looked like a sleeping kid. Bonder's mind went to his own son, and imagined him sleeping.

Flynn was dead, for sure. And this was the end of life for Bonder, too. If the law didn't kill him, prison or Potter Riley would. Something had to be salvaged.

Bonder shoved through the door and ran headlong into the watery assault.

* * * * *

Less than an hour later, Bonder shivered beside his tiny field of dead corn stalks, his pathetic effort at repentance, as the preacher called what he needed. He had sincerely hoped he could turn over a new leaf, get his life cleaned up, give Charlotte and the boy a home and be a man they both could be proud of someday. He had plowed and he had planted. And to an extent, he had harvested. But the weeds had come, just like the alcohol craving in his soul had come to ruin everything. He had pulled the scraggly invaders, crawling on his knees, hoping against hope that he could get a good crop in, a turnaround crop that would prove his good intentions. But Charlotte had mocked his skimpy patch of corn that would feed them for a few weeks at best. Something inside him had let go of the fragile hold on tomorrow's hope. And now everything was gone, the corn and the glimmer of expectation.

His lungs heaved vapor, resisting a continued headlong run. Bending over, he grabbed the tops of his knees and steadied himself, sucking air, staring at the rippling puddle of mud hiding all but the tops of his brogans. He could feel the blood surging through his chest, beating at his temples, neck and legs. He had heard bloodhounds baying minutes before. They were onto his scent even in the rain. But he had to rest and catch his breath.

During his halting run from the shed he had had time to think as blood rushed through his system and diminished the effects of drink on his mind. Maybe he could make it to the old cabin by the river, hide out there until he could figure out what to do. It was clear there would be no return to mercy. The accident had been just that: an accident. But who would take his word? Charlotte would not stand by him, the Sheriff would not hear his explanation, and Potter Riley, that old bootlegger and reprobate, would kill him in a heartbeat. No, if he lived through this, it would be behind bars. So the only hope for a future was that of his son, Adam, who would not be able to understand anything of what Bonder wanted to say, not for years to come.

He lowered his head and broke into a sprint for home. His energy left him as he neared his property and he slowed to a heavy walk.

In the opening ahead was his house. A dim light in the front room told him Charlotte had left a lamp lit for him. She did love him, probably. He suddenly realized he had not shown her tenderness since he had got out of jail and become, in her words, a hardened and embittered, no-account drunk. Too late now, he thought.

The old Double-A Ford flatbed truck sat at the near edge of the yard. It was his only means of escape. But he couldn't leave without doing something for his son that might keep the boy from following his father's footsteps. He had tried to be a better man for little Adam, but anyone could see his efforts had been too little.

His own Daddy's words were coming to pass. "The water that goes down the river today," he said, "is just following the water that went down yesterday."

Bonder was winding up just like him. The fear of that happening to his boy drove desperation into his heart.

Bonder accepted that his own life was doomed to destruction, but cringed at the image in his mind of Adam running from the law. A thought came to him, an idea for salvaging something good for the boy. He had seen something like it somewhere - in the Bible, maybe - that might serve to let the boy know his father cared about him, wanted something better for him. Maybe it was too little, but something, nevertheless, the boy could have that might guide him, someday, away from his father's destiny. He forced himself erect and ran the last hundred yards.

Bonder hurried to the old truck and, climbing inside, felt for the ignition switch. He turned it on, quickly advanced the spark and switched the gas on. The truck would be noisy, but he had to be certain it was running and warmed before doing what he needed to do. Pressing the starter, he let the motor turn a couple of times before adjusting the choke. That had been the sequence he had learned was the secret to getting the old truck cranked in a hurry. Suddenly the engine came to life in a roar. Waking Charlotte could not be avoided.

Racing toward the house, he jumped onto the porch and glanced back to make sure the bloodhounds were not near. The door knob turned quietly under his palm and his first step put an instant puddle on Charlotte's varnished floor. She worked to keep a nice house, and for once he hated himself for degrading it. Nevertheless, he had something to do and there would be no time for apologies or repair.

Leaving a trail of water behind him, he disappeared into the bedroom and, a moment later, ran out to the sound of Charlotte's confused shouts. He bounded onto the porch again and out into the beating storm with his infant son blanketed in his arms. The baby awoke as the first cold drops hit the parts Bonder could not cover, and he gave a frightened wail.

Charlotte ran onto the porch with a handful of soggy bills and threw them aside. He had emptied his pockets of winnings in apology. "What are you doing!" she yelled as he raced into the downpour.

"No! Bonder!" she screamed. "Bring him back!"

Bonder opened the truck door and climbed in, slapped the door lock behind him and felt for the gear shift lever. He had not been driving the truck because it needed brake work, and he had drunk away all the money. He kissed Adam and placed him on the floor in his blanket, wondering if his son was awake enough to smell the liquor odor that filled the cab and that suddenly seemed awful and foreign to Bonder.

"It's all right, Adam," he shushed over Charlotte's screams. "Go back to sleep. Daddy's taking you for a ride." The boy's heavy eyes fluttered and he whimpered as they closed altogether. Bonder shoved the lever into first gear.

Charlotte jumped off the porch and now ran across the yard in her bare feet screaming something unheard over the rumble of the truck, her arms outstretched. Bonder locked the other door and let out the clutch enough to move the old flatbed. He was creeping forward with the headlights cutting tunnels through the rain when Charlotte reached the truck. Her hair clung to her oval face, her nightgown pasted to her slim form.

"Bonder!" her muffled voice demanded. "Where are you taking my baby?" Her hands pounded against the door as Bonder ignored her and turned the truck slowly away from the house, she running alongside the accelerating vehicle. The pounding stopped and her scream turned into a vanishing wail.

The last words he could make out over the engine noise were, "I hate you, Bonder. I hate you, I hate you. I hope you burn in hell!" Her voice echoed in his ears even after the sound drowned away.

He was not too drunk or hardened to cry for all he had done to bring her and himself to this. If he could take care of this one thing and make his way to the cabin by the river, maybe he could figure out what to do to turn it all around again.

Rain had slowed to a steady drizzle. Little Adam was sleeping when the truck squeaked to a stop outside a converted service station flanked on the left side by a mountain of used tires. Bonder killed the motor, unlocked the opposite door and jumped out in a run to the door of the building. The only light visible through the plate glass front window was from a wall clock. A metal sign underneath it advertised Bardahl Oil. The hands indicated 11:11.

Bonder banged on the door until a light spilled through a doorway to the left. He recalled the old man had turned the repair bay into dingy living quarters and studio. In moments a flashlight beam played through the doorway against the floor where it bounced and diminished in size until the direct beam sliced across the room and caught him in the face. Bonder shielded his eyes.

"What you want?" snapped the old man, his accent amplifying his irritation.

"Open up! Hurry!"

"I don't open up. Go away."

"I need a tattoo! Now!"

"Nobody needs tattoo! Go away!" The old man turned to leave.

"I'll pay double!" Bonder felt a few remaining bills in his pocket.

The retreating light stopped and the silhouette behind it wheeled.

"Double? No, three times!"

"Okay! Open up."

The lock clacked and the door swung open.

"Through here," said the old man.

Bonder ran back to the truck and lifted little Adam from the passenger-side floor. He cradled him against his wet shirt and ran into the station. The old man looked up from his work bench, his fat face dramatized in the light of the gooseneck lamp.

"*Vas ist los*?" he frowned at Bonder standing in the doorway with the bundle in his arms.

"My boy." He let the blanket drop from the boy's head.

"A *bebe*? I don't tattoo *kinder*!"

Bonder fixed his wet, angry eyes on the man. "That's not what I hear." He stepped into the room and stood in front of the tattooist.

"I hear you did anything for money before winding up in prison," Bonder added.

The old man grimaced. His upper lip curled and his brow lowered in the middle.

Bonder took wet bills from his pocket and tossed them into a lump on the small table beside several small jars and an open cigar box littered with stained needles.

The old man eyed the bills as if he could count them, then looked back at Bonder with disgust. He took the money and nodded to a stool beside the table.

"Where?"

Bonder uncovered the sleeping boy's right hand and held it palm up.

"There." He grabbed a pencil and wrote on an envelope that lay on the table. "Do that!" he commanded.

Moments later, the baby's scream filled the room and cut through the hiss of rain outside the window and merged with a distant siren.

"Hurry," Bonder urged.

* * * * *

Loretta Slaughter, cleaning up the kitchen after a late night at church and an even later supper, called out to her husband in the living room. Henry completely missed whatever she said. He heard only the low roll of thunder and his toddler daughter's soft happy sounds, so focused was he on the moment. Loretta repeated.

"We need to get her in bed, Henry. It's late and coming a storm."

"She's gonna walk, Loretta!" Henry called. "Come here, quick!" His voice was lost under a sudden harsh pelting of rain on the roof.

He held Maisie's tiny hands and stepped backwards slowly to assist her first tentative step. His wide, expectant eyes fixed on her right foot as the heel lifted and the toes of her bare foot played with the temptation to let go of the firmament of the living room floor. He had moved no more than four inches away and allowed little Maisie to lean toward him with her tight grip on his outstretched index fingers.

"Let's get her to bed before we wake up Bosco," said Loretta wiping her hands on a towel. Nine year-old Bascomb Slaughter had fallen asleep in the car, and Henry had carried him to bed.

Suddenly, before Maisie's foot moved from its spot, she halted. Her head swung in an arc to the side as though she had heard something. Her poised body swayed as she fought to maintain balance. The transformation of Maisie's facial expression was instant and startling to Henry. She almost seemed to have been alerted to something he could not sense. Her sudden shift in attention caused him to follow her gaze, but he saw nothing in the dark window that might have scared her. Nevertheless, when her attention returned to him, her eyes were red and glistening with tears. Her lip quivered and she whimpered.

"Do you hear that, Henry?" Loretta called, moving to the doorway.

Henry bent to his daughter and pulled her to himself, lifting her in his arms.

"Oh, Honey, what's the matter?" He kissed his daughter's

cheek.

"Henry?" Loretta's voice came again, louder.

"What, Loretta? Maisie was just about to take her first step, but she started crying." He rocked the baby gently against his chest and nuzzled her with his cheek as she heaved with nearly silent sobs. "It's okay, Maisie. Don't cry."

"A siren. I think I hear a police car or ambulance!"

"A siren? I don't hear anything. Say, Maisie is just crying her eyes out, Loretta. Come see if you can calm her down. I don't know what upset her."

Loretta stood in the doorway. "You don't hear that?" she asked, her brows furrowed in concern as she stared at the window beyond Henry.

Henry cocked his head a bit. "No, I don't hear a siren. Just the rainstorm."

"Henry, are you serious? It's getting louder. It almost sounds like a baby screaming." She took a step closer to him.

Henry stopped rocking Maisie and watched his wife. "Loretta, I don't hear anything. Are you hearing in the Spirit?"

"Why, maybe I am. But it sounds so clear." She moved closer and placed her hand against her daughter's forehead. The child was genuinely disturbed at something. "I think she hears it, too, Henry."

"You think so?" He handed Maisie to Loretta and the girl instantly began sobbing loudly, her little shoulders shaking and her hands reaching for her mother's hair. Maisie always seemed to be comforted by taking tufts of her mother's hair in her hands and rubbing her face against the soft brown strands.

After nearly thirty minutes of walking and singing to Maisie, Loretta got her to stop crying. In the oak rocker beside the fireplace, Loretta rocked slowly with Maisie against her bosom. The child lay spent, her cheek against her mother's shoulder. She sighed with deep shudders, her sad eyes staring into the distance. Henry tiptoed into the room and stood looking at Loretta. He questioned her with his eyes. She shook her head slightly.

"She knows something," whispered Loretta. "Deep down. The Holy Spirit is speaking to her spirit."

"Deep calling unto deep," said Henry, kneeling to place a hand on his daughter's back. "God's given us a special child, Loretta."

Loretta nodded.

"A very special girl."

* * * * *

The burning barn would have generated alarm from as far as two miles across the flat farm country, except for the fact that the neighbors all knew why it burned. Potter Riley set it afire.

The old man sat in a chair – not the rocking chair he once favored on the three-sided porch of his house, but a hard, upright oak chair – in the yard just outside the range of singeing heat, and watched rats run for their lives. A double-barrel shotgun stood at attention on his thigh, and half a dozen spent shotgun shells lay on the ground beside his chair. The blazing structure loomed like a black skeleton shuddering against the flames of hell, and every escaping silhouette darting in fear for its life gave him a titillating foretaste of the revenge he would exact against his son's killer.

When the legs of his overalls began to steam, Riley moved his chair back a few feet. When a panicked rodent made the mistake of veering into the space before the stern, black figure in the yard, a shotgun blast obliterated it along with two inches of hard soil immediately beneath its feet. When the flames threatened to weaken, he went to the porch and dragged his best two rockers to the fire and hurled them into the inferno. Later, the shutters on his house, the screen door he ripped from its hinges and the roof over the well pulley fell victim to his rage, as his grieving wife wept and shook her head in the upstairs window.

By morning, a case of shotgun shells littered the ground around the straight-back chair. A shattered demijohn lay between there and the smoking ruins of the barn and shed. And a fire that burned out just before dawn had leapt into the heart of its host.

CHAPTER ONE

1951

Adam Woods glared at the black glove he pulled onto his right hand, the hand that had made him a freak in his own mind. He could no longer look at his hand and innocently wonder what the writing meant, the way he had so many times as a child. When he looked at his hand now, it was with hatred and bitterness. His father had done that to him, had bound him to misery and mockery, most likely to ensure that his seed would suffer lifelong bondage of the kind Bondurant Woods, himself, faced, even as a murderer.

Yes, he thought: his father, the murderer. The slight fact his mother forgot to mention to him over the years, and more, that his father had died in prison instead of in a wreck! A fact known to everyone in middle Georgia but himself, apparently! That fact, and now, its delayed revelation, contributed no small burden to his life of exile from peers. Who, after all, wanted to be pals with the son of a killer?

"How long do you plan to wear those gloves?" His mother stood in the doorway of his bedroom, showing no trace of the remorse he would have expected after the way she broke the news to him about his father.

"That glove," he corrected without looking up.

"That glove? You mean you're just going to wear one?"

He looked at her as though flabbergasted that she really needed to ask the question. He nodded.

"That'll look great! That and that fancy shirt. If you think you've had trouble before, wait till the rednecks where you've been hanging out see you."

"How would you know what trouble I've had before now?"

"I'm your Mama, Adam. You need to talk more

respectfully."

He looked at her and adjusted the tone of his voice. "All right, I'm sorry. But exactly how would you know? You and Mister Ray Lee Colbert are so preoccupied with square dancing every weekend and, glued to the radio every other night, I'm surprised you remember I have a life here."

"Stop it, Adam. He's your step-father and you need to respect him, too."

"I forgot." He stood and held his gloved hand before the mirror on the closet door, making a fist. He had not liked Ray Lee from the very first sight of him. The man had not been with his mother when Adam first laid eyes on him, but with a known bootlegger, Potter Riley, whose son, Adam had recently learned, was the victim of Bonder Woods' drunken brawling. Colbert had worn a sneer on his face that seemed to invite someone to knock it off.

"Respect is hard to come by," said Adam. "I intend to earn it. Maybe Ray Lee ought to consider the same approach."

Charlotte Woods Colbert swung away from the doorway and tramped noisily down the hall to the living room. She would have the radio on in seconds, Adam knew. It was her refuge from every storm and her soul's dry cleaner, much like the liquor bottles she had always said was the hiding place for his father, Bondurant. And likewise, nothing ever got any more resolved in her life than in the life of the deceased husband she still hated. Her punishment for marrying a drunk and murderer, Adam figured, was a life sentence with a no-good, two-timing hypocrite, and that was being kind to Ray Lee Colbert, in Adam's mind.

His mother and Ray Lee both went to church and pretended to be Christians, but displayed none of the pretense beyond the sanctuary doors. For that reason, Adam had refused all Charlotte's entreaties to join them at church; he would rather live like hell without being a hypocrite.

He had a better way to camouflage his dissatisfaction with life. It was called bar-hopping by the so-called rednecks his mother looked down on. He just went to different clubs than the hypocrites frequented. At least, he would tonight. After all, it was Saturday and it would not be pleasant to run into Ray

Lee and one of his local skanks socializing, when the man told Charlotte he was working.

* * * * *

Adam drove his rebuilt '36 Chevy through the low-water town of Odino, slowly, to avoid the well known speed traps the Ocmulgee County Sheriff used to supplement his salary. Having bought the car with money Adam earned by painting houses and doing light construction, he had rebuilt the motor and had begun restoring the interior, beat a couple of dents out of the front fenders and put a radio in it. He could not afford the customizations some people were doing with old cars, at least, not yet. For now, it was enough that the motor was strong.

At this time of day – closing time for most retail establishments – interior lights were blinking out and clerks were bringing racks of hardware and decorative florals inside from the sidewalks for the night. Downtown Odino's two restaurants, on opposite sides of the narrow main street, opened their doors to allow the aromas of fried catfish and barbecue to fight for the attention of potential patrons. His destination was neither, but a hole-in-the-wall beer joint two miles out on a county road. It relied on the patronage of sunburned fishermen, self-styled billiard sharks, a smattering of airmen from a nearby air base, migrant field workers, and back-door sales to underage clientele from every high school within thirty miles. He wasn't in high school, not since he dropped out at 16, but still, he had six months left before turning legal. Besides, he looked older than 21. And the diversity in the joint's clientele was just varied enough in appearance to afford anonymity to an unemployed high-school dropout wearing a glove on his right hand.

Adam was driving past the brick one-story post office building when he saw a tall young woman come out the front double doors of the farm supply store a hundred yards away. A bundle in her arms shielded part of her, but she looked exactly like Maisie Slaughter. Sure enough, her old red Ford pickup was at the curb. His adrenaline level jumped and he eased closer to the speed limit to get to her before she had time to get inside the truck. He could use a new lure from the fishing tackle counter; that would explain his stopping by if the question arose. He pulled behind the truck and killed the motor before she reached the door. He got out just as she was placing a large bag in the truck's bed. He had to be casual, so he let the door close by its own weight as he sauntered her way.

When she glanced up, Adam spoke. "Hey! How are you?" He smiled and halted a few feet from the truck's back bumper. "It's Maisie, right?" Of course, he knew very well what her name was. He slipped off the glove as casually as he could and stuffed it into his back pocket, without realizing why.

Her clear gray eyes and uncomplicated demeanor studied his face a moment before registering recognition and a friendly smile. "Oh, hi. Um, is it – ?" she hesitated.

"Adam," he supplied. "Adam Woods."

"Yes, how have you been, Adam?" She released the bag and dusted her hand against her jeans, then reached out to shake his hand.

He took it quickly to avoid exposing the palm, at the same time allowing his smile to be as genuine and frank as hers. She was undoubtedly the most beautiful girl he had ever seen, and that included the ones who had won beauty contests and gone off to popularity at the best colleges. Her hair was pulled back in a pony tail, which made her even more beautiful than he had remembered.

"I'm doing fine, I guess. It sure is good to see you, Maisie."

Immediately he wondered if he was coming on too strong for this quiet unassuming girl. After all, he had barely spoken to her in years past, when he had been too headstrong to admit the need for friends. Things changed when he separated himself from the pain of being among those who lived for popularity. He was truly alone after dropping out of school, and longed for a kind and friendly face in the intervening years, if not a face showing interest in him.

Maisie had been something of an anomaly during his high

school days, and, like him, she was the butt of unfair comments and condescending looks. But something about her had always seemed way different than everybody else: serious, even older than her years. But her beauty was not lost on anyone. Other girls shunned her out of apparent jealousy, and guys treated her with uncommon respect, giving her smiles that, to him, said they knew she was unimpressed by the routine familiarity they used with other girls. As for Adam, he had always admired the way she handled comments and snubs, though the outrageous things he heard about her – that she was strange, that she talked to God and could heal sick people – made her so mysterious that he had never really talked with her. Yet, to him, she was the most beautiful creature alive.

Her eyes narrowed to a keen focus on him, though her smile did not disappear.

"You know, Adam, God has spoken to me about you, as a matter of fact."

Her words stunned him, catching him off guard. He lost his smile for a split second and his eyes became questioning. Quickly, he made the decision to smile in return. He could not miss the opportunity to spend a few more moments in her presence, even in the face of her unpredictability. Was she serious or joking? He could not guess. If he heard correctly, no one had ever said anything like that to him, so he could do nothing but try to give an unsurprised reply.

"I guess you're not kidding, huh? What did He say?" He knew he sounded like a jerk, but that was the best response he could come up with. He prepared himself for anything. Besides, whatever she might say was okay if it afforded him a little more time with her.

"No, I don't kid about what God tells me." Her eyes betrayed no offense, he was relieved to see. "He said that you need a friend, and He wants to *be* that for you." Her gray eyes were electric, sparkling, but without a hint of the mystery he had accorded to her. They seemed to confirm she was being honest and sincere.

"Wow. I, uh, never thought of having God as a friend." He shifted his stance, looked briefly at his feet and rebounded with interest. "How would anybody go about doing that?"

"Start by talking to Him. Most act as though He's dead. But He's more real than anybody I know."

Adam nodded. He had no quick response, so he waited for her to fill the void.

"Hey, would you like to help me plant vegetables?"

"Vegetables?" He had heard her clearly, but once again, he was taken by surprise and could think of nothing except to echo her last word.

"Yeah," she grinned. "I'm a little late getting started, but I should still have time to get a decent crop this summer."

"Yeah, sure. When?"

"You doing anything right now?"

He quickly weighed this surprising option against hanging out at a beer joint. "Nothing that sounds half as good as that," he answered with a blush he could in no way suppress.

"Great, follow me." She turned and got into her truck and, in seconds, she had made a u-turn and was headed back through town.

Adam made a quick search for patrol cars, and followed her lead.

Wow! He thought as he shifted through the gears. Maisie Slaughter! God, I'd say that was a friendly thing to do. Wow!

Adrenaline raced. He could not believe the good fortune of just running into her, and then, to actually be going to her farm to help her garden! If he could have her as a – well, a friend – he would never go to another beer joint again.

The most beautiful girl in middle Georgia, he thought; heck, probably in the whole world! What if she likes me, say, has for a long time! Wouldn't that be something! But don't get your hopes up, Junior. They say she's not interested in dating and things like that. So who cares! Hanging out with her would be great.

A few miles north of town, Maisie turned off the highway onto a gravel road. Dust boiled from underneath her truck and engulfed his car. That meant a trip to the car wash, but that did not matter at all to Adam. A quarter mile later, she turned right onto a narrow drive that descended through a tunnel of trees and opened onto a sunny patch of grass. In the middle of the sunny opening sat a small unpainted farmhouse with a covered well to the right of the low front porch and a pasture and barn to the left.

"Have a seat on the porch," she called as Adam got out. She bounded onto the porch and let the screen door bang shut behind her as she vanished inside.

She's excited, he thought. Maybe she's happy at my being here. Not so fast, he corrected himself. She's an unusual person, that's all.

He had barely got seated in one of the two faded metal chairs when she came out again wearing a broad-brimmed straw hat and carrying a watering can. The hat had a bright yellow scarf tied around the base of the crown and trailing away behind her. Adam thought he had never seen anyone so full of life and so blasted pretty.

"You grab the seeds out of the truck bed and I'll get a hoe from the shed," she said in passing. Adam obeyed.

Maisie attacked the small plot of ground with glee, instructing Adam to dig out rocks and weeds from the long-unturned soil. They pulled straight furrows with the hoe and she posted seed envelopes at the end of each row to identify what was being planted. They drove stakes for tomatoes and strung poles for beans. Around the perimeter, Maisie planted marigolds to help keep rabbits out.

Adam let his hands get dirty enough to make wearing a glove unnecessary. He sweated through his fancy shirt. His low-ankled shoes attracted small clods of dirt that tumbled over the sides and crunched under his sock feet. But Adam grinned. Just being around this girl made him happier than he had been in months, maybe years. He could even imagine himself being a farmer, something he had never before associated with himself.

And Maisie worked happily, humming a tune that sounded vaguely familiar to him. When she looked up to smile at him, he felt stunned. He was actually here with Maisie Slaughter!

When she went inside, Adam flopped onto his back in the softened, warm dirt and sighed. His hands and back felt the tight ache of labor, but the spring sun on his face and a light breeze cooling the perspiration on his brow felt like something from another world. He might as well be in heaven.

Maisie returned with two glasses of iced tea and plopped down opposite him. He sat up and took the glass dripping with condensation.

"How do you feel, Adam?" she asked. "Is gardening better than what you were headed to do?"

He let himself take in her face as he pretended to think about the answer. She had grey eyes, auburn hair and the kind of beauty that makeup would only hide. He felt dizzy just looking at her. Finally, he had to speak. "By a long mile!" he said. "Not even close!"

"I thought so," she said lifting the glass to her lips. "I never thought it would be fun at all to sit around some juke joint drinking alcohol and watching people slowly overthrow their good judgment."

He swallowed and studied her seriously. "How did you know what I was going to do?"

"A dove told me," she smiled. "He said that you needed to make a u-turn."

"No, really! How could you know that?" He was intrigued, but somehow not surprised that she would know.

"He told me the moment you said you were doing fine, *you guessed*."

"Did the dove tell you anything else?"

"Sure."

"What was it?"

She smiled and looked down. "Maybe He'll let me tell you later."

"Tell me this, then. Why do you live out here alone?"

"My mom and dad died in an accident two years ago, and my older brother, Bosco, offered to apply for a hardship discharge from the Army to come and help me with the farm. But I told him God and I could take very good care of the place. He's a chaplain stationed in Germany. He worried in the beginning, but now he sees I'm handling things pretty well."

Adam took a deep breath before speaking again. He felt the awkwardness of what he was thinking but charged ahead. He was kicking down a carefully built barrier, he knew, but he could not resist the safety he felt with her.

22

"Have you ever thought about marriage?" Then, as though he surprised himself at actually asking the question, he quickly added, "I mean, wouldn't it be better out here with a husband?"

"I am married, in a way."

Adam blinked. His mouth opened but no sound came forth.

Maisie looked past him, her head raised and her eyes focused far away. A puff of wind played with her hair, feathering it at her temples. "I think of God as my Husband. I can't imagine loving anyone more. He is so loving, faithful, kind and gentle. And who could be a better Provider?"

Something in his heart sank. But just as suddenly, he realized he was envious of God, and rejected the feeling as crazy. His amazement at her uniqueness far overshadowed any urge to draw back at her unavailability. "I never knew anyone had those kinds of thoughts."

"I didn't always feel that way. For as long as I remember I believed in Jesus, but there came a time when I got to know Him. It was when I was down and hurting with no one to turn to for comfort. He was there for me."

"So you know Him? Like talking to Him and hearing Him?"

She nodded. "Of course. Why not?"

"I just didn't know it was really possible, that's all."

"It's not only possible; it's necessary."

Adam picked up a clod and rolled it around in the palm of his left hand as he leaned on his right.

"Maisie, I – " he hesitated, as though deciding whether to go on. "I don't think it's really me that wants to do crazy things, like drinking. I think somewhere inside I really want to have something to live for, like a compass that says where to go and what to do, and even how to do it. I don't much like the way I am when I have a few beers." He flushed again, surprised again at what he was willing to say.

"Keep talking, Adam." Maisie seemed to be trying not to smile.

He ran his hand through his hair and furrowed his brow in thought. "It's like this, Maisie. You're such a good person, I would never have thought somebody like you could be a friend to somebody like me. But when you invited me to work in the garden with you, I kinda thought – Wow! Maybe you could be my friend. And today, being here with you seems like being in another world entirely, one where I would think it's crazy to go out and get drunk. But before I saw you today, I would've laughed if somebody said I might enjoy getting dirty planting vegetables. Do you understand what I'm saying?"

She nodded. "Do you know what the difference is?"

"Yeah, you!" he grinned.

She laughed. "No, stop flirting. It's not me at all. It's the One who lives in me. He makes all things different. A moment with Him and the world is turned upside down."

Adam looked down and nodded. But he thought she was wrong. Not about the flirting. He was sure it was Maisie that made his world feel new and different.

"All I'm trying to say, I guess, is that I've never really had a friend. I just don't make friends easily. I've convinced myself over the years that I don't need anybody, but spending this time with you makes me know I'm fooling myself." He wanted to ask if she would be his friend, but stopped for two reasons: he could not ask it without sounding like a goof ball, and, he felt his throat choking up with long held emotion over his confession.

Maisie held out her hand to him. "Adam, I think you'd be a great friend to have," she said.

He sat up and took her hand. When he did, a mild jolt of something like electricity passed through his arm and something in his ears fluttered. He wanted to say something, but somehow could not. Just touching her hand was amazing. He was overwhelmed by her, he knew. His emotions wanted to break forth like a pony set to pasture. But he had to stuff the feeling rather than risk ruining the moment. He thought of saying he thought she, too, would make a good friend, but still he could not speak. So he simply nodded his head.

She nodded with him.

For once in his life, Adam Woods had a friend. And more, he felt he could possibly begin to live.

CHAPTER TWO

Potter Riley had aged tremendously in the years since Flynn's death. He had been forty-eight then. But to the mirror across the room from him, forty-eight and eighteen equaled something like ninety. His hair was gone except for a few white strands on top of his head, his face had grown jowls that sagged, his skin looked like it had been molded from dirty wax, and his eyes, nearly always bloodshot now, had shrunk to the size of double-ought buckshot and receded into the puffy folds that once were eyelids.

He cursed the image mocking him from across the dim room. All the hatred and will power and money he had invested in killing the man who killed his son had not been able to accomplish so simple a task. The only redeeming fact remaining was that he still had more money after all he had invested. And he would spend it all on whatever it took to see Bonder Woods dead.

The first attempt on Woods' life, years ago, took only days to arrange, but because the killing was to occur between the jail and the courthouse, where Bonder's trial was to take place, Potter had had to wait more than six months for the opportunity. In the end, the bungling new Sheriff, Ott Mobley, who had replaced longtime Sheriff Lucius Fanning, stepped in the way and almost got himself shot. The shooter was spotted and caught with his rifle, but lied his way out of an attempted murder charge, with the help of the Sheriff. The man claimed to be returning from a hog hunt on posted land and was playing around when he aimed the rifle at Woods from across the road. Mobley said the man was a known poacher and didn't have sense enough to hatch a plan to murder a prisoner in county custody. Charges were dropped due to lack of evidence and provable motive. Riley had the man beaten severely and dared him to show his face in the area again.

A year later, when Woods was serving a life sentence in prison, the convict who agreed to the job was, himself, killed before it could be done. To Riley, it seemed impossible that a killer could lead such a charmed life. But two attempts had failed flat. After that, Riley had what doctors called a nervous breakdown. He spent months in alcohol rehab and when he returned to Odino, his farm was run down and his bootlegging operation in shambles. He could not rub two nickels together and got no respect from his former cohorts. Sheriff Mobley had even become antagonistic to him. Without money, Riley was nobody.

The climb back to power was slow and arduous. Riley had to get a job and embezzle enough money to get started again. When the bootlegging operation resumed, so did Riley's drinking. And with the alcohol came more demons than he had ever accommodated before. The growing rage inside the man made him twice the terror he had been. While evading the state and federal lawmen was as great an obstacle as before, the greatest danger facing anyone working for him was from Riley himself. He had become so intense and impatient, few could stand to remain with him. And with the fall from his former glory had also come a dramatic plunge in his health and mental stability.

Potter Riley picked up the phone and dialed the number of the only man he could lean on for dirty work. The man had shown himself gutsy in running liquor, and thorough in convincing people who needed convincing, but for something as risky as murder, Riley needed more leverage against him as well as confidence that the man would not cave. Riley had decided to test him with a little project. He had approached Ray Lee Colbert with the idea of courting Bonder Woods' ex-wife and convincing her to marry him, as an opportunity to ruin her financially. To Riley that would be only partial payback against her husband. Little more than a month later, Colbert had married her and settled in quietly. The next part of the test was to bleed her finances so she could not make payments on the property. She would not know that Riley would hold the mortgage. Eventually, Ray Lee would lead her into alcohol and dope, drain any savings she might have –

which Riley said he could keep for himself – and divorce her as Riley called the loan. That was the plan. She and Woods' boy would be out on the street and Colbert would have enough inside information on Bonder Woods to arrange a successful hit on him.

Ray Lee's phone rang for the fifth time before he picked up. Riley spoke immediately.

"What are you doing, Colbert?"

"Well, hello, Mister Smith."

"Is the woman with you?"

"Yes sir, Mister Smith, I put that oil pump on your tractor."

"Get over here," said Riley.

"Yes sir, I was just having an early supper at home with my lovely wife, but I'll be glad to come take a look at it."

"Don't overdo it, you fool."

"No sir, she doesn't mind. I'll be right over. Good-bye."

Riley shook his head and slammed the receiver down. Colbert was annoyingly smarmy, like a metal pan sliding across pavement. But the man would have to do; no one else was as willing and available as he was. Riley picked a glass from the telephone table and turned it up. Hundred-proof liquor went down as easy as ice water these days. He had begun an early supper of sorts himself. He went to the kitchen counter and poured the glass full again. It was time to see how confident in crime Colbert had gotten with this new venture.

* * * * *

"I have everything under control," insisted Colbert twenty minutes later as he stared at Potter Riley's red, scowling face. "She's about ready to turn the house over to me, so why shouldn't she trust me with managing the money?"

"Forget the house," snarled Riley. "Spend her money however you want, but I take the house."

Colbert's face reddened, and he blurted, "What? Why?" He did not remember that being part of the deal. Riley had said he could have whatever he could get out of the deal.

"I'm paying you for this job, that's why. I own enough shares in the bank I can take over her mortgage as soon as she's in arrears on the payments. If I can't kill Woods yet, I want him to suffer, knowing his wife and kid will be out on the street. And I'll make sure he knows I'm the new owner."

Colbert settled a bit. Riley had told him to bleed the woman dry, but he should have suspected the old man wanted the house and land out of it.

"All right, all right! No big deal. Take the house," Colbert said.

"I've got something else I want you to do," said Riley.

"What?"

"Kill the boy."

Colbert's mouth dropped. "Kill him? Why?"

"Woods killed my boy. An eye for an eye."

Colbert squirmed and picked his glass up. "I didn't sign on to do no murder, Mister Riley." He took a small sip to maintain an appearance of calm resolve.

"I pay you, Colbert. You know you could go to prison right now, if I told the right people what you've already done?"

Colbert laughed nervously. "Well, you'd go to prison right along with me."

Riley's eyes gleamed maliciously as he shook his head. "Won't happen. I've got the Sheriff in my pocket, and half a dozen character witnesses who will say whatever I pay them to say in court." Riley leaned back in his chair, satisfied he had the man over a barrel.

Colbert thought for a moment. Probably, the old man was bluffing. "No. I won't kill the kid. Do what you aim to, Riley. I ain't going to sit in the electric chair for you nor anybody else." Colbert slammed his glass onto the table, splashing clear liquid onto the surface. He stood and made as though to leave, pulling at his pants waist. "No sir. I won't kill for you."

"So be it!" said Riley, setting his glass down. "Don't bother with the rest of the deal. The Sheriff will be out to see you tomorrow morning, Colbert." Riley stood up and smiled confidently. "You're not the only one I can hire to do my bidding."

"Now, just hold on, hold on." Colbert blustered. "Just what do you think you've got on me?"

"Remember Tolleson?"

"That was a fair fight, Riley. And Tolleson ain't dead."

"Tolleson's as good as dead; he can't even put a whole sentence together." Here a wicked smile crept across Riley's face. "I had you followed, Colbert. My man brought me the tire iron. It's got your prints and his blood."

Colbert wilted. He stepped forward and grabbed hold of the chair. "You..." He bit off what he wanted to say. His eye-lock with Riley faltered when the man shrugged and turned his concern back to his drink.

"L-let me think about it a couple of days." Colbert muttered after a moment.

Riley did not bother to turn toward him. "What's to think about? You do it and you get paid handsomely. You don't do it and you go to prison. Sounds like a fool's dilemma to me!"

"I can't just go shoot the kid in the head or stick a knife in his back. I got to make it look like somebody else did it, or make it look like an accident."

"Figure it out, then. Monkey with the brakes on his hot rod, or rig dynamite to his gas tank. I don't care how you do it. Just do it, and I'll make sure the Sheriff steers the newspapers and the DA away from you."

"All right. I'll figure out something."

"Make sure you do." Before Colbert could slink away, Riley pointed at him and growled, "But listen, Colbert, if you try skipping out, I'll have the Sheriff on your tail before you can get out of the county."

Colbert studied the man's evil eyes. He knew what the man said was within his ability. He jammed his cap on his head and hurried to the front door. With his hand on the doorknob, he hesitated as though to speak again, but suddenly jerked the door open and left.

* * * * *

Colbert slouched on the sofa in the living room trying to fight off the fog in his head long enough to come up with an idea. How could he make Adam Woods' death appear to be an accident? He had just enough to drink that he did not have to pick a fight with Charlotte in order to get some private time to think. The mere sight and smell of him was enough to start fireworks. He had the radio on, with some crime drama playing.

Charlotte sat in the kitchen muttering about having to leave her supper on the table. When Adam came in the back door, she was ready to aim her frustrations at him.

"Where have you been?" she demanded of him, her anger already near a boiling point.

"What's eating you?" he asked, closing the door behind him. Adam was used to strife in the house, but it was not usually so sudden and without any apparent reason.

Charlotte looked away and shook her head. "Oh, it's not you." She cocked her head toward the living room and motioned with her thumb in that direction. "I'm just mad. I'll get over it."

Adam leaned far enough to the side to see bare feet extending from the sofa in the next room. He nodded.

"You look unusually happy today," she said. "What've you been drinking?"

"I've got to be drinking if I'm happy?"

"So what is it?"

He shrugged, consciously making himself look more serious. "Why shouldn't I be?"

"You weren't very happy when you left earlier. I seem to remember you were aggravated I told you about your father."

"Not that you told me! That you didn't tell me years ago!"

"You met a girl."

He feigned irritation. "Here you go! You think you know me when you barely know I exist."

"I do know you, and you're hiding something. What's her name?"

He shook his head and rolled his eyes. "If I had met a girl, why would I talk to you about her? Looks like you failed twice at picking a mate for yourself." He turned toward the other end of the house, where his bedroom was.

"Ooh, that was nasty. I guess you're not so happy after all."

"Kind of like accusing me of being drunk."

"I take it back. You haven't been drinking. And you must've met someone really special to keep you from your redneck buddies." She had been casually flipping through a copy of Life magazine, and now turned her attention away from him as she examined a page.

"Okay," said Adam, giving in to her and lowering his voice. "Do you remember the girl they call 'Gal'? Her parents died a few years ago in a car wreck."

"Yeah, the Slaughter girl. She lives out on that farm by herself."

"Her name's Maisie, Mama. I've never seen anybody as pretty as she is, and she's –"

"Crazy?"

"No! She's not crazy; she's the most interesting woman..."

"Woman?" Charlotte raised her voice an octave. "I've heard she's some kind of wild heathen gal, doing witchcraft out there! People say she dances alone in the woods at midnight, singing and twirling and speaking to spirits. She goes barefoot and wears blue jeans like a man, and lets her hair fly loose. And they say she knows things about people that she ought not know."

Adam shook his head. "That's what's crazy! Not her! If she's crazy, everybody else in the world is a bunch of idiots! She's intelligent and wise!"

"You've come under some kind of spell, Adam. You didn't go out to her old house, did you?"

"Mama, believe me, she's as straight as a line. She just loves God."

"Ha! Not from what I've heard! More likely, she loves the devil, out there dancin' in the moonlight!"

Adam turned crimson. "What do *you* know? Have you ever met her?"

"Don't need to meet her. I've heard she heals people and conjures."

Adam threw up his hands. "Where'd you hear stuff like that? Some of your old gossip buddies?"

"Stop it, Adam. It's not gossip when it's true! You can't be in love with a witch and wart conjurer."

"If she does heal people, what's wrong with that?"

"It's just not done by regular Christian folks."

Adam stood suddenly and shoved his chair back. "I should've known I couldn't have an honest conversation with you! The Sunday saint!" He glared at her. "Who judges people from her dirty ivory tower!" He stalked out of the room shaking his head and passed through the living room without looking at Colbert.

* * * * *

Colbert watched the boy march through the room without looking his way. He smiled to himself as he replayed in his mind the conversation he had overheard. The boy is hot on Gal, the crazy girl living on that farm she got when her folks got killed. On hearing that, the idea had jumped right into his mind. A lunatic woman might be prone to do anything. How hard would it be to make a killing look like some spooky devil work?

Suddenly, in a satisfied mood, he turned the power knob off and the radio faded.

"Charlotte, Honey," he called out, satisfied with his solution. "I'm sorry I made you mad," he said as he appeared at the kitchen doorway. "I don't know what got into me, drinking alone like that. Just hearing how that boy talked to you makes me want to apologize. Why don't you let me buy you a couple of drinks?"

She moved toward the door. "Are you feelin' okay, Ray Lee?"

"As okay as I've ever been, Baby. You were right to be mad at me, and I'm sorry."

Charlotte smiled and came to him. She hugged him and laid her head on his shoulder as though he were the only comfort in her life.

Just exactly the way Ray Lee wanted her.

CHAPTER THREE

The roads in Odino were always desolate before 9:00 on Sunday mornings, spiking with a brief frenzy of traffic between 9:45 and 10:05, and returning to relative quiet until 12:05PM. At 10:01, the doors of the Vine Arbor Church closed and anyone standing outside heard the reverberating voice of the choir director intone with practiced enthusiasm, "Good morning! Open your hymnals to page 301. Everyone stand with me and let's sing 'Standing On The Promises'!" The piano sounded out an introductory bar and the choir burst forth with zeal.

Services at Charlotte's church were pretty predictable to Colbert. He and she sat in the same pew every visit to avoid ticking off the people who guarded their regular seats against all challengers. They sang the same five hymns to the sound of the same out-of-tune piano. The preacher preached what, to Colbert, was pretty much the same heavy message every week. And then they all stretched, smiled, formed an exit line and shook the preacher's hand as they hurried out the door and drove in the direction of the same tired mom-and-pop for lunch.

Today, he did not have to work hard to stay awake because he used the time developing a plan he considered nothing short of ingenious. In fact, he was looking at the very man who could make it work like a charm.

* * * * *

Adam sat two rows behind his mother and her new husband. His price for forgiveness from his mother was his attendance at this service. He had given in to the blackmail in order to keep peace. But aside from that, his visit with Maisie had got him thinking about God. If Maisie was the most wonderful person he had ever met – and she was – maybe God had something to do with it. She had said as much. Maybe it wouldn't hurt to listen to what the preacher had to say.

Charlotte was sitting unnaturally erect and stiff, as usual. Her way of looking pious, he thought. Ray Lee, on the other hand, was amazingly alert today. He was not nodding off at all. If the way he was eyeing the pastor meant anything, Colbert was even engaged in the sermon. Something told him, however, that Colbert would not be one of the humble converts responding to the call today. The man always had the look of someone with something up his sleeve, but today even more so.

When the service ended and Charlotte and Ray Lee made their way to the exit, Ray Lee leaned over to whisper something to the pastor. Adam's suspicious mind alerted. Since Charlotte and Ray Lee were the last in line to shake hands, the pastor nodded for Colbert to come with him. The two appeared to be headed toward the pastor's office. Adam wanted very much to find out what was on the mind of his step-father. He went to the water fountain in the hall outside the church office and leaned down as though getting a drink.

The pastor's voice reverberated clearly.

"...the girl they call Gal?"

Adam was startled. They were talking about Maisie. His heart raced. What could Colbert be saying about her? As far as Adam knew, the man had never seen her before.

"That's the one, Pastor Moncus. She lives out on County Line Road on a run-down farm her parents left her."

Run down? The farm was well kept and the house much cleaner than the one Colbert and Charlotte shared.

Colbert continued talking. "I've heard the poor girl is as crazy as a bat, and involved in all kinds of things out there – conjuring, fortune-telling, doing some kind of moon worship at night, dancing around a hilltop."

Adam seethed. Lies! Colbert was embellishing on what he probably overheard Charlotte say the night before. What was the point of this?

"Are you serious!" asked the pastor, with sincere concern.

Pastor Moncus was buying everything Colbert said! Adam balled his fists and ground his teeth. He was tempted to break through the back door and put a stop to the liar's accusations. In his distracted anger, he missed the next exchange in the conversation.

"...out there tonight and see for yourself."

"That poor girl. I wonder if the death of her parents sent her over the edge."

"I wouldn't doubt it a bit. She's probably a danger to herself and to the community in that kind of state. I've heard some folks are afraid to go around her place."

"A danger?" The pastor paused a moment, apparently thinking about the idea. "I guess she probably is a danger, now that you mention it."

"Wouldn't it be the Christian thing to do to go out and...?"

"Confirm the rumors?" asked the pastor.

"Yeah, yeah. To see what the devil is going on out there."

"The devil? I hadn't thought of that, either. But it could be the work of the devil."

"Well, sure. You're probably right. I wouldn't put anything past Old Slewfoot."

Adam stepped closer to the doorway. He wanted more than anything to open the door and drag Colbert out. But he knew that would not help.

"...meet you here at nine, just after dark, and we'll ride out together. How's that?"

"That's fine, Mister Colbert. I guess we – somebody – needs to do something. Look, thanks for bringing that to my attention. I sure hate the thoughts of what could be controlling that girl's mind, if what you heard is true."

Adam hurried away and left by the back door, determined to do something himself, either to stop them from spying on Maisie or to warn her against their outrageous talk.

* * * * *

Driving home, Colbert could barely suppress his glee at having the preacher go along so easily. The man had been easy to convince once Colbert used a few words that preachers love to hate. It had been a stroke of genius to lure the pastor out to the girl's farm to confirm she was crazy enough to be dangerous! Colbert suddenly felt like a mover and a shaker. Right up there with the likes of Potter Riley!

It was just his good fortune that the girl really was crazy. As Charlotte, herself, had said, "If it ain't the devil Gal is out there dancing for on that hill at night, who the heck would it be?"

That was a good question, from Colbert's viewpoint. Nobody in their right mind would be outside dancing anyway, unless they were drunk as a skunk. And even then, they wouldn't be dancing alone.

CHAPTER FOUR

Stars sprinkled the sky like pinholes in a black velvet coverlet. Neither moon nor clouds intruded. Only a hint of low, shadowed hills and trees confirmed that the earth met the rest of the universe in the middle of the horizon.

Adam shook his head in disbelief that he was here, spying on two spies. He had been unable to find Maisie in the afternoon, and convinced himself he might be able to spoil Ray Lee's plan before he could carry it out. He had pulled the coil wire on Ray Lee's truck, but Colbert popped the hood and spotted the problem in a couple of minutes. Adam had not even slowed Ray Lee down. So he decided to be in the woods before the two spies got to Maisie's farm; maybe he could do something to scare them off.

If everything failed, he would have to convince the preacher that Maisie was just a normal happy Christian girl. All he needed to do was to arrange for the pastor to sit down and have a conversation with her. She was so easy to talk to, and she had a peaceful way about her that made Adam enjoy being with her. Naturally, he was biased, but if Ray Lee was too dense to pick up on her qualities, the minister would undoubtedly see right away that she was normal and it was Ray Lee Colbert that was crazy.

He admired the beauty of the Slaughter farm at night. It lay submerged in a sea of navy light as though engulfed by a quiet flood. There, barely visible in the distant background of the inky image stood a field, now neat rows of turned soil and soon, bristling with new corn stalks. To the left, bordering a small pasture that once held half a dozen red cows, stood a weathered barn and scattered sheds, including an outhouse retained from earlier days. Two of the three front windows in the farmhouse shone with light through wispy curtains. The front door stood open behind a screen door, testifying to the openness and, in Adam's mind, the harmlessness of the lone inhabitant.

The scene was so inviting and pleasing to him that he could almost forget the reason he had come and the men he expected to make their way into the trees at any moment. He set his ears and eyes on alert. He did not know what time it was, but he was sure it was past nine.

Moments later, he heard a car door shut in the direction of the road. He squatted to his knees and did his best to blend with the shape of a honeysuckle bush he had found near the front yard of Maisie's farm. Soon he made out the shapes of two men moving slowly between the trees. Recent rains kept the base of leaves from making racket, but nevertheless, the two were not very good at stealth. He could hear their whispering even before they found a place to stop.

"Here's a good spot. Get by that tree." Unmistakably, the voice was Ray Lee's. Even whispering, it was raspy with the hint of years of cigarette smoking and whiskey drinking.

"Oh my, I feel strange being out here! I've never had to sneak around to find the devil's work. It's always come by on its own."

"Well, I wouldn't be surprised if old Slewfoot hisself would show up out here."

He has, Adam thought to himself. Too bad the preacher can't recognize him.

Adam watched the two shapes, trying to discern facial features, but the darkness in the trees was too thick, even over the thirty or so yards separating them. One of the men appeared to be sitting on the ground while the other remained standing. Before the men spoke again, a noise took Adam's attention back to the house.

His eyes locked on the female shape that filled the open doorway and moved outside as the screen swung open with a screech before closing silently again. Maisie's bare feet stepped soundlessly across the worn porch, quick but confident in the near absence of light, to her rendezvous. Her pale skin was ghostlike and her cotton nightgown trailed luminescent, encouraged by a touch of mid-spring air. Suddenly, Adam was completely immersed in the scene before him.

* * * * *

Maisie walked swiftly across the porch. The grass was cool
when she left the bottom stair, sending a rush of excitement up
her legs and setting her into a tiptoe run along the all-but-
invisible path ahead. She breathed the briskness in, let her
head reel back and opened her eyes to the stars. A giggle
escaped and her run became a skipping, a dancing of forward
motion.

After twenty years, she knew the home place so well she
gave no thought to where her feet might land. This was her
land. Grief over her mother and father, the fear of loneliness,
the anxiety at keeping up the farm – they were long gone. The
Lord God had enabled her. He had made Himself known to
her since her first heartbroken night out, when she could no
longer endure the heaviness of her circumstances and the
resistance of the farm house to her need for release.

She swept past the dark shape of their old well, her arms
now moving to an inner melody. When her feet found the
higher grass of the unplowed meadow, ungrazed by cattle for
years now, she began her dance with a leap and a call.

"I'm here!" This was both an announcement and a song
that morphed into a wordless melody.

Delight carried her voice to the distant tree line where it
was instantly absorbed. The nearest neighbor, almost a mile
distant, would never hear her. She was alone with her love.

This was her "garden," her private Eden, the overlapping
of heaven and earth. Here she had found freedom. She had
found her Father's Spirit. And in this garden had come an
unimaginable harvest. Fruit the Bible said was of the Spirit.
Her songs to Him had plowed and sown. And from
somewhere, somehow, amazingly, had come more than she
could possibly have planted.

"I love You!"

She leaned into the swirl, losing herself in the vortex of her
dance, resting in the growing presence of the Spirit. Images

came to her, spreading her already pleased smile. She envisioned the first hesitant time she awoke and came from the house, not knowing where to go to find peace and comfort. Knowing nothing of the One to whom she had committed herself as a child. Knowing only that she had read or heard or dreamed that she was to draw near if she wanted His nearness. Later she had realized that it need not have been outdoors, away from the stifling, man-made enclosure she knew as home. But by then, she loved to meet Him outside.

Who knew how long her visits with Him lasted! She felt as though she could dance in His presence forever. She seemed never to run out of strength. Only when she realized she had work to do come daylight, or at times, when daylight itself commenced, would she relent and return to the house. Already, mid-May as it was, she dreaded winter, when she would have to meet with Him in the cramped confines of the front room before a hastily started fire, or in her bedroom, wrapped in blankets.

She whorled and wished for an echo, so that she might imagine it as His voice in return.

She sang. Her voice turned soft, melodious, exuberant in its elongated words. She twirled like a child, her arms out in openness and balance. Her gown flared lightly and her feet arced across the tender grass.

* * * * *

"Sounds like she's singing," whispered the reverend.

Colbert shook his head as he watched. "Reckon she might be on some kind of dope. Or she might be trying to conjure up spirits."

"Heaven only knows! But you're right about one thing: she's certainly not up to any good."

"What else'd make a gal act that way, other than dope or the devil?"

The minister only sighed. Why had he agreed to come out here with Colbert? He had no experience dealing with spiritual things like actual devils and such. Something would need to be done, and now he was right in the midst of the issue, a first-hand witness. He had been handed this rural mission in spite of his request for a congregation in a larger city where people were better educated and had regular jobs, with steady incomes. Had they sent him here to punish him for some infraction or failure? This was not the kind of situation he should have to deal with. Seminary had not prepared him for this kind of aberration. If the law was brought in or it went before a judge, he was stuck as a witness. No way out of that. And sure as the world, something would need to be done. For the girl's safety and for the safety of the townspeople.

As if reading his mind, Colbert spoke. "What if she was to go berserk?"

The minister gave an audible groan. "I suppose we'll need to tell somebody." He thought of newspaper articles with his name mentioned prominently. "Maybe we can convince the authorities to keep it quiet."

"No way to keep this kind of thing quiet!" said Colbert. "This'll be all over town in no time. It might even make the out-of-town papers."

"She's crazy all right!" said Reverend Moncus, leaning toward his associate without taking his eyes from the strange scene. "Look at the way she's carrying on, and without a soul in sight."

Starlight filtered through the myriad pine brushes overhead, leaving the limp fedora on the minister's head the only shape graced with a hint of color. Beside him, leaning his shoulder against the opposite side of the same tree, was the informer, Ray Lee Colbert.

"I never would've believed it, Mister Colbert," said the preacher leaning around the tree trunk, as he placed a palm against his cheek in wonderment and turned to his acquaintance.

"Kinda spooked me, seeing her act that way."

"She ain't right, Reverend," Colbert answered, his tone communicating satisfaction at having proved his claim true. "I told you she was peculiar. Maybe when her mamma and daddy died, she went all the way crazy."

The preacher seemed worried. "I heard of the Slaughters. Good folks, people said. I'd heard of somebody people called 'Gal,' but didn't know who they were talking about. It just doesn't seem right they'd have a crazy daughter."

"Well, I guess you saw it with your own eyes. Don't you think she could be a problem – I mean, in the community?"

"What about her brother? The Slaughters had a boy, older, I think."

"I heard he went off with the Army – who knows where – a year or two before his Mama and Daddy passed. He probably don't know about this dangerous situation."

The pastor spoke. "Maybe I'll have a talk with the sheriff tomorrow. He'll know what ought to be done about crazy people. Don't know as she'd be a harm to anyone."

"You don't ever know, though," Colbert hastened to add. "She sure could be a danger to herself. Or somebody else."

The preacher studied the dark spaces where Ray Lee's eyes were. He slowly nodded.

Colbert continued, encouraged by the agreement of the man, "Young gal out here by herself. Farm to take care of. Ain't no man gonna marry a crazy woman and take care of her and what all."

The preacher shook his head in sadness. "The devil might have her, sure enough."

* * * * *

"All is not right." Maisie's eyes came open at the voice in her heart. Her awareness returned to the present. She had never heard His voice that clearly before. Was that Him? Had she actually heard it or had her thoughts manufactured the supposed sound? She gradually allowed herself to stop the dance. And when she stood still and made her bearings clear in her mind once more, her arms flagging involuntarily to her side, she set her ears alert.

The sound of it was fresh in her head: "All is not right."

Standing stone still, Maisie listened. Despite the fact it was not yet the time for crickets, a lone chirp arose far back in the trees. Not enough breeze stirred to make a noise with the barn door or the tin roof on the house.

"Tell me again," she whispered, closing her eyes again to focus her attention.

She waited for a minute or two, finally realizing He was not going to speak again, which meant to her that she had heard what she heard. Something was not right.

She remembered something her mother used to say: "There's a time to cry and a time to laugh, a time to mourn and a time to dance. You don't do anything all the time. But do what the Lord puts in front of you to do." She knew it was time to go inside and listen.

Maisie wrapped her arms around her mid-section, suddenly feeling a chill, but hesitant to take the first step away. She had had too much of mourning and crying in recent years. Why couldn't the laughing and dancing be always? "No use whining," her mother would have said. "Doesn't God say the rain falls on the just and the unjust alike? Rain grows crops just like sunshine does."

Maisie nodded and headed toward the house. She estimated it was not even midnight. Not very late at all, so she might open the Bible for a while. That was where God usually explained what she did not understand.

* * * * *

She had stopped dancing and had gone inside. A dim light came on in a room to the right of the front door.

"I wanted you to see it for yourself, Preacher," whispered Colbert.

"You did the right thing, Mister Colbert. Why, if I'd known that – you know – the Slaughters had left a feeble-minded gal..."

"She might've hurt herself, or somebody. Who knows if she can even fend for herself?"

"You're right." The preacher ran a hand through his sparse

hair and shook his head again. "My oh my! You're sure right about that."

"Whatta you think the sheriff'll do about her?" Ray Lee prompted.

"Mid-State, more than likely," he said. "Take her down there."

After another anxious look at the house, the preacher retrieved his snake stick from the back side of the tree and straightened himself.

"Guess we'd better get on," he said. "There's nothing we can do for the poor girl standing around here."

"Crazy as a loon!" said Ray Lee. He turned with the preacher to leave. "Nice piece of property here. Wonder what'll happen to it, with her down in Mid-State?"

The preacher cut his head sharply around to Ray Lee, frowning, and swatted at briars with his stick. He saw nothing in the man's face, the trees making night darker as they had.

With his eyes to the ground, Colbert missed the look.

"Lord have mercy!" said the pastor just above a whisper.

Ray Lee smiled to himself. "Poor girl," he said.

* * * * *

Well hidden from the sight of the two men, Adam Woods watched the shapes skulking away in the dark of the trees toward the road. He had been too caught up in watching Maisie to try to thwart the men behind him. And she had gone in after only a little while. He was stunned at what he had seen and heard. There had to be some reasonable explanation why Maisie was dancing outside in the middle of the night. Surely, Ray Lee Colbert was wrong in his assertions that she was insane. The man was up to no good, Adam had no doubt, but the last thing he expected to see was some confirmation of his evil stepfather's claims.

While he had more questions now than he had before following the two men, he had learned that night what treachery and stupidity were. Colbert had defined both for him. But now he needed to know how to deal with them.

Despite what he had seen and heard, he would not give up what he felt inside: that Maisie Slaughter was in no way crazy, as they had said.

If anyone was crazy, it was the two in the woods that night, crazy for thinking Maisie was out of her mind. He had never seen anyone more sane and wonderful and beautiful than she was. He had never met anyone with a more honest and more genuine love for God, a love that just flowed right out of her without stopping to stuff itself hard-like in a small box they called church.

The volume of the tree frogs' cry seemed to ratchet up now that he was alone. They seemed to be screaming, "Seee! Seee!" as though they had known all along that evil had come to entrap Gal. And it was supposedly good people who had come to accuse her so wrongly!

CHAPTER FIVE

Anyone who might have been able to see Bonder Woods could have believed he was dead. No one slept sitting up. Not in this place. And if they could sleep like that, they would look asleep, with head lolled to the side maybe, mouth slack, shoulders slumped, and not like sudden death had taken him and rigor mortis had locked him in place.

That is what Bonder Woods looked like.

He was aware, but not of his immediate surroundings. His awareness was consumed by the vastness of the Spirit of God.

The soft light by which he was enveloped was big, very big. Yet it was near. And the nearness of it extended even to the very extremities of it. Unlike the darkness of his surroundings, opaque deadness that had consumed and overtaken him in his pathetic history, causing him to lose all sense of being and life, this was a light that had come into darkness and neutralized it. It was a translucent space of composite colors softened with peace, as though by a thousand successive silk canopies floating overhead and draping to the corners of infinity, canopies of every hue, held aloft with some pervasive flow of delicious air.

He sat in it, alone but not lonely. Conscious but detached.

Sounds in the distance were under his control to the extent they were not at all distracting or even vaguely interesting at the moment. He heard them with other ears and let them remain beyond the protective veil swaddling him. It was as though he sat at the bottom of a crystal clear river deep as the sky and wide as the horizon, looking up at a translucent night with no end. Not drowning in the soft, gentle flow. Already drowned, yet more alive. And completely aware, unthreatened, unresistant – a willing and happy participant in the concert of felt silence.

Thoughts came and hovered like tiny fish in the flow. He

watched them more than heard them. Observed their content and considered their purpose or need as though they belonged to someone else.

As he sat he occasionally spoke, without effort or sound.

Thank you. Thank you. Jesus. My all, in all.

This transparent space was where he came often, and at least a couple of hours ago this time.

He sensed the long time of his past as a flashing moment in the immensity of the present. A single raindrop on the surface of the stream above. Its fading ripples gradually moved as a cloud in the sky sweeping from his peripheral vision into the vast upstream existence behind him.

A thought buoyed before him. Are my eyes open or closed? He let it swim away unanswered.

He saw the face of the young man as a panorama above the watery veils. Flynn Riley. Forever positioned the same in his mind. The thought came as it often did. Not accusing, but reminding. Flynn's options are ended. And with it came the feeling of grief, long-spent grief, like one more veil. And then the panorama ascended until it merged with the translucent flow.

Thank you, he said silently, for forgiving me.

He allowed Charlotte's image to materialize before him now. And Adam's. Little Adam, as he had last seen him. Asleep as he had been before Bonder took him from the crib; Charlotte had almost the same smile she wore on their wedding day. With only a hint of sadnesses seen. The baby lay in her arms. Oblivious. Though surely he was not now oblivious, after so many years. He knew his father was a killer. What had that knowledge done to him?

God, please fill the empty space. Teach him what he needs to know.

Bonder dwelt with the image of Adam for some time, attempting to convert the baby's face and stature into that of the young man he must have become, but without success. Finally, the image of Adam drifted into the colors of the slowly flowing crystal stream.

And there was God. Invisible in the stream. An undeniable presence that had no need to speak, but poured waves of inexpressible knowledge into him. So powerful as to be pervasive, and yet so contained as to be only there. With him, despite the facts of his past and the fact of Flynn's death, both lost in the pages of an old book. Odd how he knew God had forgiven. Amazing how God had made entrance into the monotonous series of failures known as Bonder's life, bringing heart-wrenching sorrow where little feeling had ever found foothold. Amazing how He had made His way into solitary confinement, though not even a mouse had found its way there over the seeming eons of lights on and lights off, of seasons recognized only by the change in temperature, of meals shoved unannounced through a slot with such predictability he had known the second each would arrive, without sounds for clues.

God had come and saved him from the long journey into insanity everyone said was inevitable in solitary. That is what they, the guards and the other inmates, predicted. Whether he had completed the trip and was now back, or whether that destination had been preempted he might never know. If the killers and thieves could see him this moment, for all observance asleep or comatose, they would assume he had arrived where so many others had gone and remained. They would assume he had succumbed to the inevitable, total insanity.

But Bonder knew better. He was with the Creator. He had been alone long enough to sense, blindfolded and deafened to sensory input, the presence of another living entity. On the other journey, his former life, he had sensed very real entities of a different nature, also unseen. No one could persuade him either was imaginary.

After what had seemed days or seconds, he decided to return to the temporal and eat this meal, which he realized without thinking, would be breakfast.

He thanked God again and willed his eyes to open, his body to stir. A second later, the light fixture bolted to the ceiling flashed on in all its forty-watt splendor.

A covered tray slid through the slot in the door and stopped on the abbreviated steel shelf.

His friend – the guard he called Foster because he had had a friend once whose last name was Foster – drummed his fingers quickly on the outside of the door. Bonder leaned over and duplicated the sound as his appreciation.

His conversation with a mortal for the day. The only one, if he did not count those tête-à-têtes with himself.

"Let me guess," he said, his eyes fixed on the gray concrete wall before him, his hand hovering above the tray lid. "Unsalted scrambled eggs, dry toast, a four-ounce cup of lukewarm black coffee and a toothpick."

He lifted the lid.

"Ah! Just the way I like it. No surprises.

"Thank you for this. Please bless it. And don't forget to bless Charlotte's and Adam's food."

The thought of Charlotte reminded Bonder of all he owed her. He owed her a huge apology for marrying her in the first place. He should have known it wasn't right. She had pretty much thrown herself at him, maybe thinking she could tame him. He was vain enough to think it was love. But his condition had been down, so down, after loving and, as they say, losing, that his compass was broken. That was what had sent him into a tailspin of drinking and gambling. Charlotte had been attracted to the danger in his life, what looked like brave and daring recklessness, but was in reality grief. He would try to make up some of the badness by praying for Charlotte.

He set the thoughts aside temporarily. No use in re-hashing all of that. He had done what he had done out of stupidity, out of not having his heart filled by the Holy Spirit of God.

That was the sum of it.

He forked a lump of eggs onto the dry bread and took a bite.

A plumbing pipe in the tier above flooded with rushing water as it did every morning at this time.

"The guy's regular. You can say that for him."

Six minutes later, he returned the tray lid just as Foster tapped on the door. He slid the tray out and watched it disappear. He saw a flash of the cart and Foster's gray trousers before the outer flap of the slot slid shut.

He had one hundred twenty minutes before activity yard,

if this was a weekday as he supposed. He would have thirty minutes there. Alone. The yard was forty-seven steps in each of the four directions and caged with a heavy-duty chain-link ceiling atop an eight-foot concrete wall that permitted no view of the general exercise yard two stories below. The floor of the solitary yard was swept concrete. Once it had been covered with two inches of sand. That was removed two years earlier because inmates left messages in the sand for each other.

He would go to the sunny patch and stand, and pray. If it was raining a little, he would go to the same spot and feel the uniqueness of the moisture. If it was raining hard, he would stand in the downpour long enough to be saturated with the experience and then sit on the bench underneath the overhang to the right of the door and watch raindrops pelt the puddles.

"I've got a little more time I can spend with you," he said to the Lord, and placed his toothpick on the shelf of the door.

Bonder closed his eyes and hurried into the peaceful space.

In the moment before his conscious awareness shifted locations, a flood of memory reminded him of a darkness that held him not many months ago.

* * * * *

How could he ever forget that morning?

Bonder had awakened at a shriek. His own shriek. His heart fought its confinement the way he had pounded desperately on the unrelenting walls hours earlier. Because he had also heard another voice.

The voice was not one of the many he had heard before. The others had been random scraps, some barely intelligible, speaking nonsensical phrases or the names of obscure people. He had ignored them for as long as he could. But there was nothing else to which he could fix his attention. The numbing silence of solitary confinement grew to mammoth size, spreading to fill the emptiness, filling and overflowing it, becoming loud itself, more insistent, finally transforming itself from harmless emptiness to screaming madness.

No, this is not real.

Oh, yes it is! I am very real!

No. No, I'll wake up.

You are awake, and you can't stop me. I'm in control. Of you. Of this place. I can make daylight dark, and I can make night light up like noonday. I can fix you or mess you all up, get you out of this place or destroy you completely. Give it up.

Hands gripped his throat suddenly. Hands he could not see. The sudden force made him gasp. The hold was overwhelming. He reached to pry loose the fingers but felt none. Panic consumed him as the pressure increased exponentially. His head was being forced off his shoulders. His eyes bulged in their sockets as he struggled in vain to free himself. Grey gas clouds flooded into his mental view, quickly blocking all awareness of who he was, where he was, what the voice had just spoken to him. He fell limp into deep, unending blackness.

Do you believe me now?

The voice echoed inside his failing brain. The grey fog dissipated slowly, and the words he had just heard began to register meaning. He faced something he had never imagined and could not now quite understand, except that the disembodied voice was a very real presence, a dangerous one. This being was murderous, whoever he was. Bonder would have to do what the voice said.

Do you?

Bonder nodded. He found that he was on his back on the floor of the dim cell, pressed into the corner with his shoulders hard against the stainless steel toilet. He saw that his sock-covered feet were moving frantically, pushing in vain against the smooth concrete to get him away from the place where the voice seemed to originate, the pale grey wall opposite his bunk.

His struggling mind worked at processing what he heard and felt. Despite the cold fear gripping him, he saw a scene replayed in his mind. He was very young, sitting close beside his mother on a worn wooden bench under a shelter with no walls. People had been singing. Church songs. But now they were crowded around a figure that writhed on the dirt floor of the place. Mostly men crowded close around the person on the floor. They were muttering in a forceful monotone, gesturing toward and staring at the person, whose eyes were slits riveted on one of the men, a man holding a book toward the rafters and, smiling, speaking as though he was talking to someone up in those rafters. The person on the floor screamed and clutched at the air violently before falling limp. Low eddies of dust boiled around the still body. Bonder thought the person had died.

Make a rope!

The voice startled him out of the mental scene.

Two sheets. Tear long strips and twist them into a rope. You're a worthless murderer. A baby mauler. A drunk and robber. You deserve to die for all you've done. Charlotte was right to turn you in, you piece of trash! She was right to divorce you without a word!

Bonder glanced at the bed. The sheets were rumpled from his tossing and rolling through fits of troubled sleep. They were old sheets and would easily tear.

The cage around the light. Stand on your bunk and tie one end around your neck. Tie the other end to the steel cage. Tighten it until you're on your tiptoes.

Bonder eyed the steel cage surrounding the now-dark light bulb.

And jump off the bunk. Get it over with, for your kid's sake. He hates you anyway. Just like Charlotte hates you. Pay for the Riley boy's life with yours.

A trickle of brine ran down Bonder's face. His vision filled with the sight of Flynn Riley lying on his back, his eye sockets puddling with rain water, a jagged tree limb growing from his midsection.

He grabbed the sheet from his bunk, stifling sobs that might be heard, and ripped long strips from it. The resolve had been clear and firm. His hands shook little compared with his quivering lips and flickering eyelids.

He was already standing upon the bunk, trying to thread the twisted end of cloth through the steel cage fashioned around the light fixture, an oversight prison officials might purposely have let remain in solitary confinement as concession to compassion.

It was in the moment before he knotted the shortened length around his neck that he heard the word. Two syllables, spoken in the voice of his mother, somehow. She had spoken in answer to his defiant seventeen-year-old demand why he should not drink the glass of moonshine whiskey in his hand, the sound and syllables reverberating across nearly thirty years of empty space to find him.

"Jesus."

It had been a simple answer he had thought stupid until he heard it atop that bunk, with his hands gripping a homemade rope.

Somehow the word cleared its way through layers of darkness and isolation and managed to seem like an actual answer.

So much so that within another minute, he was sitting on the bunk, using the untwisted fabric of the sheet strips to wipe his cheeks of inexplicable moisture.

Those two syllables had sparked a quiet revolution of sorts that had become a four-year dawn breaking unto daylight.

Bonder had returned from his trip to insanity.

And no one knew. Not even Foster.

Only the Son of God knew.

CHAPTER SIX

After watching Colbert and the preacher slip away, Adam had walked back from Maisie's farm to the spot where he hid his car, and had driven home in a confused stupor. His anger and determination over Colbert's apparent scheme had transformed into a heavy, sinking feeling that occluded his every thought. The need to protect Maisie was unfazed; an inner, urgent unction to do anything necessary to keep Colbert's evil intent, whatever its form, from harming her, still dominated his own mind and heart. His failure to understand what she was doing on that hill in the dark had simply defused or delayed his response, which, he had previously considered might involve some physical force against Colbert if needed.

He parked his car in the yard in front of his mother's house, deciding to spend the night in it rather than go inside and wake her and Colbert. The moon had risen and its light shone through the rustling leaves of a pecan tree, played against the curved dash as he lay on his back in the front seat of his car with his feet propped on the brow of the door's open window. A soft breeze nuzzled through the window and kept the interior of the car cool. The broad cloth seat was pushed away from the steering column and, with his head resting on the armrest of the passenger door, he was reasonably comfortable.

One part of his mind wanted to barge into the house, drag Colbert out of bed and force him to tell what his intentions were, why he hatched some off-the-wall plan to prove Maisie was out of her mind. What on earth could he gain by doing something like that! As far as Adam knew, Colbert had never seen her. The whole idea seemed linked to Adam's interest in her, but it was inconceivable that the man even knew of it. Unless he overheard Adam's conversation with his mother two nights before. But even then, what would be the point? Did

Colbert hate Adam so much that he would concoct some tale to tarnish Maisie's reputation, or worse, simply because he showed interest in her? The whole circumstance made no sense.

The other thought occupying Adam's mind was what he might do to protect Maisie. She was as innocent of wrongdoing as she could possibly be, he knew, even if he could not understand what she was doing outside at night. He knew there must be some explanation. Maybe it was some form of communication with God that she was doing out there. He wished he could have heard what she was singing, but he was distracted by hearing Colbert and the preacher, and the sounds of the wind in the trees and the tree frogs so near him obliterated her words. He allowed himself the thought that, no matter how impossible the idea seemed, he would take Maisie far away from any danger, if she would allow him. Or maybe he could just talk to Maisie, ask her straight out what she was doing – he would have to apologize for snooping, of course – and explain everything to the preacher, so he would not think she was some danger to herself. That would not neutralize Colbert, but it might thwart his scheme, whatever that was.

If anyone was genuine, Maisie Slaughter was. The way she spoke of the Almighty made Adam confident that God was alive and real. In her a fire burned that illuminated her eyes and her speech. God was with her. Of that, Adam was convinced. And what could be wrong with that, after all, even if her communication with Him took on some strange expression neither he nor Colbert nor even the preacher had ever witnessed? Adam readily admitted he was no saint, and certainly no student of the Bible, but who was to say she could not give worship to God in that way? He rejected the thought that she was doing anything other than worshipping God out there.

Maisie Slaughter was, to Adam, beauty and peace and everything that happiness meant. Yes, he was influenced by her personal beauty, and, yes, by his own loneliness, he admitted, but there was something about her that went far deeper than beauty, something that made it impossible that her love for God could lead her into insanity. That just did not add up.

* * * * *

Monday morning, after Colbert drove away, Adam went inside to clean up and change clothes. Charlotte confronted him, accusing him of staying out all night with some girl, and, when he denied that, of laying drunk like his "worthless" father had done time and again. Adam dodged her assault as best he could and went about cleaning up. He had decided to drive out to Maisie's farm and have a talk with her. It was vital that he understand what she was doing, and that she understand why he was out snooping. He had overcome the fear that she would be angry at him for sneaking around, watching her, by rationalizing that if he lost her new friendship because of it, at least he would be doing something to protect her. Maybe she would come around later and forgive him.

Growing in his awareness was the realization that what he was experiencing was love, at least some seedling form of it. He spent half the night fighting the ridiculousness of the idea, attributing the sensation to some immaturity in his own lonesome life. In the end, he decided it did not matter what motivated him, or whether anything would ever come of it; he would not deny to his own mind the love and admiration he so quickly found for Maisie. She was one of a kind. Something about her spoke so loudly of kindness, gentleness and genuine sincerity, he would be crazy not to admire her. Anyone would. That would go halfway in explaining Colbert's motivation: he was simply crazy.

* * * * *

Adam stood on Maisie's front porch, opened the screen door and knocked softly on the wooden door. The sun had risen over the eastern trees an hour before and now promised a beautiful, warm day. He heard no sound inside. Realizing that he was being timid, a bit shy about broaching the question he had to ask and admit his forwardness in the events of the night before, he braced himself with the knowledge it had to be done, and knocked louder.

"Good morning, Adam!"

He turned to see Maisie leaning against a rake near the porch steps. She wore jeans and a man's shirt over worn out white sneakers, Her auburn hair was disheveled and fell beautifully, he thought, to the side of her face.

"I was in the barn and heard your car. I'm thinking of buying a calf, so I had to do a little prep work." She smiled at him. "What brings you out so early?"

Walking toward her, he smiled back in an apologetic way. "Hi Maisie. I apologize for coming out again, but I need to talk with you."

She leaned her rake against the house. "Oh sure. Why don't you have a seat here on the porch while I make some coffee?" She gestured to one of the metal chairs.

"No, Maisie, I need to ask you something before I lose my nerve."

"Okay, Adam. Want to sit here on the steps?" She sat on the top step with her back against the side of the house. He joined her, unable to hide his discomfort.

"Maisie, somebody's been out here spying on you, and they're trying to say you're crazy."

"Crazy?" She laughed softly. "I guess that wouldn't be the first time. I've been called that a few times."

"First, I don't think you are. In fact, I know you're not. From the little time I spent with you, I know you're more sane than I am."

"Thanks – "

He continued before she could finish. "I was out here last night."

"You were?"

He nodded. "I'm sorry, but I promise I wasn't out here to spy on you, I was following two men who were. Ray Lee Colbert and the Preacher Moncus."

"What in the world – ?"

He interrupted her. "I overheard Colbert telling the preacher you were doing some kind of witchcraft or devil worship, and offered to bring him out here last night to prove it to him. So I followed them."

"They came out here spying on me?"

"Maisie, Colbert is up to something. I don't know what, but he seems to be on a mission to prove you are crazy and a danger to yourself."

"Who is this Ray Lee Colbert? I've never heard of him."

"My mother's husband." Adam blushed at what he was about to say. "He might have overheard me talking about you to my mother." He paused before continuing and shrugged as if to apologize for seeming to care. "Maybe he hates me enough to want to hurt you because I said you were my friend."

Maisie smiled and touched his hand briefly. "It's not your fault, Adam. Don't worry. I am your friend."

"I hope you will be when I tell you I saw you dancing out there." He nodded toward the pasture.

"You saw that? Why would that be a problem?"

"You're not mad at me?"

"Mad? No, you were looking out after me. God warned me that something was wrong last night so I came in. Regardless of what their motives might be, God watches out for me, too."

"Well, what – uh, what were you – ?"

"I was worshipping God." She grinned and his heart eased. "He loves it!" she said.

"I knew it had to be something like that. I just wanted to, you know – "

"To hear me say it?" She almost laughed.

"Yeah. I mean, I've never seen – "

"No, even if you went to church, I don't think you would. If other people do that, they probably do it at home, just for Him. I got the idea from King David. He did that in front of his people and it really made his wife mad." She laughed aloud. "Maybe it'll make my accusers mad."

"That's what I'm afraid of, Maisie."

"Don't worry. To quote my Daddy, 'They can't kill me and eat me, too.'"

"Well, I don't want them to do either one," said Adam. "You're the only friend I've got."

"I'll tell you what, Adam. When you give your life to Jesus, you'll be welcome to come out here and worship Him with me."

Adam did not know how to respond to that so he kept his silence. He held out his hand. She shook it and stood.

"You feel like working on my barn?"

"Well, I don't have to be at work until this afternoon. I can't imagine getting a better offer than that today." He began rolling up his sleeve. "What will we do?"

"I really need to tear down a rickety old tool shed in the back, but if you've got to go to work later, why don't you help me rake the barn stalls?"

"I'm your man!"

"Here." She held out the rake to him. "See if that'll fit your hand." Maisie turned toward the barn and marched off, turning her head to speak. "We've got work to do, Adam. Come on!"

Adam was thrilled. Another opportunity to spend time with the most wonderful creature on God's earth!

"Okay, okay! But I might want that cup of coffee after we're done."

"I'll make it as soon as we're done!" she called.

Adam noticed as he followed her up the incline toward the barn that the heaviness and anxiety of the last ten or twelve hours had disappeared within the last few moments. How could anyone dislike Maisie Slaughter? She was truly amazing. And it didn't hurt that she was gorgeous to boot!

CHAPTER SEVEN

Bonder did not know what day this was – maybe day 2,000 or 2,100 in solitary, it did not really matter – but he knew that the thing sliding through the slot in the cell door was lunch.

Odd. Foster did not drum his fingers on the door. He glanced through the small space in the slot to the side of his tray. He saw nothing except the concrete floor.

Something else was different. A folded piece of paper peeked from underneath his bologna sandwich. He plucked it free. Handwriting on it said, "Flush after reading."

He opened the fold and read.

"Out of solitary tomorrow. Back in general population."

He could not believe his eyes. Reading the words four times made them no less incredible. Worse, he did not know what to feel or think. Solitary had been hell until six or seven months ago, when his eyes and heart were opened.

He wadded the paper and aimed for the commode. He stopped at the heavy idea that maybe he had misread. He found the edges and pulled it straight again.

"Out of solitary," it said, "tomorrow."

Possibly, it was a net, a trap set for his mind. Someone hoped he was so near the end he would buck himself up with expectation, and finish the trip when he found out the lie.

That probably had happened before. Men, too far gone to see the lie, had taken the bait like a starving dog. Only to see their guts rip open and hope jerked out backwards.

Bonder wadded the paper and tossed it.

Solitary confinement was his inn, his oasis from the worst of prison.

General population was a wilderness.

He would not fall for a trick that tempted him to see them as the reverse.

---

* * * * *

The note had been real.

He was supposed to feel freer now that he was out of solitary confinement, but walking back from chow, Bonder felt far more confined than he had in months. It did not fit, this so-called release from Administrative Segregation, or Admin Seg. He had been in population for less than three hours and it felt as though it was his first day in prison once more, like the end of his life.

Something else was not right. He drew no attention at all wherever he was. No one looked at him. Most had never seen him; to them he would be a new inmate, a fish. If not an attraction because he was presumed to be a fish, at least he expected inmates would be staring at him because he was fresh from the hole. Prison was that way. Everyone knew what was going on. Word got around.

But none of this was happening. He might as well be invisible.

A guard outside the mess hall had told Bonder to go by the Laundry to pick up his bed linens. He rounded a corner down an unfamiliar narrow corridor. But of course, most everything was unfamiliar, he had been out of it for so long. A small white metal flag mounted to the wall halfway down the corridor indicated the Laundry. As he neared, a short white man with close-cropped red hair stepped into the hallway with a stack of linens in his arms.

"You Woods?" he asked. Something was wrong with the man's eyes, Bonder thought. He was zoned out.

"Yeah," said Bonder.

He was five feet away from the man when a door opened inches to his right and something hit him in the back. His head was jerked backward and something locked around his neck, squeezing off his breath. The last image he saw was of the red-headed man looking quickly behind himself and turning back to fix his wild eyes on Bonder before throwing a sheet over his head.

For a split-second, he had the sensation of flying. Then suddenly he landed with a jolt on the concrete floor.

Bonder lay still, unable to move. Were they still there, whoever grabbed him? Everything was dark. He hurt everywhere, especially his back, where something warm flowed down his right side and under the curve of his body.

He tried to speak, but only an awkward sound came forth. No words.

Bonder Woods lay bleeding and wondered if there was even any point in calling out for help.

The moan Bonder heard was his own. It was serious, he knew, not just because of the cramping pain or because he felt the warmth of blood spreading under him, but also because of his shortness of breath. Probably his lung had been punctured. He drew his left arm tight against his side, instinctively, before realizing he would not be able to stanch the flow from the wound. He relaxed it a moment later.

He always wondered what death would be like. Would he panic and cry? Would his life flash before his eyes? Would he think of Charlotte and little Adam – who wouldn't be so little anymore – would he see the face of Flynn Riley taking his own last breath? Or would his last thoughts turn to the God Whom he had forsaken long before, but to Whom he had recently turned for peace?

His thoughts fluttered like pages of a book until he saw in his mind, the young man, Potter Riley's son. Lying below him, just beyond Bonder's rain-spotted brogans. The boy might have tried to move his lips, but only for an instant. Then they were still.

Now that death was coming for him, Bonder realized all of the anticipated images crowded his thoughts. God, Flynn, Charlotte and Adam – all rushed for first position in his mind. He had done much wrong to all of them, but he knew he had gotten right with God in the months past. Even though he had killed a man in a drunken fight over a few measly dollars.

He had treated Charlotte like a servant girl, had not even given her the respect of explaining his actions when he stole Adam from her and left her frantic in the rain. He regretted making no attempt to write to his son, even with the certain knowledge that Charlotte would have torn the letters to shreds. He wished suddenly he had not assuaged himself with the lie that someday he would explain everything to Adam. Some day when he was free. He knew he couldn't count on ever being free. He had committed nearly every crime a man could do. And his own wife did not even come to his trial. Her last words to him were that she wished he would burn in hell.

No one deserved to pay that ultimate price more than he.

The thought that that penalty had already been taken was the most comforting realization now, far outweighing the strong possibility he would never see another day on earth.

He wondered if Charlotte was at church tonight. If she had reared Adam in church. If Adam would have forgiven him had Bonder ever asked.

Hot tears streamed down his cold cheeks. Don't be a hypocrite in your last moments, he thought to himself. It would take a lot of gall to pity yourself after what the Savior did for you!

Even so, he could not help thinking forty-eight is too soon.

Well, it could have happened years before. That was pure fact. Only grace had kept him alive long enough to know the truth.

When he heard footfalls echoing down the corridor, nearing at a fast pace, he tried and failed to wipe his eyes. Even dying, he could not let anyone see him crying. He closed his eyes. Maybe he would check out quietly before they reached him and he would not have to endure their efforts to save his life.

"There he is!"

"Get him on his left side," someone said. He vaguely felt hands shoving and pulling him, felt his torso twist until he lay atop his left arm.

"Hold that rag against the hole! Tight! Aw man, there's more wounds! Go get some towels in the laundry!"

Nobody deserves this more than me. But, God, have mercy on my soul.

The last sound Bonder heard was footsteps receding in a hall. He felt awareness slipping into a cold dark flood. He took a quick breath. Then he saw her. A young girl dancing in a field of flowers before a brilliant sunset. Or was it a sunrise?

He drew closer, but still too far to know for sure. He decided to find out.

"Charlotte!" he called out. "Charlotte! It's Bonder!"

CHAPTER EIGHT

Reverend Howard Moncus had brooded over the problem of the Slaughter girl. The thing that kept haunting him was that she might hurt herself or somebody else in her altered state of mind. He knew the devil was capable of influencing people to do some awful things, and he surely did not want an incident on his conscience that might be prevented by doing the right thing. That was what brought him to the Sheriff's office unannounced so late in the afternoon.

He hesitated before the door of the small building behind the post office. He had parked his car at the corner on Main Street so that no one would see his car in front of the Sheriff's office and start some silly rumor. He had learned to be careful in everything he did; one never knew what a flock of "sheep" would do left to their own imaginations. What halted him was the thought that he might have failed to put a dime in the parking meter before walking the block to the office. Wouldn't that be great! Getting a parking ticket while he was in talking with the Sheriff! He was turning back toward his car when the door opened and a hefty uniformed officer stepped out.

"Yes sir! What can we do for you today?"

Caught off guard, Moncus stammered a bit before getting his response together. "I was coming to talk with the Sheriff. Is he in?"

"Yes sir," said the officer, who was holding a paper cup of coffee in one hand and the door with the other. His voice sounded raspy, as though he had a cold. "He's interrogating someone at the moment. What can I do for you? I'm Captain Lowe." The man let the door swing shut and propped his hand on the heel of the revolver positioned at his hip. The movement got Moncus' attention and he suddenly felt nervous.

"Well, I'm Pastor Howard Moncus. I haven't broken any

laws or anything," he laughed unconvincingly. "But I do need to speak with the Sheriff about a matter of importance."

"All right." The officer said, unmoved by the attempt at humor. He pushed the door open again and tilted his head in its direction. "You're welcome to have a seat and wait. Come on in."

Moncus followed him inside where a window-mounted air conditioning unit had the small waiting area at least fifteen degrees cooler than the outside temperature. He took the seat pointed out by the officer and declined his offer of coffee. After ten minutes of waiting, the Sheriff's office door opened and a man of medium height but expansive girth stepped out. He hitched up his gun belt and spoke before Captain Lowe got his attention.

"I'll tell you, Wayne, that Smith woman is – !"

"Sheriff Mobley," the Captain interrupted. He cut his eyes to the side of the room and nodded toward a bank of chairs. "Reverend Moncus, here, has come to speak with you about a matter of importance, sir."

The Sheriff blushed but recovered quickly. He turned with outstretched hand and a big smile. "Well, certainly, Reverend Moncus. Glad to meet you."

Moncus stood and took the offered hand.

"Sheriff, I have a situation that needs quick attention, and I felt I'd better speak with you about it."

"Of course. Of course. Something gone wrong at your church, Reverend?"

"Would you mind if we talked privately?" Moncus cut his eyes toward the Sheriff's office.

"No, not at all, sir. Come on in." He turned and held the door open for Moncus, shutting it behind them. Moncus took the seat in front of the desk, noticing as he did, the fragrance of strong perfume and whiskey. Since he saw no one leave the Sheriff's office except the man himself, he looked around the room. A back entrance solved the question in his mind.

"Now what can I do for you, Reverend?" The Sheriff asked, taking his seat behind the desk.

"I'm afraid we have a woman in the community that is suffering from some kind of demonic oppression, Sheriff."

The Sheriff sat up as if he had been jolted awake. "A what?"

"A young woman they call Gal, she's doing strange things back in the woods at night. I've been told she's – well, she's insane – a danger to herself and maybe to others."

"The Slaughter girl?"

"Yessir."

"What d'you mean, demonic? Like devil worship?"

"I'm afraid that could be the case."

"Well, I've heard the Slaughter girl was a little off, but I had no idea she was into that kind of thing."

"A fellow in my congregation – a Mister Colbert – warned me about her, and took me out to her place last night. We actually saw her cavorting in the moonlight on a hill behind her shack. Dancing and carrying on." At the mention of Colbert's name, the Sheriff seemed to become more alert.

"Ray Lee Colbert?"

"Yessir. He told me some people have become afraid, either for her or of her."

"Is that so?"

"Yes sir, and I tend to think the poor girl needs to be in an institution before something happens."

The Sheriff leaned forward with concern evident on his face. "So, Mister Colbert put you onto her, is that it?"

"He did. He seemed to be very concerned, himself. Both for her safety and that of the community in general."

"I see." The Sheriff picked up a pen and scribbled something onto a legal pad. "I take these kinds of things very seriously, Reverend Moncus," he said looking up. "I plan to call Mister Colbert myself and investigate this thing in detail. What's your telephone number, Reverend? I'll get back with you as soon as possible and let you know what we can do."

When Moncus gave that to him, the Sheriff scribbled it down and rose with the pastor. They shook hands and the Sheriff affirmed again that he would follow up quickly and decisively.

Outside, Reverend Moncus breathed a sigh of relief. He had done what he could, passed the problem on to the proper authorities. He was satisfied the girl would get the medication and treatment needed to keep her and others around her safe. And besides, if anything happened now, it would be off his shoulders. No one could blame him. He had done the right thing. Let the law handle those kinds of things.

He hurried up the street, again wondering if he got a parking ticket while he was in there doing his Christian duty.

* * * * *

Riley picked up the telephone on the third ring.

"Yeah?"

"Riley, this is Ott. What have you and Colbert got going on that involves that crazy Slaughter gal?"

"What the devil are you talking about, Mobley?"

"There was a preacher in here just now saying Colbert told him how crazy and dangerous Gal is and that she ought to be put away."

Riley swore. "No telling what that idiot Colbert is up to. I give him a simple project and he always turns things into acts of Congress. You're the Sheriff, do your duty. If she's crazy, send her away. Simple as that! Don't get me involved in that stuff!" He slammed the phone down.

* * * * *

Sheriff Ott Mobley swore to himself and set the phone down. Why did these problems have to turn up just when things seemed to be going fairly smoothly? The election was seven months away and he knew there was talk of cleaning up the office. He had a hard time putting down talk about ties with Potter Riley, but if he didn't, he could be looking at the need to find a job somewhere. If the community was all up in arms, afraid of Gal, then he'd better do something to calm them down. He didn't need some preacher saying he had gone to the Sheriff to warn him of possible danger, only to have the law do nothing about it. But what could he do, legally? It would be just as bad to haul off and take Gal over to Mid-State if the law didn't allow that kind of thing.

He picked up the phone and dialed quickly.

"District Attorney's office, Millie speaking."

"Millie, this is Ott Mobley. Let me speak to Warren." Warren Staples had been the D.A. for twenty-five years. He had steered Mobley through a couple of possible problems in the past. Only trouble was, he was one cantankerous, self-important mongrel. Mobley hated talking with him because he was unpredictable. No one ever knew where he stood with Staples. One minute he could be strict with the law, but if he saw some advantage – usually for himself – he could find a way around the law.

Staples came on the line. "What is it, Ott?"

Warren Staples was in an impatient mood today, Mobley clearly discerned. He would package it as tightly for the man as he could.

"Warren, I need your opinion on the involuntary commitment of a mentally unstable person,"

"How old is this person?"

"Say, early twenties."

"Any relatives in the picture?"

"None."

"Is he or she a danger to self or to others?"

"I believe both."

"Any bizarre behavior?"

"Yep."

"Mid-State is just down the road, Ott. You'll be doing the person and the community a service, my man. Anything else?"

"I just pick her up and take her down there? And they'll take her?"

"Call Judge Satterfield first. Tell him what you told me, and ask him to sign an order of committal. Give him the name and other details. Don't call Judge Banks if you're in a hurry. He'll take a week to think it over. Satterfield will get right on it. Okay?"

It was obvious the conversation was over. In a way, it was better if Staples was in a hurry like this. No beating around the bush. You get it and go.

"Okay, got it. Thanks, Warren."

The telephone line clicked off before the word, "thanks."

The phone call to Judge Satterfield led to his requirement that a psychiatrist sign an affidavit affirming the patient's mental illness, and for that purpose the judge recommended a poker-playing buddy, Dr. Cal Holcomb, who, he was sure would be familiar with the Slaughter girl's situation.

Growing irritation plagued Mobley, but he made the next phone call promptly.

"Gal Slaughter? Of course I know of her," the doctor said. "I've never treated her, so don't hold me to anything."

Mobley had given thought as to how to word his request. "Would you say she could benefit from professional treatment, Doctor?" The Sheriff was hoping to find a way to solve the issue with as little trouble as possible.

"You and I both probably could, Mobley. I think she actually did well in public school."

"It's pretty well known that she's out there alone, kind of a loner and non-conformist, and a lot of folks think she could be a danger to herself or somebody else."

"I suppose the sudden, tragic loss of her parents could have had a traumatic effect on her."

"Would you sign an affidavit stating that she could benefit from professional psychiatric evaluation?"

"Evaluation? Sure, no problem there. I couldn't go so far as to say commitment was needed, but evaluation wouldn't hurt. By the way, contact Vernon Blanchard at the State Hospital; they call him 'Doc' because he's up on all the latest treatments. He's a big believer in *parens patriae* care."

"In what?"

"It means the government is the ultimate parent in taking responsibility for the care of its citizens."

"Right! That's why I'm trying to help the girl," he lied. "I can come by in an hour if you can put the thing together."

"I'll leave it with my receptionist."

* * * * *

It was past five in the afternoon already and Colbert spun a quarter on the rickety kitchen table while Potter Riley spoke in covert tones into the telephone across the room. Excited and successful. That is what Colbert felt. His hands were calm, his head did not ache, he felt like he had passed a big test. He had accomplished much, and the old man would be pleased. Maybe even pleased enough at Colbert's plan to throw in a bonus. Another day or so and he would spring a trap that would show him to be a regular genius.

He had seen Adam out at the girl's place, watched them talk before heading toward the barn. He had seen her handle a rake and later a hoe. Her hands seemed strong enough to wield a hoe pretty fast and furious. Adam was so absorbed with the gal that he would never know what hit him. The Sheriff would find him in the barn with his skull split open, and blood on the girl's work gloves, hoe handle, barn door, and even on her own hands if his plan worked the way he expected. All he had to do was to dribble some blood on the front door knob and screen door handle, then make a racket that would wake her up and send her running in the dark toward the barn. No jury in the world would suspect she was set up. Especially with a bona fide preacher testifying she was out-of-her-gourd crazy. He just had to act before the preacher could have her sent off to some asylum.

He stopped playing with the coin. What was taking Riley so long? The man acted like it was more important to be talking with somebody on the phone than with him. He whispered and grinned like he was the one with a great trap about to spring. Colbert could hardly wait to tell the old pig what he was going to do. And yet Riley was treating him as though his presence was completely irrelevant. He was getting a little frustrated, waiting. His irritation began to surface and he decided not to squelch it.

With a show of his impatience, Colbert stood abruptly and pushed the chair back noisily on the rough hardwood floor. He shoved the coin in his pocket.

"Riley, I can't wait around all night. I'm leaving," he

announced.

He thrust the chair under the edge of the table and walked to the door. The fact that Riley still was not ending his conversation ticked Colbert off even more. With his hand on the door knob, he turned and glanced at the man. The grin was gone, replaced by an angry red scowl. Riley's eyes were glaring at him and his mouth had stopped working. Colbert was satisfied he had got the man's attention. Maybe now they could have a little conversation that would prove Colbert's worth, and shut off the old man's grousing, ungrateful demands on him.

He waited, expecting Riley to hang up the phone and demand he come back. When a couple of seconds passed and Riley only muttered something into the phone without breaking his stare, Colbert decided to push a little further. He was tired of being used, abused and ignored. To heck with Riley!

Colbert opened the door and slammed it behind him. He strode across the front porch and stepped onto the dirt yard with determination, half expecting the door to open again and to hear Riley bellow some furious demand. When that did not happen, he got in his truck and roared off. In the seconds that passed from the house to his truck he had made up his mind to act without Riley's knowledge or input, He would go back to the house and find out what Adam was up to. Maybe he could come up with a way to lure him out to the girl's farm tonight. If not, he could do the deed wherever necessary and haul the body out there. It was time for action, with or without old man Riley's involvement.

CHAPTER NINE

Adam had just come from the bathroom after bathing off the grime of auto repair work. His mother was due in from work any moment and Adam wanted to go over to Pastor Moncus' house for a little talk. He wanted to find out what Colbert was up to and convince Moncus not to take the man's accusations seriously. The telephone rang and he picked it up.

It was Colbert.

"Adam, you're just who I wanted to speak with."

"Yeah? What's up?"

"Your Mama's not around, is she?"

"No."

"Good! Don't mention anything to her if you see her, but I need your help. I've got her a little surprise and I need you to help me get it in the truck."

"A surprise? What've you got?"

"Just a surprise. Now, here's what I need you to do."

"Look, Ray Lee, I've got plans for tonight. Why don't we make it some other time?" Adam really wanted nothing to do with Colbert.

"No, now, Adam. This is important, and it won't take long. We can get it in the truck and you can go about your business."

Adam shook his head. "What is it?"

"Meet me out at Cooley's old farm on County Line Road. I've dug up an apple tree and want to plant it in the yard for your Mama. You know how much she loves apples."

"I've just taken a bath, Ray Lee, and I don't want to get sweaty again." If Ray Lee was actually treating his wife like he loved her, couldn't he find somebody else to help him load up his surprise?

"I'm telling you, it won't take hardly a minute or two. No way will you get sweaty. Just come on out here and let's get it done. Can't you do something nice for your mother this one time? She's got a birthday coming up next month."

"It'll be fully dark before I can get out there. Can't we do this tomorrow?"

"Look, I've spent an hour digging this thing up and if I don't move it tonight the roots will dry out. I've come all the way to the crossroads to call you for help. Come on, Adam. I'll have my headlights on the tree so we can see what we're doing. It won't take any time."

He took a deep breath and gave in. He could stand being around the man for a minute or two. "What part of Cooley's farm?"

"There's a little creek on the north end and a turn-off before the fence line. Pull right back there in those trees. I'll be waiting."

Adam hung up. He would rather do just about anything than help Ray Lee Colbert, the man who was scheming to send Maisie to an insane asylum. The only way he could do this favor was to get out there, help him load the tree up, keep his mouth shut and leave. He had nothing good or friendly to say to him. No off-hand comments about how heavy the tree is or what a good idea it is to get it for his mother, nothing.

He pulled on his glove, ran a comb through his hair and grabbed his car key. On the way out the front door, he switched on the front porch light for his mother. She had almost tripped on the stairs a week or so ago.

* * * * *

Ray Lee Colbert steered his truck off the paved road onto the narrow trail behind Cooley's farm, followed it about one hundred yards and turned the vehicle around so as to direct his headlights toward the approach. That would prevent Adam from immediately seeing there was no tree, and give Colbert the chance to stand behind the beams of light with the hoe he had taken from Gal's barn.

Darkness had fully descended on the grove, and a dirge composed of crickets and frogs rose from the creek. No more than five minutes passed before Colbert heard the sound of an approaching car. He switched on his high beams and flooded the trail with light. The vehicle coming from the north slowed almost to a stop and turned slowly onto the trail. The car had its high beams on as well. Colbert could imagine Adam stubbornly refusing to lower them or switch to parking lights. If he had to have high beams in his face, apparently he was determined to give like kind again. That was okay. If he wanted to play a little game, it would make the job Colbert came to do that much more pleasant. The game would soon be over, and it would be Colbert one, Adam nothing.

The car stopped thirty feet away and the driver side door opened and shut, but Adam seemed reluctant to come forward. Maybe he suspects something, thought Colbert. He anticipated that could happen. He leaned the hoe against the side of the truck and stepped forward into the light. He wore work gloves to enhance the appearance he had been out there laboring over a tree, but for the actual purpose of keeping his prints off the hoe handle.

"Come on, Adam!" he called, pointing with his thumb to the darkness behind him. "The tree's right over here. Let's get this over with." He turned as if to go back to work, but waited for Adam to come forward. He held a gloved hand to his brow to shield his eyes from part of the light. "Hurry up! I thought you had someplace to go."

Finally, he saw movement in the dark nearer the front of the car, and was about to return to get the hoe.

"Ray Lee!" The voice was a warning.

"Huh?"

The blast from the shotgun tore into his knees and Colbert fell, bleeding. He cried out in pain, and Potter Riley stepped into the light, a shotgun angled toward the ground between them.

Colbert gasped in the midst of hyperventilating. He grimaced and squinted to see better. "Riley?" he shouted.

Riley broke open the breach, pulled a spent shell from the chamber, fished in his pants pocket and brought out another. "That's right, Colbert."

"Why, Riley?" he yelled. "Why?"

Riley thumbed the second shell into the chamber and jerked the weapon upward enough to snap the barrel closed. "You crossed the line, Colbert. You don't talk to me that way and get by with it. Who do you think you are?"

"I'm sorry, Potter. Don't kill me, please!" He screamed.

"Yeah, now that's more like it, Colbert." He lifted the weapon higher. "Only you're just a little too late." The second blast tore up the ground around Colbert and blew out the headlamp nearest him. Colbert pitched over and jerked a couple of times before falling still. Smoke from the gun swirled in the light. The crickets and frogs were silent.

At that moment, another car approached from the north and braked suddenly before swinging in a quick arc onto the trail. The headlights illuminated the entire scene, as Potter Riley turned fully into the beam.

* * * * *

As he approached the turn-off, Adam saw lights flicker and blare through the black tangle of trees, and as he braked hard he heard a blast. He swung right, thinking his car backfired, and swerved onto the narrow trail before coming to a sliding stop. When he slammed on his brakes he saw old man Riley standing in the headlights of one car, holding a shotgun, and what looked like Colbert lying on the ground in front of a truck with one headlight on. Fear swept through him at the realization of what he was seeing.

Before he could jam the transmission into reverse, Riley threw open the breach of the shotgun and scrambled to find another shell, apparently for a single-shot weapon. Adam jammed the shifter into reverse gear and gunned the car backwards, all the while keeping his eyes fixed on the old man. Riley found a shell and managed to get it into the weapon. The barrel came up and Adam instinctively got himself as low in the seat as he could. His tires were spinning. He let off the clutch slightly until the tires gripped, opened his door and ducked his head out to see where he was going backward.

Simultaneously with the report of the gun, the passenger side of his windshield became a mosaic of concentric cracks around half a dozen tiny holes. Somehow, he was able to steer the careening car onto the roadway.

His back tires broke free of the wet dirt and squalled as they hit pavement. He forced the wheel in an arc that pointed his car north again, and ground first gear before the car could stop. Again, the tires protested violently as he slammed his door, floored the accelerator and got one more glance of old man Riley running toward the road before his tires caught and sent him roaring away.

His only thought was to get away as fast and as far as he could before the old man could get his car out and chase him. He was maybe half a mile away when he looked back and saw Riley's car bound onto the road backwards and gyrate through the motions of orienting itself in his direction. He had a couple of miles before reaching an intersection that would give him a chance to lose Riley. Trouble was, this was a straight road and a rebuilt 1936 Chevrolet could not last long against the new car he saw Riley was driving. He had only one chance.

Adam switched off his lights, trusting that he would be able to see the road well enough to keep off the low shoulders and stay away from any car he might encounter on this desolate stretch of county highway. With no rearview mirror, he was forced to turn around to check out the back window for the position of Riley's car. The headlights were still about half a mile back, so the old man had not hit his top speed yet. Adam had to act fast. He let off the accelerator, realizing he could not risk being seen braking, and watched for any place he could swerve off the road. His eyes gradually adjusted to the darkness and he saw a field and what appeared to be a stand of corn just ahead. The ground was just moist enough to avoid dust and the shoulder just near enough to the same elevation as the road that he would not risk a rollover. With another look backward, and a quick scan ahead, he picked an angle that would take him into the flat field toward a backdrop of trees a few yards beyond. His hope was that the field would be level enough and he could coast far enough without bouncing dangerously to make the tree line before Riley caught up and passed.

He made his move with a slight angle off the road and a tight grip on the wheel. He had slowed to maybe thirty miles per hour as he hit the grassy shoulder. The car swerved wildly, but he managed to steer it into the shadows of what now proved to be corn. The urge to touch the brakes was powerful, as the car bounded and bounced. Instead, he downshifted to second gear and the car slowed dramatically as the engine revved high.

The ground elevated a bit as he hit the corn stalks, and it bottomed out on the furrows, but continued at a fast clip – slow for normal driving, but fast for the irregular surface. He looked back again. Corn stalks fled past the side window, not tall enough to hide his roof from the road completely, but dense enough to forbid any sight other than a lucky glimpse down a makeshift path of prematurely harvested stalks.

Feeling more confident as he progressed into the field, Adam accelerated a bit to put more distance between himself and the road, but not enough to raise the noise level of the engine. The ground level began to decline, so he took his foot off the accelerator again, switched off the engine completely and shifted into neutral as he steered slightly to his right. Gradually, the car coasted to a stop.

He sat in silence daring not to open the door because of the dome light. After a few moments, he pulled himself out the open window and stood on the ground, motionless and calming his erratic breathing enough to hear any noise that might indicate he had been caught. No breeze moved amid the stalks. No lights made any glow over the direction of the road. Only his car ticked and sighed with settling.

He picked his way carefully along the path his car had come, far enough along its destructive course to see the point at which he had entered the field. In the dim, moonless night he saw nothing except corn stalks and tree shapes. Nothing moved. He had eluded Riley. At least until and if the man might realize he had been tricked, and might backtrack to find a possible escape route. Certainly he could not risk remaining here as long as daylight. He had to move quickly, decide whether he could drive away or had to leave his car behind.

He returned to the car, used his hand to examine the hood and headlamps. Small holes and dents peppered the hood. A parking light lens was broken. The tires had not been damaged. He raised the hood and, daring not to touch the hot radiator, settled for listening and smelling for leaking water, again without discovering a problem. He pressed the hood closed again with as little noise as possible and climbed back through the window. He engaged the starter and was glad to hear the engine crank without hesitation.

As he moved the car slowly away, he came to the realization of what had just happened. Potter Riley had just shot Ray Lee Colbert and tried to shoot him. Colbert was probably dead. Should he risk going back to check him? Riley did not appear concerned that he had not finished the deed. The body Adam saw was completely still and Riley seemed completely unhurried in the moment before reacting to Adam's arrival.

Nevertheless, Adam could not just drive away, He had never liked Colbert, but if the man was still alive Adam had to do something to help him. He would not be able to live with himself if he later learned he left the man bleeding with life still in him.

Against all his urges to distance himself from the scene, Adam drove slowly out of the corn field and onto the road toward the Cooley farm. He switched on his lights. He had to do it, so he might as well go into whatever awaited with eyes wide open and a clear path ahead.

CHAPTER TEN

Dawn was nearing, Adam knew, because the interminable darkness was gradually faltering. Sleep had completely evaded him after he returned to the cornfield – the only place he felt he could go and not be spotted immediately. He would eventually go to the old cabin where his father used to go to fish, according to his mother. But before that, he had to speak to Maisie, to make sure she knew he was not guilty of the murder, and to urge her once more to be watchful for someone trying to have her committed, even though the instigator of that plan was now dead.

Fear had grown in Adam's chest since the events of the night before. He had driven back to check on Colbert; he did not need a medical degree to know the man was dead, so he did not stay long. Seeing Colbert's body and passing the patrol car on his way north again sparked the fear that had been a mere ember before. His situation was dire.

Potter Riley was closely enough aligned with the Sheriff, Ott Mobley, that it was highly likely the old man stood in less danger of being accused of the crime than he, Adam, did. After all, to Riley, Colbert was a faithful employee; to Adam, he was a thorn and a source of constant contention. Riley knew or eventually figured out it was Adam who had driven upon the scene. After all, how many people among those who knew Colbert drove older model cars around Odino, Georgia? On top of that, he had no one to stand for him. Anyone to whom Adam might be able to tell his own side of the story was either on Riley's payroll or prone to suspect that the rebel boy, school dropout, who wore one black glove, and who despised his stepfather, would be the killer. In his eyes, the deck was stacked against him.

A chill had settled on the hour before dawn, and Adam leaned against the front fender of his car, his arms crossed against his chest to stave off some of the cold. He watched the eastern horizon with anticipation. With sunup Maisie would be awake, and he would risk driving the short distance to her farm. He would need to be alert, in case it had become known to the Sheriff that he had been visiting Gal. No doubt, his mother had already been visited, assuming the patrol car he saw last night was en route to check out a report from Potter Riley.

He shook his head briskly, not so much for the cold as for the thoughts threatening to overtake his temporary calm. Thoughts of never seeing Maisie again, of being thrown into prison for something he did not do, of thereafter living out his father's fate – as he had once heard, a river only flows from its headwaters.

Where was the future he had hoped would find him and shine upon him? Just as he was cresting a hill from where he might get a glimpse of his destiny, there lay a cliff, beyond which was certain destruction.

Yes, he had been foolish enough to think, to hope, Maisie might be a part of a good turn in the road. And, truth be known, inside him was a glimmer that a word from her, a last word, as it were, might be a life-giving breath for his dying hope.

Finally, a cloud on the horizon thinned enough to allow a hint of dawn. That was enough. He jumped to his car, cranked it and made his way back to the road. Rather than drive right up to her farm and have only one way of escape in the event something happened, he would find a place nearby to hide his car and walk through the woods.

* * * * *

Maisie washed dishes in a pan set in the sink, the kitchen light on overhead. The sun would be up in another hour or so. She had boiled a mess of green beans with a piece of ham and baked a pan of cornbread the night before. Although she could talk herself out of eating, Maisie felt it was important, now that her parents were gone, to neglect no opportunity to live life as she might if she had others around her to care for. A husband, a younger brother, an ailing parent at home or a neighbor in need – these were not to be neglected by Loretta Slaughter. Maisie's mother always had food ready to warm up in case a neighbor or family member dropped by.

When she set the wet dishes into a rack on the sink counter to dry, she wiped her hands on the dish towel and slipped onto the porch where her Daddy's old wooden rocker waited next to the metal chairs. She sat and watched the sky over the trees as the coming sun began to lighten it. A breeze caressed her and gave her limbs a sense of ease. She commenced rocking slightly, keeping time with the pulse of her heart, that seemed to permeate her consciousness..

Gradually, a melody rose in her throat and she sang a hymn. Her eyes closed and she envisioned the face of the Almighty, sitting on the great white throne, smiling at her. She knew the smile was too similar to her father's smile, but she would not consciously change it to something else. It was what it was, and she knew she was not worshiping her earthly father, who had been a God-worshipper all his life and was, without question, in the very presence of the Almighty now. No, she knew she was worshipping the only God and Father, the God of Abraham, Isaac and Jacob, the Father who had given up His Son for all. Whatever the face looked like, her imagination could never capture the majesty anyway. So she focused all her love and devotion to Him, the best way she knew to do that.

Her voice rose in volume and beauty so that it almost sounded angelic. And did she not hear angels accompanying her? The sound seemed to be joined by a choir of multitudes. She did not even care to wipe the tears of joy from her eyes, so caught up was she in her praise to Him.

Had anyone else felt the presence of God so closely? She presumed the great apostles of the faith had, and members of the first church in Jerusalem and Asia Minor. Why was it that when she spoke of the beautiful presence of the living God to people in the churches she had visited, they all looked at her blankly and nodded vacant assent before finding an excuse to walk away? She, if she had encountered someone who remarked about such wonder, would have taken the occasion to jump with joy and hug that person, for she would have found someone with whom she could relate. As it was, life was lonely in man's churches. Everyone she met in them seemed to worship God at a distance, or to treat it as a formality. How she longed for the affinity of one like-minded person!

After a while, the Spirit of God urged her to go inside and take up again the task of cleaning. Reluctantly, she obeyed. She dampened a mop and danced with it about the living room floor. On moving to the kitchen, she heard a light tapping on the front door. Setting her mop aside, she hurried to open it. To her surprise, there stood Adam Woods, looking disheveled and bothered.

* * * * *

Adam had walked a few hundred yards through the woods along the road. Now he stood on Maisie's porch to see if she was awakened by his knock. When he heard footsteps, he breathed a sigh of relief.

"Adam, what in the world have you been doing?" Maisie opened the screen and stepped onto the porch, placing a hand on his shoulder in a sisterly way.

"I need to talk to you, Maisie. Can you sit with me out here for a few minutes?"

"Of course! Is anything wrong?" She pulled her father's rocker closer to the metal chairs and gestured for Adam to sit.

"You'll probably hear," Adam began as he sat, "that I killed a man."

When Maisie gasped, he quickly added, "But it's not true, Maisie."

"Who? And what happened?" The concern on her face only intensified his urgency to tell her.

"I was meeting my stepfather last night out by the old Cooley farm a couple of miles from here, and when I drove up, I saw Potter Riley with a shotgun, and my stepfather lying on the ground."

"Oh, no! Had they fought?"

"I don't know. As soon as I stopped, old man Riley tried to shoot me, but I was able to get away."

"He didn't hurt you, did he? Did you go to the Sheriff?"

"Maisie, the Sheriff is so close to Potter Riley, if one sneezes, the other wipes his nose."

"So what did you do? And how do you know your stepfather was dead?"

Adam spent the next few minutes giving her all the details of checking Colbert's body and spending the night in a corn field. All the while, she listened intently. She seemed to accept his supposition that he would be blamed.

"What will you do, Adam?" Was that moisture in her eyes, he wondered.

"My father had a place down on the Ocmulgee River, where he would spend a week at the time fishing, and whatever else he did. I know how to get there. I'll stay there as long as I can."

She leaned toward him. "Adam, you've never known God have you?"

He shook his head. "But Maisie, I need to tell you. Don't be careless just because Colbert is dead. He might have already talked with the Sheriff – he or the preacher – and they may still be trying to make out that you're crazy."

"Adam, you're evading. Will you listen to me?"

"Okay, but you've got to listen to me, too."

"No matter what the circumstances look like, Adam, you've got to turn your life over to Jesus. We were born sinners and God sent Jesus to change us. Life will always be hopeless without Him."

"Okay."

"Does 'okay' mean you will?"

"It means I'll try. I'll think about it."

"Adam, you're my friend. Do you remember, I said I might tell you what else the Holy Spirit showed me about you?"

"Of course."

"He said, you belong to God."

Adam blanched. He sat forward in the rocker and looked

at her intently without speaking.

"He said you will swim where your father waded, and you will find footing where he sank. Do not be afraid of the river."

Stunned a second time, the blood that rushed from his face now rose in his neck until it flushed his cheeks. Still, he did not speak, his eyes holding fast to hers.

"Do you understand, Adam?"

He blinked and looked away quickly. Rising to his feet, he took a step away, trying to process what she said, as well as the fact that God had apparently spoken it to her. The evidence that God was intimately aware of him, though the thought of it was something he would, a moment before, have possibly agreed was true, now hit him like a splash of water in the face. It had the effect of placing God in the midst of his real circumstances, not just in a theoretical role.

Maisie stood also and stepped closer. She placed a hand on his shoulder again. "You've been through a lot, Adam. Don't go through it alone. God will go with you if you will let Him."

He nodded. The last thing he wanted was to remain alone, but he could not tell her that he wanted her to go through the difficulties with him. And he knew she was right. From the moment she spoke God's words to him, he knew that what he really needed was God Himself. He just did not know what to do about it.

A noise near the road distracted him. Maisie saw it first.

"Adam, the Sheriff's car is turning down the drive."

He saw it as she spoke, through the trees a white sedan with a glint of red on its roof, just turning off the road. The morning light was still dim enough in the shadow of the trees to obscure visibility. He turned to her wanting to say a hundred things to her, but knowing he could not express them.

"Why don't you go inside?" she said. "I'll see what's up."

He slipped inside, closed the door and moved to the curtained window to see the car pull slowly out of the trees onto the grassy yard in front of the house and come to a stop beside her red truck. The door opened and a man of medium height stepped out. He recognized him as Sheriff Mobley.

Maisie walked to the edge of the porch and placed a hand on the support post. "Good morning, Sheriff," he heard her say.

"Miss Slaughter?" He walked toward her holding a folded paper. He stopped five or six feet away and cocked his western hat slightly back on his head. "Ma'am, I have an order from Judge Horace Satterfield remanding you to the State Hospital in Mooresville for evaluation."

Adam flinched. The unthinkable had happened. He immediately grabbed the front door knob and pushed his way onto the porch, slamming the screen door behind him. The Sheriff turned his full attention to Adam.

"Are you Mister Woods, Adam Woods?"

"I am," he snapped. He pointed at the officer. "The thing you have in your hand is bogus, Sheriff! Maisie is smarter and a better person than you and that judge will ever be."

"Well, I didn't expect to find a murderer and a crazy gal at the same time, but you're under arrest, Mister Woods." He took a step forward before Maisie's voice split the air.

"Sheriff!" Her hand shot out as if to stop him. "'I know you,' says the Lord. 'I know you when you take money to make a mockery of justice.'" The Sheriff, obviously startled, stopped in his tracks and riveted his stare upon Maisie. "'I know you when you commit adultery in the very office you occupy. And I know you when you receive false accusations of murder.'"

Maisie showed no evidence of being shocked by what she said, nor any hesitance in speaking it. "'You think you serve because of your ability or your own strength, but you serve at My pleasure,' says the Lord. 'I lift up and I pull down,' says God. 'Get your house in order.'"

The Sheriff's eyes were wide. He stood as a statue and shook visibly. He neither made a move toward either person on the porch nor took his eyes off Maisie. Adam saw the man as though he stepped onto a high voltage wire, shaking without ability to move. The lawman remained as he was for perhaps half a minute before the electrifying effect of the words appeared to relent.

Slowly, the Sheriff turned his eyes toward the ground. "I haven't seen either of you," he said. "Go away until all this blows over." He stuffed the paper in his pocket and turned slowly away. Adam's mouth dropped open. The Sheriff walked toward his patrol car. He appeared to be a beaten man.

"Sheriff," said Maisie, softly. He stopped and turned to her, his eyes red and glistening. "Let me do a few things in the house and I will go with you," she said. He appeared as shocked at this as he had before. His mouth moved but he said nothing.

"No," said Adam, stepping toward her. "Maisie, he said he would let us go."

"I know, but I've had people saying things like that about me for as long as I can remember. I'll clear my name, Adam. If they want to evaluate me, I'll go and let them see for themselves I'm sane."

"I'll go with you, then."

"Adam, from what you've told me, your life is in danger here. You should go away like the Sheriff says, until it all blows over. Besides, wherever I go, I go with God. You need time to hear God's voice, and you won't be able to if you stay here. You'll be looking over your shoulder every minute."

Now it was Adam's turn to stand in silence.

"It's okay," added Maisie, "he said this was just for evaluation. Isn't that right, Sheriff?"

The Sheriff stared blankly. Nevertheless, he nodded, apparently completely unhinged and growing more so with each moment.

Maisie stepped to Adam and took his hand in hers. "Trust me, Adam. It's not just your life that's in danger. Your very soul is at stake. I have nothing to fear from those who can only harm the body and do nothing to the soul. You go and do what is needed to draw near to God. No matter what happens to me, I will be near Him."

She hugged him.

"Now, please, go." Her eyes directed his attention into the woods.

"It had better be just an evaluation," he said softly to her. "Or I will come after you."

"Then you will come with God." She smiled and his heart fluttered. "Won't you?"

He smiled back at her and, as if impulsively, kissed her on the cheek.

"Yes." He nodded and locked his eyes with hers. "I will."

CHAPTER ELEVEN

Maisie took the time to set her cat outside the back door. He was a good mouser and could fend for himself very well outside. She made sure all windows were tightened down, the bed made and the clothes brought in from the line. She would have to postpone buying a calf or two, but maybe not for long. She locked her truck doors and the front door to her house. Even if they kept her at this hospital for as long as a week, her place would be fine when she returned.

In the patrol car, she turned in the back seat so she could see her new friend – actually, her only human friend – sitting on the edge of her porch, apparently very disheartened but refusing to leave until she had. She leaned against the back of the seat not to lose sight of him, though he blurred through her tears. She waved at him, knowing it might be the last time she would see Adam.

The car swept around the corner of the house to make a loop through the back yard. When it completed the circuit to the dirt drive, Adam stood at the side of the house. He moved closer and briefly placed his hand against the side window. As the car crept cautiously past, Maisie held her hand at the same place on the window. For a split second, she felt as if glass did not separate them, an infinitesimal moment of connection. Then Adam's hand was gone, and his image, receding into the background.

The car bounced up the hill and her farmhouse disappeared behind the trees.

She fell back into the seat hurt and distressed. Why had all this happened? Adam said they thought she was crazy. Because she danced in the night? The thought was too bizarre to accept. She began to pray silently.

What if, her mind suggested to her, this is not really just an evaluation, but a trick? Or what if the people evaluating me come to the conclusion I'm insane? What if this is the last time I see my farm? Why did I agree to submit to this? Yes, it seemed to be the right thing to do. But will the Sheriff still come back for him? Dear God! Be with me. And be with my friend Adam.

Her heart felt grief, much like the deep and overwhelming grief she had endured when her mother and father died. And it was brought on by her neighbors, who were supposed to love her as she loved them. She had done nothing wrong that she could identify, but she was being put on trial, in a sense, for the crime of loving God with all her heart, mind, soul and strength. For worshipping Him outside the dictates of tradition.

Maisie buried her head in her hands and wept.

God, give me more of Your grace. I believe I will need it dearly.

* * * * *

Adam drove southward from Maisie's farm, still astounded at what had happened. He was numb with questioning how she knew what God wanted to say to the Sheriff, as well as what she said He had told her about Adam. He could not very well question whether she had quoted God, because she related things she could not have known otherwise. The Sheriff denied nothing, and in fact, looked as if he had been caught red-handed. What, other than that kind of hard truth, could have made him wilt the way he did and totally give up the mission he had been sent on? As for her revelation about himself, he was stunned. The overwhelming conclusion, in Adam's mind, was that God is real and He talks to Maisie.

Despite Maisie's nearness to God, Adam was worried about her. His heart and mind felt heavier and heavier, as though he had lost her. Why had he let her go? She did not need to prove her sanity. She, the sanest person he knew? And why should she have to endure some senseless evaluation by a shrink from the state? He should have stayed and persuaded her not to be concerned about what people think. Surely the preacher, Moncus, could be convinced that she worshipped God, and not devils. But all his arguments eventually came back to the same place: Potter Riley intended to kill him.

As it was, there seemed to be no way to go back to Odino soon. He would have to hide away until the truth somehow came out. If the Sheriff changed his mind and came after him, Adam would have to figure out a way to convince a jury that Potter Riley was the real killer. If Potter Riley found him, he would have to fight or die.

But two big concerns were uppermost to him now: he had to find a way to keep track of Maisie's hospital evaluation. He absolutely meant what he said. If they did not release her, he would go after her and somehow get her out. And somehow he would keep the rest of his promise to her: that he would come with God.

With that recollection, he prayed silently. Help, God. I don't know how to begin knowing you or how to follow Jesus. I don't know how to find out about Maisie's evaluation. Will You help me?

His prayer was brief and did not feel very holy. But somehow, he believed that God had heard it.

* * * * *

Sheriff Ott Mobley stared at the road ahead without seeing detail. A concrete block seemed to occupy his midsection ever since Gal said what she did. One moment he wanted to throw up; next minute he wanted to turn around and give up, never to see Potter Riley and never to wear the Sheriff's uniform again. He had been a fool in so many ways, not the least of which was in his taking money from Riley. He had been raised better. He knew better. He owed better to his wife than what he had given her over the years. But while the office of Sheriff gave him all the notoriety he currently wanted, it gave him little of the monetary reward he had hoped to come his way. Thus, he had justified taking money on the side. It had allowed him to drive a better car than he could have otherwise afforded, own a nice fishing boat and a pretty piece of hunting land that might be worth a fortune some day.

The biggest way he had played the fool was in thinking he could fool God. What had happened to his life to take him so far away from God? As a kid, he knew God was real. He had even made a confession of faith in Jesus Christ. But somehow, he had drifted away - so far away that he supposed God had quit paying attention. Inside, Ott Mobley shook with fear that God had not only *not* been fooled, but He had called him out on his sins.

Every mile he drove, when his eyes strayed to the rearview mirror and saw the young woman in the back seat, alternately wiping her red eyes and muttering soft prayers, he felt the concrete block grow in his midsection. What he was doing just did not feel right. But he kept telling himself, Okay, this is just an evaluation; if there's really nothing wrong with her, she'll be back in a few days. He might even suggest that the administrator call his office when he's finished with the tests or whatever. Bringing her back home would at least help him feel a little better about all of this.

On the other hand, he wondered if he would really ever feel better.

CHAPTER TWELVE

Maisie sat on a hard metal stool opposite a tall counter, behind which sat a nurse of about fifty. All she could see over the top of the counter was a starched white cap pinned to the back of the woman's grayish brown hair. A sign fixed to the front of the counter read, "ADMISSIONS." Sheriff Mobley had gone inside an office behind the nurse with a very tall man wearing a starched white jacket. She had thought at one point the Sheriff might turn around before reaching the hospital and take her home. He seemed to be under some heavy conviction. Several times, she saw him staring at her in the rearview mirror. Each time, he looked away with apparent shame, seemingly unable to fix her with his troubled eyes. Once inside the admissions area, he spoke softly to the nurse. She heard him say the word, "evaluation," and repeat it with emphasis as the nurse walked into the office beyond.

Maisie wore a plain white blouse over a full, blue cotton skirt, a grey sweater folded in her lap, from which she was nervously picking tiny balls of loose wool. She was praying under her breath when the door to the office opened and the man in the white jacket came out walking briskly and barged through the opening in the counter front to come to an abrupt halt a few feet away from her. The Sheriff followed close behind him.

"Doc Blanchard, that's Miss Slaughter," said the Sheriff catching up to the man and gesturing toward Maisie.

Blanchard merely stood and stared at Maisie. She raised her head and returned his gaze. Her eyes were red and she looked very tired. After a moment, she returned her attention to removing fuzz from her sweater. Blanchard's eyes studied her coldly, fastening on her hands. He lifted a clipboard and wrote quickly on a sheet of paper.

"What is her first name?" he asked.

"Uh, it's Maisie," he said, and turned to her. "Isn't that right, Miss Slaughter?" His voice was conciliatory.

"It's Amaize," she answered. "My parents spelled it A-M-A-I-Z-E."

"How old?"asked Blanchard without taking his eyes from the chart.

The Sheriff looked to her.

"Twenty," she said. Then she added, locking her eyes on Blanchard. "As in twenty thousand, the amount of money someone stole from the hospital's general account."

For a moment, no one spoke. The nurse leaned over the counter to stare, and Sheriff Mobley raised his eyebrows toward Blanchard, who kept his eyes fixed on Maisie.

"Does she often spout nonsense?" asked Blanchard, turning to him.

Mobley shrugged, red-faced.

"Thank you very much, Sheriff. We will take it from here." Blanchard extended his hand to the Sheriff, who shook it tentatively.

"As I mentioned, Doc, I don't think she's – "

Blanchard interrupted with a mechanical smile. "We'll determine that, Sheriff, with a thorough evaluation."

"Well, you will call my office when you've finished the evaluation?" Mobley asked.

"You may call here next week and speak to Nurse Proctor if you like." He spoke louder, directing his attention to the nurse behind the admissions counter. "Nurse Proctor, you will speak to Sheriff Mobley if he calls, correct?"

"Yes sir," called the nurse, raising her head above the counter only high enough for Maisie to see her dispassionate eyes.

Sheriff Mobley, glanced at Maisie as if to speak, but quickly looked back at Blanchard, who only enfolded the clipboard in his arms and maintained a steady, officious expression that seemed to say, "We are finished."

Mobley looked from Blanchard to Maisie again, as if deciding whether to say more. Finally, he turned toward the foyer door and walked away. Before exiting, he turned to Maisie once more.

His eyes were moist and reddening.

"Miss Slaughter, I, uh..." He removed his cap. "Thank you for saying what you did."

Maisie smiled at the Sheriff and nodded.

When the door closed behind the Sheriff, Blanchard turned to his office again. As he passed the nurse's position he passed the clipboard to her and said, "Find her a nice jacket, Proctor."

"A jacket?" Nurse Proctor sounded surprised.

Blanchard stopped and stared at the nurse.'"Did you not understand, Nurse Proctor?" He spoke in a condescending tone.

"I thought you said 'a jacket,' Mister Blanchard," she replied.

"Then you understood me correctly," he snapped and strode into his office, closing the door promptly behind himself.

Nurse Proctor rose from her desk and looked across the narrow hall at Maisie.

"Miss," she said mechanically. "Would you mind coming with me? I'll introduce you one of our nurse matrons who will get you ready for your evaluation."

She came from behind the counter and extended her hand to Maisie, who smiled at her and, rising, took her hand. Maisie noticed that the nurse's hand was cold.

* * * *

Vernon Blanchard, the interim administrator of Mid-State Hospital, shook off the girl's frightening comment. It was virtually an accusation. She was not the first lunatic to show up at MSH with strange psychic ability. But fortunately, he had the means to deal with people like that. Perhaps it was good to know so soon that she was one of the freaks, so he could take care of her before anybody took her comments seriously.

He picked up the report he had been reading earlier and settled behind his desk, a very small desk for the administrator of one of the largest asylums in the world, to his way of thinking. The three large stacks on his desktop – one of patient files, one of staff assessments and requests, and the third, of studies detailing the latest techniques in patient treatment – virtually covered its usable surface. No question about it: the desk was inadequate for his needs and position. As soon as he was named permanent administrator, he would rectify the situation. In fact, the office, positioned at the massive and stately entrance to the MSH's main building, was still a bit modest and might need some renovation.

He had been named interim administrator a year earlier, after the death of MSH's beloved iconic leader, H. Paul Weston, M.D. The "M.D." after his predecessor's name was a thorn to Blanchard. Though he had long – even before Weston's passing – cultivated the image and persona of a doctor for himself, and encouraged the nickname he had given himself – that of "Doc" Blanchard – he had never even applied to med school, much less attended. A minor issue, in his mind. He was smart, well read, insightful and a very capable leader. Why could he not overshadow Weston's image in due order! To Blanchard's way of thinking, Weston was a lax administrator, who had let the reputation of the hospital fall into disrepair. Blanchard, on the other hand, considered himself a master of control, with unwavering attention to the needs of the facility. Popularity with staff and peers was nothing compared to the status awaiting the man who turned this hospital into the epitome of psychiatric care hospitals with cutting edge methods and efficiency.

Blanchard flipped through the report until he found where he had been reading earlier. He placed a finger on the page and read aloud to himself:

"...At the time of the first EEG, the patient manifested some of the behavior recorded in her October office visit, specifically, wringing of her hands, unintelligible muttering and peculiar jargon of speech. These manifested as she walked into the laboratory, but oddly enough, were not exhibited once recording commenced. When the second and third electro-encephalographic studies were made later in 1950, the patient presented, as she entered the EEG lab, significant increase and exaggeration of her earlier behavior manifestations..."

He moved his finger down the page and found the place he was searching for.

"...On February 8, 1948, Dr. R. Burson Munter performed a bilateral frontal lobotomy similar to the operation used by Freeman and Watts. Dr. Munter states that 'holes were drilled in the bone approximately 3cm. posterior to the edge of the orbit, and the frontal lobes were sectioned on each side by sweeping a blunted gespatula upward and downward in the white matter.' The frontal cortex was thus undercut.

"On March 20, 1948, approximately seven weeks after the lobotomy, the formerly thin, nervous woman with a halting gait, jaws champing, and a nervous picking at the skin who had been evaluated before the operation now presented herself as one who had gained weight, enjoyed healthy color, exhibited a casual manner and was even somewhat charming in her endeavor to cooperate with the hospital in having a subsequent EEG taken."

Blanchard closed the report, set it atop one of the stacks and leaned back in his chair. He had met Dr. Munter at a conference, heard him speak on the origins and successes of an improved procedure that required no drilling into the skull, using only a long, sharp ice-pick like tool, developed by the daring and bold neuropsychiatrist Dr. Walter Freeman, formerly of George Washington University Hospital. Opening his desk drawer, Blanchard retrieved a long flat, black case, unsnapped its cover and opened it. Against its black velvet interior were strapped a pair of long, shiny and sharp leucotomes. He had ordered the instruments from Europe months before, in the hope that he might enlist the aid of Dr. Munter in performing a lobotomy, or leucotomy as it was called in the more sophisticated hospitals. In the event Dr. Munter might be unavailable, Blanchard thought, what would prevent himself from performing the procedure at MSH? If such a step was called for, of course. He had read quite a bit and, in all honesty, he saw nothing so complicated about the procedure that a layman could not handle it easily, especially one who was very knowledgeable on the subject. In fact, Freeman had trained others in the procedure so that, within a short period, they could perform pre-frontal lobotomies as effectively as he could.

Successful leucotomies at MSH could mean a lot of publicity for the hospital. And it might even have the effect of catapulting him into arenas more suited to his skills and abilities. He needed one good, healthy subject to get things started and convince state medical authorities he could turn the affairs of MSH permanently around.

Blanchard smiled to himself. What good fortune that, just at the right time in his career, a backwoods Sheriff would dump in his lap a patient reported to be a danger to herself and her community, and that, at least on initial observation, manifested some of the classic signs of eligibility! How she happened to know about the temporarily misappropriated money was freakish, to be sure. But weird things happened with some of the mental cases at MSH. That was just one more good reason to make her the first lobotomy recipient on his watch. Perhaps he was only one evaluation away from securing the path to medical prominence.

* * * * *

Three hours later, Sheriff Mobley was in agony as he sat behind the closed door of his office. He had been the one to personally deliver, the night before, the tragic news to Charlotte Colbert that her husband had been murdered. He had also been the one to find her son, a supposed murderer, and let him go, risking retaliation by Potter Riley. He had been the one who had had to drive that beautiful young woman – who seemed to be as sane as anyone he had ever met – to an insane asylum to satisfy some needlessly worried preacher, and, in fact, into the hands of what at first glance appeared to be a certifiable zombie maker. Now, after all the weight that had been dumped on him, he got a telephone call from the state prison in Jameston saying Bonder Woods had been killed, and would the Sheriff notify the next of kin?

What had ever caused him to imagine the office of Sheriff would be a lucrative and easy stepping stone to higher political expectations? And what had ever caused him to think Potter Riley would be anything but trouble and tragedy? All of a sudden, the man's money and power meant very little to Ott Mobley. While Riley did not come right out and admit killing Colbert, Mobley knew enough to suspect he was the killer. Knowing that and doing nothing would make him an accessory to murder.

Mobley had a choice to make. Would he go out to the Woods place and tell Charlotte that, not only was her son the prime suspect in her husband's death, but her first husband had been murdered in prison – likely the same prison where her son would end up? Or would he tell her that he had reason to believe her son was not a killer, but that his life was probably in danger? Did he really have to do any of that? Couldn't he simply lay down his badge and disappear, so he would not have to face the barrel of Potter Riley's shotgun?

He knew the answer. If he chose to protect Riley while prosecuting Adam Woods, he would be Riley's lackey for the rest of the old man's miserable life.

If he found evidence of Potter Riley's guilt, and arrested him, he would be setting himself up to be murdered.

If he chose to run away, Riley would not rest until he had made an example of him.

All of the three scenarios had unsatisfactory endings. The only choice, if he wanted to retrieve what little might remain of his integrity, would be to do everything he could to protect Adam Woods and see that Potter Riley paid for his crimes. If he lost his life in the process, at least he would not leave his wife in shame.

Ott Mobley decided he had to reverse course and do what was right. After all, he had learned something earth-shattering: God was real and He had his number. The words spoken by the girl when he went to pick her up had cut him to the innermost parts of his soul. God was aware of him. For some reason, that fact was something that had not occurred to him in a very long time.

He did not know where Woods had gone. Charlotte most likely did not know, because she had asked him, when he came to report Colbert's death, if he had seen anything of her son. And that was before Adam knew that his life might be in danger. But he was sure the girl knew. If he needed to question Adam in private, while allowing him to remain in hiding, he would have to return to the State Hospital and question the girl first. But before that, he had some business to take care of.

He dialed Potter Riley's number. As soon as the man answered, Mobley spoke.

"All deals are off. I am no longer on your payroll. From now on, watch your step in this county. Do you hear me?"

"I hear you but I don't believe you."

"Believe me."

"You have a lapse of good sense, Mobley? Do you have any idea what – ?"

He hung up the telephone and stood. Now for the next thing.

CHAPTER THIRTEEN

The jacket Maisie wore made her arms cramp, pulled, as they were, across her midsection and bound in that position. But that was not the entire cause of her tears. She had begun crying the moment the matron, a kindly nurse named Caldwell, pulled the unbleached canvas jacket from the cabinet in the treatment room. The matron had called it a jacket when she gently coaxed her into it, with its incredibly long sleeves. But Maisie knew its purpose was not warmth and comfort. She had heard of the purpose of a straight jacket.

The nurse continued to speak gently, almost lovingly, presumably thinking Maisie was not so aware of reality that she would object to the instrument of torture if she was given it gently. But it had been deception. Maisie had read of men fighting against the confines of strait jackets, screaming and writhing themselves into total exhaustion, to no purpose, and ending up deeper into any mental oblivion they might have formerly possessed. The nurse had remained gentle to her, but it had been a lie from the beginning. More than the dread of wearing the straight jacket was the sudden grief at knowing she was being betrayed by a fellow human being to whom she had given her trust, and that she was given no credit for her clarity of heart and harmlessness.

"It's going to be all right, Honey," the matron, Nurse Caldwell, had cooed. Maisie had thought Nurse Caldwell was someone who cared, one she could share truth with.

"But when will I be evaluated?"

"Soon, Honey. Soon."

The nurse went about her routine with practiced focus.

Maisie's arms were pulled into a cross in front of her and the long sleeves were strapped and buckled behind her. Her tears quickly stained the front of the jacket. She looked at Nurse Caldwell through watery swells.

"Why do I have to wear – ?"

The nurse stopped her in mid-sentence.

"Mister Blanchard said – " She turned her eyes upward and halted at the sight of Maisie's face. Redness flooded her own cheeks and some feint realization passed before her eyes.

Maisie's lip quivered and tears rolled down from her beautiful wet lashes. She looked into the eyes of the nurse.

"Oh, don't do that, Honey," the matron whined. "I've got to do this."

The voice inside Maisie's heart was louder than that of Nurse Caldwell.

"Don't despair. I will be with you. Don't let fear or discouragement in. Stand strong and I will help you."

Maisie nodded to the voice. Nurse Caldwell took it to be understanding toward her task.

"There, there, Honey," said the matron, composing herself and giving comfort to Maisie with the loosening of a strap buckle by one hole. "I'll keep an eye on you, Dear. Soon, you'll be all better."

The matron led Maisie back to a ward, a long, dingy gray room filled with the sounds of patients muttering, crying and banging their limbs against hard surfaces. Bed after bed occupied by women, mostly old, gaunt-eyed and weary, some rocking back and forth in their habitual boredom, others still as portraits of the dead in their insulin–induced calm.

"After I give you some medicine, Honey, we'll get that ugly old jacket off of you and put you to bed, okay?"

Caldwell guided Maisie to the side of the bed, injected her hip, and, as Maisie began to relax and drowse, removed the straight jacket and eased her onto the bed. She quickly removed Maisie's clothing and wrapped her in a faded hospital gown. Then she eased her onto her back and strapped her into the bed.

* * * * *

Adam had got lost a couple of times, being confused by the

development of a new road. He had no idea of the time, but he knew it must be pretty near midnight. He drove slowly, watching for the dirt road on the right that led to the cabin. He had only been to the cabin once before, when he was about twelve years old, with his father's uncle, who was the only connection he had ever had with his father's family. The stay was supposed to have been a fishing trip. And it was, for the first day or two. When the old man learned he could buy whiskey at a bait store, the trip turned into a nightmare, with the old man raging at one thing and then another, throwing empty bottles in the river and shooting at them with a pistol, trying to cook fish in a raging bonfire. Adam had never wanted to come back to the cabin as long as the uncle was alive. After his death, he had toyed with the idea of leaving home and living in the cabin, especially after Colbert married his mother, but he had never taken the step until now.

Finally, he identified the road and made his turn, bouncing a couple of times as his tires hit washouts. Barely wider than a trail, the road was obviously seldom traveled. Mailboxes on leaning posts indicated that shapes barely visible through fleeting shafts of moonlight were actually cabins. When he got a glimpse of the river as the path bent southward to parallel the waterway, he breathed easier, confirmed in his hope he had found the right road. Some of the winding drives that veered off the road were overgrown, suggesting the cabins might be abandoned. He ventured down one driveway until he saw the cabin was not the one he remembered, then backed out to the narrow roadway again.

He stopped at a drive nearly grown over with briars. A rotted log lay across its entrance. That was it. He had forgotten his uncle dragging the log across the drive when they first got to the cabin before, to keep intruders away.

He moved the log and pulled the car onto the long winding trail to the cabin, his headlights illuminating a tunnel through the trees. A seam of tall weeds in the middle of two long unused tire ruts rustled and rubbed underneath his car. Puddles from a recent rain filled low spots and water dripped from low-hanging limbs. A low fog drifted among the trees and, in places, partially obscured the rough roadbed.

Someone would have to know exactly where this place was in order to find him. Adam knew the Sheriff would not be able to put off Potter Riley for long. The killer surely knew Adam had seen him. With or without the Sheriff's help, the old man would come looking. The advantage Adam had was that his mother was the only person who knew where he might be and how to get to the cabin. He had not taken the time to call her, but he would need to do that in the morning. Surely she would know about Ray Lee, and would not believe the lie that Adam had been his killer. At that moment, the thought struck him that his mother was potentially in danger. He would need to warn her about Potter Riley. And with that, he knew he would appeal to her to also come down to the cabin until something happened to convince people who the real killer was.

The path emerged from the trees into an opening with the cabin on the left, merely a dark angular shape amid tree limbs that stood against a blackish blue sky and a dark chasm that was the Ocmulgee River. He parked his car, pulled a flashlight from the dashboard and made his way toward the cabin's front door. He had come with almost nothing that he needed. No clothes, food or money enough to buy anything. Yet he hoped he would find fishing gear inside with which he could at least obtain food. But for now, he would settle for a place to get a decent night's sleep. If need be, he could spend the night in the front seat of that big old Chevy. He had done that before.

He played his flashlight beam across the front of the structure. The graying, unpainted lap siding and rusting metal roof had not changed. He half expected the structure to be falling down, but the cabin looked as though it had weathered well. Large limbs lay around the yard as evidence of storms. One lay against the covered front porch, its brown pine needles having shed themselves onto the warped flooring and blended with the layer of needles carpeting the yard below. Tall, rangy weeds had found their way through the needle carpet. On the river side of the yard, about forty feet from the porch, was a cutting table with a rusted pail overturned beside it. It was the surface his father used for cleaning fish, he knew.

Beyond the table stood a row of high hedges that obscured sight of the river, except for a three-foot opening where the path ran down to an old dock. He could not see the dock over the berm, but he knew it was there. He recalled having tied the old flatboat there, which meant it was probably long swamped in the shallows.

Adam stepped over the limb by the porch. He climbed the frail-looking wooden steps and fished his pocket for the key he had long kept in his car. Finding it, he fit it into the padlock that held the steel hasp against the doorway. It opened as easily as it had years before and he pushed the door inward.

Inside, the place was remarkably the same. A dim glow of moonlight filtered through the dirty windows, some shaded with thin, dingy curtains. The cabin had just the one main room, with a rudimentary bathroom partitioned onto the middle of the back wall. He studied the paneled wooden bathroom door, remembering that it latched with a thumb-bolt inside. The floor was covered with a large square of old, scarred linoleum with some obscured pattern, tacked down at the tattered edges. To the left of the bathroom, a metal cot sat against the back wall, topped by a stained mattress, and to the right of the bathroom door was the kitchen area, which consisted of a sink and counter against the right wall and a three-foot-by-four wooden table pushed against the front wall.

A disturbed wasp buzzed above him and he swatted at it, sending it toward the open front door. He let it fly out before shutting the door. The inside air was musty and warm. He crossed over to the window above the sink and drew back the tea-colored curtain. After a couple of useless attempts at lifting the window, the flashlight beam caught a nail in the wooden track. It slipped cleanly out of its hole and he raised the sash to the fine grid of a steel wire screen. Successfully repeating the maneuver at the window directly across the room resulted in instant movement of air. The action brought memories of his having done the same thing on his first visit. He recalled the night-time cross-breezes that caused him to seek cover under an old blanket that had been stowed on a shelf in the bathroom. He found a kerosene lamp on the small table in the middle of the room, tilted the lamp until the scant fuel in the base saturated the wick, and lit it with a match. A soft yellow glow revealed the entire room for him.

Something drew him to the kitchen counter, where it stopped short of the back wall. Instinctively, he leaned down and looked into the opening of the unfinished left wall of the counter cabinet. There was the fishing rod he had used before, stashed in the dark innards of the cabinet's base. He retrieved it and, just to the right, his hand went directly to the small glass jar holding cork bobbers and a variety of hooks. Adam smiled. There would be fish to eat at some time this day, even if he had to roast them over an open fire. Before standing, his eye caught a glimpse of a cloth wrapped around something. He retrieved it and before unwrapping it he could tell it was a pistol. Laying the cloth aside, he found a snub-nose .38 caliber pistol. It had a little rust on the barrel but the cloth had been oily at one time, sparing the weapon from major corrosion over the years. He slipped it into his pocket.

He was very tired. But before settling in he had to do a little cleaning. The mattress needed a good beating. And somehow, he had to get his car closer and bring his few belongings inside.

He gave the old place another brief review. It felt good. Maybe he was meant to be here. Eight or nine years had left it almost totally unchanged. The cabin felt as if it had been waiting for his return.

He would work hard after daylight, cleaning up, then fish for a meal and, after that, find out what he could about Maisie.

It wasn't much of a plan, he knew, but it was the only one he could come up with in his weary and worried state of mind.

He would find a telephone somewhere; there had been a bait store not far away. If he could determine when Maisie's evaluation would be complete, he could pick her up and drive her back to her farm. That would be a risk, he knew, but making sure she got home safely would be worth that risk.

After beating both sides of the old mattress with a two-by four, he pulled a blanket from the bathroom shelf, extinguished the lamp and lay exhausted on the cot.

The last image that came to him before sleep was that of Maisie's beautiful, sad face in the side window of the Sheriff's patrol car, and her faithful hand still upon the glass.

An odor that smelled strongly of body waste and scorched food filled the room lighted only by daylight streaming through the few windows. A large male ward attendant in rumpled whites pushed a stainless steel cart toward the double doors to the hall. A heavyset matron in starched whites unceremoniously set food trays on top of swing-arm countertops mounted on stands beside each bed, moving quickly and efficiently from one to the next.

Maisie had been weeping and praying for an hour, upon waking and finding herself immobilized in a strange bed with a cacophony of unfamiliar sounds filling the then-dark ward. Gradually, recollection of her whereabouts came to her, but none of the peace she had acquired en route to the hospital. The realization that she was not free to move about frightened her.

Now, into her tear-blurred vision walked a nurse carrying a tray of food, the second nurse she met the night before.

"Hello, Miss Slaughter. Do you remember me? I'm Nurse Caldwell. I hope you don't mind if I call you Maisie."

Maisie wanted to say no, but quickly realized she might have misjudged this nurse the night before. She nodded.

"Will you be conducting the evaluation this morning?" Maisie asked.

"Evaluation?" repeated Nurse Caldwell. "I haven't been told about that, Maisie, but I'll go check for you." She unstrapped Maisie from the bed and helped her sit up. "Here, take your medications and then have a bite of breakfast."

Maisie cheeked the pill Caldwell gave her and held it there as she swallowed water. When the nurse left, she took the pill out of her mouth and wadded it into a paper napkin. The breakfast was a rubbery fried egg, a pale, dry biscuit and a small glass of tomato juice. She made it through a bite of the egg and biscuit before downing the juice in two swallows.

The nurse returned with a pleasant expression on her face. "Doctor Mason and Mister Blanchard were in a meeting, so I asked my supervisor, Nurse Proctor, about an evaluation. She only said you were due for one today." At that Nurse Caldwell gave her a friendly smile and said, "That's all I can tell you for now, Maisie."

Maisie moved to get out of bed and realized quickly that she was wearing only a thin gown. "Where are my clothes?" she asked.

"Oh, we usually place them in a locker for safe keeping." She leaned closer and spoke as though confidentially. "I'll get you a robe so you don't have to walk around uncovered in the back."

The nurse picked up a small metal pan from the breakfast tray and held it up. "It's kind of an unpublished procedure among some of us to give patients a sugar pill the very first time, Maisie. I'm guessing you wadded it up in your napkin and it's right there on the tray." She smiled at Maisie.

Maisie blushed and smiled back at her.

"The real medication is here. I hope you won't mind the trick."

"What is that?"

"A light dosage of insulin to help you relax."

"But I am relaxed," she objected.

Caldwell straightened up with the realization. "You know, I can see that. Why don't we dispense with the medication? Do you mind?" She put the pan back on the tray.

"Not at all," she said, looking on the floor for something to put on her feet.

"We just won't tell Mister Blanchard, okay? He tends to get very angry at breaches in procedure."

"Your secret is safe. Do you have any slippers for me?"

"I'll see what I can find." Caldwell hurried away carrying the tray. After a few minutes she returned with a light cotton robe and a pair of slippers.

"Would you like to sit and read before your evaluation?"

Maisie agreed, and Caldwell led her to a far corner of the long ward, where sunlight flooded through tall windows whose glass was strengthened internally by thick woven wire, and beneath which was positioned a small desk of the kind used in elementary schools – an immoveable wooden seat on a steel frame with an equally immobile writing surface fixed inches from the seat back. The nurse pointed her to a bookcase littered with old magazines and a few hardback books, and said she would come back for her when it was time for her evaluation. Maisie sat and studied her environment.

A few elderly people in hospital gowns sat statue-like in chairs positioned at intervals in the sunlit space. A frail, weary looking man walked slowly around the perimeter of the open area, careful not to step on the long rectangles of light spreading from the windows across the floor. A woman who appeared to be in her early thirties sat in a wheel chair, rocking her upper torso and moaning as she twisted a finger-thick strand of her matted brown hair. Her gown was stained about the neck and speckled with bits of food.

Maisie wanted to call out to Nurse Caldwell as she walked back through the ward, her white uniform melding into the mottled grayness of the room's distant interior. She had the urge to get up and follow her. But this was her trial. The Holy Spirit had said to be strong. She would have to find a way in this strange environment to get in communion with Him until she could get back to the farm.

Shifting her attention once again to the young woman in the wheel chair, Maisie was struck by the apparent lack of control the woman seemed to have. It seemed almost as though she was occupying a body with which she had no identification, as though she did not feel at home in it. She appeared to be imprisoned, and her body was the jail. Instantly Maisie knew the woman was the victim of intimidation, not from people but from spirits. Somehow, the woman had fallen under the control of evil spirits and could no longer live peacefully in her physical shell. Maisie rose and went to her, kneeling beside her chair. The woman's body odor was strong, but Maisie dismissed the urge to react.

"What's your name?" Maisie asked.

The woman moved her head in slow motion until she found Maisie's face a few inches below her own. Her eyes took several moments to gain focus. She squinted as though she was not quite sure what she was seeing.

"What did you say, Miss?" The young woman's voice

creaked like flexing leather, perhaps through disuse, her words, slow and deliberate as though individually considered before using.

Being called 'Miss' by a woman not much older than herself touched Maisie's heart. "What is your name? My name is Maisie." Maisie was smiling at her, her eyes appealing an aware response.

"My name?" She hesitated a few more moments. "Sarah," she said finally.

"Sarah," Maisie repeated. "That's a lovely name. Where do you live, Sarah?'

She blinked twice. "Why, right here." Sarah appeared almost astonished at her question. As she spoke her frail index finger stopped twisting her hair and traced a small circle around the room.

"Don't you have a home somewhere?"

Sarah frowned. Her eyes changed focus and wandered upward. She might have been watching a gnat navigate tough air currents, though Maisie knew she was calling upon her memory.

"Somewhere, Miss," Sarah said. "A white porch." Then her eyes watered, brimming until they dripped tears. "Mama. Daddy."

Her mind was locked somewhere in childhood, thought Maisie.

"Do you know Jesus, Sarah?"

Sarah's head returned quickly to face her interrogator, her eyes a mixture of intense interest and fear, red and moist at the thin, awakened eyelids. Her breathing suddenly became noticeable. Her lower lip trembled; a saliva bubble formed at its middle.

"I can't know Him." The words were painfully drawn.

Maisie was shocked. "Can't? Sure you can. I've never heard someone say they can't know Him."

"I can't." She shook her head sadly and took hold of the wheels and pushed away a few inches. With another absent-minded effort she pushed the wheels again, making her way out of discomfort.

Maisie slowly returned to the reading area and sat in the

tiny desk, praying for the woman. After a while, her thoughts drifted to her circumstance again.

As undesirable as was the breakfast, she found it difficult not to wonder if she would eat again today, or if they would release her before lunch. She had not had supper the night before and her stomach was protesting.

Before she finished the thought, something broke the shaft of sunlight in the window and, simultaneously, she heard a thump. A dove fluttered before the window and fell to the ledge, jerking in spasms. It had apparently flown head-on into the window, though its glass would hardly be mistaken for open space, with wire and perhaps decades of accumulated dirt and dust disguising it.

"Mrs. Caldwell!" she called before she realized the matron was nowhere near, and that nothing could be done for the injured creature. The windows were sealed shut.

She rose with difficulty in extracting herself from the too-small desk, and moved forward to see better. "You'll be okay, little bird," she said as loud as she could without drawing unwanted attention to herself from the patients nearby. The bird settled, stopped its spasms, dropped to the sill and lay motionless.

"No!" Maisie almost shouted in her concern for the bird. "Don't die!" She now stood directly in front of the window.

"Get up!" she spoke more softly. Again she spoke, leaning next to the lower edge of the glass. "Get up."

In a moment the bird revived, fluttered its wings again, and shuddered to its feet, working its visible eye in jerky movements.

"Oh, thank you, Lord!" Maisie whispered.

The bird, fully revived now, warbled closer on the narrow ledge and appeared to stare into the window.

"Are you looking at me?" asked Maisie, leaning forward. "Don't look at me. I didn't do it." She cut her eyes upward for a second. "He did healed you."

The dove pecked at the window.

"If you're looking for food I can't help you. As you can see, this glass is pretty thick." She chuckled at herself. "You wouldn't want the food here, anyway. You wouldn't be able to eat it unless you could pinch your nose."

She held her hand to the window in front of the bird, palm up, and motioned upward. "Go ahead, fly home," she said.

As if the bird had heard and obeyed, it hopped halfway around, toward the outside of the ledge, and flew away.

"That was quick, Father," said Maisie. "You care about the sparrows, too." Looking up, she corrected herself. "A dove, in this case." She smiled to herself. "I'm not as crazy as they think."

When Maisie turned from the window happily, she almost bumped into someone who had been watching over her shoulder.

"Oh, I'm sorry," she apologized before looking up.

"So, you think you have no need to be here."

Startled, Maisie looked up to see Vernon Blanchard scowling above her left shoulder. She realized he had to have made a wide arc in approaching her so as not to be noticed in her peripheral vision. He remained in place, forcing her to contort herself in order to see his face.

"Talking to ourselves, are we?" He allowed his face a malevolent grin.

"Evaluation complete!"

Turning, he stalked away.

CHAPTER FOURTEEN

The transorbital lobotomy had, since the 1940s, been considered a respectable medical procedure, by some, at least. Disingenuously termed psychosurgery, perhaps to allow it some degree of acceptance in medical circles – which it did attain for an amazing period of time – lobotomy in its several forms might better have been recognized as butchery. At its most hideous, an ice pick – euphemistically called a leucotome – was inserted under the patient's eyelid, above the eyeball, and maneuvered to the portion of the skull that protects the foreword lobe of the brain – the frontal lobe. There, when the physician was fairly confident of probable placement, he would drive the pick through the bony mass into the brain with a small hammer, and, with all the skill and dexterity of an untrained mortar tender, would wiggle the ice pick around until he was satisfied he had sufficiently damaged the brain to cause the desired result in his patient. That desired result was often no more than that the patient become calmer and less annoying to others.

Vernon Blanchard had been reading extensively about lobotomies. His late hour in the office tonight was not unusual. He set the medical journal on the book shelf behind him and thought about what he might do to increase the prestige of Mid-State Hospital. He knew that lobotomies were somewhat controversial and that many professionals wanted them banned, but he had expressed his well weighed opinion among his staff members that such a judgment was extreme, considering the good that might come to insane asylums - not to mention, to patients - by their continuation. Why, many facilities were overcrowded and understaffed, as well as underfunded. How little those outside the medical community knew about the trials of treating and confining the mentally disturbed! Maybe lobotomies had passed into disfavor in some sectors of the medical community, but Blanchard insisted they held great promise for many patients when performed well. And he knew how to perform them.

Much had been written about the procedure, both in medical journals and in popular journalism. Physicians had become famous and wealthy performing them, to the awe of their peers and the press. Blanchard had read enough about those performed by the well known surgeon, Walter Freeman, and studied the photographs showing the precise placement of the pick. It was said that Freeman had performed as many as fifty in one day, and had done two simultaneously on side-by-side patients. Blanchard had no doubt that he, himself, could perform at least a dozen or more in a day, starting out.

As for the respectability of the much maligned surgery, he knew for certain it had been acceptable to many well heeled families. None other than the daughter of Joseph Kennedy, of the Massachusetts Kennedies, had undergone the procedure. Those who claimed it was a botched job were likely Republicans, envious of the wealth and power of the Kennedy clan. Blanchard had read enough to know that old Joe Kennedy had made a wise move for the Kennedy family. The girl, Rose Marie, had been somewhat mercurial as a child and teen, prone to causing embarrassment. The lobotomy had saved the family a great deal of heartache, no doubt.

Certainly, lobotomies had been given a bad name. However, the right administrator might return it to respectable use if he could demonstrate the cost savings and the minimized stress on staff members charged with worrying over troublesome patients.

Take the Slaughter patient. The girl was obviously a hopeless case, talking to a bird and then imagining she was telling her father about it, nitpicking her sweater, not to mention the fact that she was brought to the hospital because she was a known danger to herself and her community. And she had a high resistance to the normal dosage of insulin, exhibiting absolutely no sign of its influence in his earlier encounter with her. Plus, she seemed to have some sixth sense that could make her a danger to him.

As much as he wanted to actually perform a lobotomy on

someone, he would have to defer to an actual psychiatric surgeon, at least for the first few attempts with the procedure. And that surgeon would need to concur with Blanchard's own course of action. Quite possibly, in her present state of resistance to a normal dosage of insulin, some surgeons might not fully agree with him. That little issue, however, might be easily resolved.

He picked up a piece of paper and wrote quickly.

Nurse Proctor, increase the insulin dosage immediately for the Slaughter patient to 400 units. Further, I want her at 450 units by the end of the week, at which time we might proceed with Electroconvulsive Therapy. Also, place a call first thing to R. Burson Munter at the phone number below and ask him to call me with his itinerary over the next week. He signed his name, Doc Blanchard.

If he had to wait on performing a lobotomy, at least, he would ensure the patient presented with symptoms calling for further measures.

* * * * *

Sleep fled Adam as the sky was dawning. He wandered absently into the yard and over the berm above the river. A light breeze wafted up from the flow, the water's surface somewhat obscured by a foggy gauze. He let gravity pull him down the embankment onto the weathered dock, where he walked to the river-side edge and sat cross-legged. The old platform, its wavy, graying planks resembling whitecaps on a wintery sea, swayed and creaked with the gentle surge of the current against the pilings, instantly having a peaceful, almost hypnotic effect on him. He stared through the fog at the brown ripples and suddenly felt a sense of floating in nothingness in this new noplace.

After a while, the sun, rising behind him, cast fingers of light against the pine horizon beyond the opposite bank, and slowly the great shade of night reeled toward him like a giant's window shade opening, even as dark clouds rolled up from the southwest. The fog dissolved into the warming light, awakening his thoughts to the needs of his immediate future.

After the phone call he would make, the day promised hours of cleaning the old place, dragging limbs away to a fire pit, and getting a little fresh air into the cabin. He would open the faucets and let the rusty red water run out of the pipes, and clean the sink and toilet. He noticed his willingness to work long and hard here and was amazed; he had experienced no similar urges at home.

But, who knew? This might represent his new life, one into which he wanted to expend himself. Beyond the danger seeking him in Odino and the concern over Maisie, he felt as though this could be the beginning of a journey from his old life to a better one. He realized the circumstances of his lonely life made him susceptible, but he also knew that if he ever loved anyone, he felt love for Maisie. Just as clear was the fact that Maisie saw him as only a friend. Once she returned from the hospital, his role would be to encourage her and, if he could learn how, to pray for her.

He wondered what Bondurant Woods had done during his forays to this world-forsaken spot. Had he only lay drunk, as was depicted to Adam all his life? Or had he come here to sober up and get his mind right, away from what might have been a life of continuous accusation and prophetic doomsaying?

He chastised himself for the thought.

Maybe his mother really had been more the effect than the cause of his father's waywardness. He had no reason to suspect Bonder Woods was a saint in disguise. He knew part of the truth was that he, Adam, had always wanted to get inside his father's head to understand what motivated – or de-motivated – him. He wished there could have been a time when his father appeared on the front porch of their house, called through the screen door and asked for Adam.

"Hey, Adam? Are you in there? It's your old man, come to make your acquaintance. I want to explain why I killed that young fella and put that tattoo on your hand. Got time to go fishing and talk some?"

Adam smiled sadly to himself. Wouldn't that have been

perfect?

Surely his father had a nice agreeable side to him. He couldn't have been unwaveringly the murdering monster Charlotte Woods and Odino, Georgia, made him out to be. Why would she have married him if that was so?

Maybe Bondurant Woods sat right here on this dock wondering about his own Daddy, of whom Adam knew nothing. Maybe he just floated down the same river his old man had disappeared down, the way Charlotte Woods said Adam was destined to go. Was it inevitable that a man would be just like his father? Somehow, he didn't think so. Adam did not even like the taste of whisky. He had tried it and gagged. Beer was really little better. Gambling was a waste to him. There was nothing in him that wanted to fight people and hurt them, not really.

But people always said a river's just a cycle of the same old water over and over again, running down to the sea, evaporating up to heaven and raining down to the river once again. And it's the same way with people and their kin. You can't ever get away from what they were before you. A river always returns to the place it started. Adam had never thought of it before, but that seemed to be the driving force behind not only the expectations of others toward him, including his mother, but, in truth, behind his expectations for himself. Was he really destined to flow in his father's path? Was there not a way to short-circuit the process?

The thought came to him: Maybe that was why he could not quite see himself deserving the love of someone like Maisie, or, for that matter, deserving the love of her God. These were things too high, too elevated above his river-bottom destiny. And the pathetic irony of it all was the engraving, the permanent mark his father had tattooed on the palm of Adam's hand. The thing that, maybe, was intended to reverse the flow of the river had become a stigma that bound him to his father's destiny. What had the man been thinking?

Somehow, Adam had to find a way to shake this open casket that had been built for him, and that everybody seemed to expect him to climb willingly into.

As long as he was consigned to hiding for a time, he would

try talking to the God Maisie knew. Maybe he could find out what was down this river for him. Was there a future for him upstream, if he could somehow reverse course?

A drop of cold rain struck him like a slap on his forehead.

* * * * *

Sheriff Mobley spent the morning in the archives of the Clerk of Court. When he walked out into the blinding sunlight he felt somewhat better than he had the night before. After hours of searching, he had found what he was looking for. Now he had to go back to his office, hoping to duck every effort by Potter Riley's thugs to press him for Adam Woods' location. He had to make a telephone call that might set into motion the only real opportunity he knew of to get Maisie Slaughter out of Mid-State Hospital. He had heard stories of people being committed to an asylum and never coming out, for the simple cause that someone wanted him or her out of the way. Somehow, he had to do what he could to prevent that from happening to this young woman. Not to act, he knew in his heavy heart, would be a much worse sin than all those he had amassed to his slate already.

According to his wristwatch, the time was 11:23. In thirty minutes or so the courthouse square would be populated by lawyers and mechanics and bank employees heading to lunch at Marty's Diner or to post mail on their lunch hour. He would hurry in order to avoid those who wanted to chit-chat or to get the latest gossip on whoever got arrested. He briskly walked the two blocks to his office watching every human movement, every window and door, with the knowledge that Riley's henchmen would probably not want to stop him for a friendly chat. An older woman he knew to be a court reporter exited the county prosecutor's office and headed straight for him.

"Sheriff Mobley, I – " She began addressing him when she was within ten feet of him.

He was glad he was walking fast enough to convince someone he was on a mission. "Morning, Miz Holloway." He held up his hand and did not slow his pace. "I don't have time to talk right now."

As he passed her, she continued speaking. "It's about my son's traffic ticket, Sheriff."

He continued on, speaking over his shoulder. "Come by my office tomorrow morning. We can talk about that then."

He made it to his office, moving into and through the dispatch area without looking at Lowe. Once inside with his door closed, he retrieved his pocket notebook and flipped to the page where he had jotted notes.

His door opened and Captain Lowe filled the space with an ominous expression. He was always serious these days, but now he appeared more so.

"Potter Riley's called four times, Sheriff. He's drunk and ugly – well, uglier than usual. Do you want to call him back?"

Sheriff Mobley waved him off. "Tell him I'm out on an arrest."

"He's making threats."

"No surprise there. Keep your gun belt on. If he comes in here making trouble while I'm out, do what you have to do."

Lowe's eyes widened. He had never heard the Sheriff say that about anyone, much less Potter Riley. In recent years Mobley had been only peripherally involved with law enforcement, and very secretive about contacts with Riley.

"I'll take that as a warning."

"It was meant to be." He nodded to Lowe, who closed the door.

He dialed the phone number he had found, and while the line made connection and began to ring, he opened his middle desk drawer and retrieved a snub-nosed .38 he sometimes carried. He slipped it into his pants pocket. Later, he would shove it under his car seat.

* * * * *

Potter Riley had been expecting the call. He picked up the telephone and spoke without greeting.

"Has he left?"

The man on the other end of the line answered in the affirmative.

"Did he take his patrol car or did he walk?"

"He drove."

"Did he seem in a hurry or was he moving slow?"

"He walked fast to his car and drove off pretty quick."

"Call me when he comes back."

* * * * *

Art Lowe was in a foul mood. He had been on the staff at the department through three different Sheriffs. He had been promoted to Captain during the term of Lucius Fanning, the Sheriff just prior to Mobley's election. Fanning had been a good man who should have been reelected, but was beat out by the slick talking, tall and – some said – good looking Ott Mobley. Fanning had been a real Sheriff. Mobley clearly had his eyes on the state legislature. He had acquired a good bit of under-the-table benefits, but he had not been generous to Lowe. No promotion. No special privileges. None of the extra funds were ever channeled his way. Lowe had made up his mind that he would run against Mobley in the next election. With everything he knew about Mobley's abuse of office, he should have no trouble winning.

He sat at the dispatch desk, pencil in hand, calculating how much he might earn as Sheriff. Honestly, for starters.

The telephone rang.

"Sheriff's office, Lowe speaking."

The voice of Potter Riley was unmistakable. Lowe could almost smell the alcohol through the line.

"You don't make enough money, Captain Lowe." Riley emphasized the word, "Captain."

What a coincidence, thought Lowe. He was just thinking the same thing.

"What's your point?" He was still irritated by the brusque manner in which Riley had spoken to him earlier.

"You could make a lot more if you worked for me." Riley waited half a second before adding, "As Sheriff."

Lowe was completely stunned. Had the man somehow been reading his mind? His heart began racing, and his mind passed it like it was sitting still. He was too conflicted between irritation and intrigue to speak.

"Are you still there?"

"How much?" Lowe was surprised at the interest revealed in his voice. He felt a little like scum for even entertaining the question, but there it was. He was as good as bought. He had taken the lure like a hungry catfish.

Riley laughed sadistically. "A lot, son. A lot!"

"Don't mess with me, Riley. I won't play ball as easy as Mobley does."

"Double what you're making now, and money to back you as a candidate."

"What's the gimmick?"

"All you have to do is help me find somebody."

'Who?"

"The man who murdered Ray Lee Colbert, my finest employee."

CHAPTER FIFTEEN

Nurse Proctor often talked to herself. After all, there were so few around her with whom she could converse. The other nurses disliked her for the confidence Doc Blanchard placed in her, but overlooked it for her loyalty to the hospital. Many patients were so doped up or comatose on insulin injections that it was useless to try relating to them. Others were in their own world, completely out of touch with reality. And Doc Blanchard, with whom she had most contact at MSH, did not have patience for small talk. He was strictly interested in running the hospital. At least, that was what he called it.

"What in the world does he want to do to the young Slaughter woman?" she muttered to herself as she laid out the morning's tray of insulin injections in the medications clinic. "We always increase dosages gradually. And if he puts her on ECT right away, what's that going to do to her?" She shook her head in resigned confusion. "Sometimes I don't understand what goes on in his head." She plucked a slip of paper from her clipboard, unfolded it and re-read it.

"Says four hundred units, all right. Lord, I sure hope he knows what he's doing. Doctor Weston ordered injections, but he was an M.D. Surely, Doc Blanchard is working through a staff physician."

She slipped a needle into the insulin bottle and drew in the prescribed amount. "Still, she doesn't seem at all like other patients, even our best ones."

She stopped muttering when she heard movement in the hall.

Nurse Caldwell entered the room and Proctor turned to her.

"Medications are almost ready, Caldwell." She finished her preparations as Caldwell waited dutifully beside her.

"By the way," she continued. "Doc said something about

the Slaughter patient having no response to the insulin yesterday. Did you inject her?"

"I did not," replied Caldwell without remorse. "She was as lucid as anybody I know."

Proctor whirled on her. "You don't have the authority to make those kinds of decisions."

"That's true. But neither does Blanchard. He acts like he thinks he's a doctor, and it appears some staff members think he is. At least, I have a conscience."

"Are you implying I don't?"

"If it fits. It's obvious to me the Slaughter woman has no business being here."

Proctor fumed and stared at her.

"That, too, is no decision of yours." She turned back to the cart. "Do not ever take it upon yourself again to withhold medications from a patient. See that she gets her dosage today. Is that understood?"

"Perfectly!" Caldwell said.

Proctor stepped away from the cart on which the medications rested, and pointed at the array of cups and needles individually identified by patient. "If you fail to do your duty this morning, don't blame me for the consequences."

"I'm more concerned about who will get the blame if I do perform the duty you've assigned me."

Caldwell moved quickly to the cart and steered it toward the door.

* * * * *

Adam ducked underneath the shallow covering over the pay telephone, his hair dripping rain over his face. He was soaked, but focused. He had driven around for more than an hour trying to find a pay phone that worked. The first one he found ate his change when a call to his mother's house failed, and he had been forced to break another dollar bill and resume his search a phone that worked. This one stood like a bored sentry at the edge of the gravel-covered parking lot of a run-down bait and tackle store. Twenty feet from a paved road, Adam could see about a mile in both directions. A cornfield behind the phone seemed to stretch on as far as the visible roadway.

After letting his mother's phone ring a dozen times, he hung up and dialed Information. On speaking with an operator and jotting down the phone number of the Sheriff's office, he inserted the coins and dialed. The connection was made almost immediately.

"Sheriff's office, Lowe speaking."

"Hello. I'd like to speak with Sheriff Mobley, please."

"The Sheriff's not in. Who's calling?"

"Adam – " He hesitated, afraid he had done something wrong by revealing his name, but quickly realized that even if he was wanted for Ray Lee's shooting, no one knew where he was anyway. "Adam Woods," he said.

"Well, Mr. Woods. I'm sure the Sheriff will want to speak with you. Give me the phone number where you are and I'll have him call you when he comes back in."

"I'm at a pay phone right now, and might not come back to this one. So it's best if I call him again. Can you tell me when he'll be back?"

Now the officer hesitated. "Well, uh, he said he was going out of the county today. Maybe he's headed in your direction. Why don't I tell him to meet you somewhere?"

Adam did not like that idea. "That's okay, I'll wait, and call him back tomorrow."

"Well, look. He might come back in, I don't know. Why don't you call back in an hour?"

A loud rumble of thunder obscured the last few words.

"Call back when?" asked Adam.

"In an hour."

"Yeah, okay. Maybe I'll do that. Thanks." Adam hung up the phone. The rain had become so heavy he could barely hear the last few words of the officer. He took a step back from the phone and hesitated. His car sat thirty or forty feet away. He had intended to make a dash to the car, but the phone call had done nothing for the anxiety he felt about Maisie. He needed to settle something. At the least, he ought to call the state hospital, he thought. Maybe he could find out how long Maisie would be there. Or maybe he might even get the chance to speak to her. Somehow, she was the only person in the world he really wanted to speak with anyway.

* * * * *

Captain Lowe held the line as he waited for the radio station's receptionist to find someone who could answer his question. Too bad Woods was so cautious. With a little luck, Lowe might have made the fastest money of his career. As it was, he might have to do a little sleuthing to find where the man was.

He scribbled a note: "pay phone...heavy rain...thunder...might not come back to this phone."

Finally, a man's resonant and carefully articulated voice came on the line. "Good morning, Officer Lowe! This is Bobby Baker of the Afternoon Show. How can I be of service to you, sir?"

"Mister Baker, I'm investigating the whereabouts of a suspect in a serious crime. The suspect made a telephone call moments ago, and in the background was clearly audible a thunder storm and heavy rainfall. Can your weather reports give me information about the location of a storm anywhere in the middle of the state at precisely 1:14 to 1:17?"

"Weather reports," he repeated. "It might take me a few minutes, Captain Lowe, but I'll be happy to assist in any way I can."

"Can you call me back in five or ten minutes with that information?"

"I will do my best, sir. Give me your telephone number."

Lowe gave him the number and hung up, feeling satisfied with himself. If he could pinpoint a tight geographic area, a phone call to the local sheriff's office in the area of that storm could prove very useful. He had the make and tag number of Woods' car. And an APB could extend his net a long way. It was possible the man could be in custody and ready to pick up before mid-afternoon. That might mean Lowe would be a wealthier man before nightfall.

And to think: his day started off lousy.

$$* * * * *$$

The warden at Jameston Prison was 46-year-old Sonny Ingles, an ex-Marine Major who fought at Guadalcanal and earned the Purple Heart for a bullet wound to the leg. Major Ingles, as the press and the governor called him, walked with a pronounced limp. He maintained the same close-cropped hair style to which he had become accustomed in the military. And Major Ingles had the great misfortune to be liked by almost everyone who knew him, with the exception of members of the State Pardons and Paroles Board, who considered him far too lenient. And he was someone who, in their opinions, did not follow the rules, despite his military training.

When he learned that one of the inmates had been stabbed, he took the attack personally. Within twelve hours after his investigation began, he had personally interviewed seven inmates. Two of them gave him the name of the likely attacker, and a third suggested who might have paid for the hit. One of those three also named a Sheriff who might have been complicit in withholding evidence at trial that could have made the difference between a life sentence and a five-year stretch for the victim.

Ingles knew well enough not to place much value in prison accusations, but he also knew that when he received independent, voluntary information corroborated by two sources who had nothing to gain by the giving of it, he needed to look further into the matter at hand. Thus, when he visited the victim in the hospital next morning, and was able to speak with him briefly, he learned enough to take a calculated risk that he hoped would help his critically wounded charge. With the cooperation of hospital staff and the local police department, he leaked word that an inmate had been killed. Then he had Bonder Woods, under another name, transferred to a medium—security facility with adequate medical staff, where he was expected to fully recover from his wounds. Since the other facility was a two-hour drive away, he was able to make two trips and several phone calls that had the effect on him of confirming that he had made the right decision. He had done nothing yet about the named attackers or those on the outside who might have had a hand in the attack. Ingles was also a patient man.

Today he sat with inmate Woods, aka Lester Hunter, and listened as the man spoke in a whisper between what appeared to be painful efforts to refill his lungs. The shank had been fashioned from a pair of steel straps removed from bed springs, welded together, probably in the prison shop, and sharpened to a dagger point. The piece had pierced Woods' right lung, coming very close to taking his life.

"Take your time, Woods. I'm in no hurry," he said, cringing inside at the man's struggle. Bonder had been describing the night when Flynn Riley had been killed.

"He accused me of cheat..." Woods took another slow breath. "Cheating...he knocked cards out of my hand."

"And you hit him?" Ingles asked.

Bonder nodded.

"He fell into..." Here, Bonder's eyes moistened and he stopped. He closed his eyes and drew in more air. "...an old limb holding the ...the roof. It fell...the limb stuck in his chest."

"Did he live long?"

Bonder shook his head, no.

"So, there were no witnesses?"

Bonder held up two fingers. "They knew...it was an accident."

Ingles nodded. He placed a hand on Bonder's shoulder and stood from the metal folding chair. "Look, Woods, I'm not gonna bother you more today. Get some rest, and I'll try to get back over here in a couple of weeks."

Bonder looked up at the man, and nodded. He smiled faintly.

"Take care of yourself. I want you to be sitting up, strong enough to fill in the rest of the blanks next time, okay?"

Ingles lifted the fedora he held in his hand and tapped it

onto his head as he left the room.

Bonder Woods closed his eyes and silently thanked God for the amazing turn of events that had piqued the interest of Warden Ingles. But he cautioned himself not to expect too much. After all, he had already received far more grace than he could ever have asked for.

CHAPTER SIXTEEN

Nurse Proctor looked up from her typewriter when Vernon Blanchard's door opened.

"That Sheriff from Ocmulgee County called a few minutes ago," she said. "He wanted to know when the Slaughter patient will be released."

"He did, did he?" Blanchard was pulling on a white clinical coat.

She nodded at him. "He sounded like he wanted to come down here to get her."

"Well, he'll have to wait a long time. Miss Slaughter has some serious issues that need treatment."

"That's what I told him. I said – "

"What exactly did you say?"

"I told him the evaluation had been completed and she would be undergoing treatment."

"And?"

"And that's all."

"You failed to tell him she would not be able to have visitors?"

"Oh, I forgot that. But he didn't actually say he was coming down here."

"Miss Proctor, when I give you instructions, I expect you to carry them out explicitly. She will have no visitors. Do not fail to make that clear if he calls again."

"Yes sir," she muttered before returning to her typing.

Blanchard remained, towering over her. "Has the patient been administered the insulin increase I ordered?"

Without taking her eyes from her work, she answered. "Yes sir, about an hour ago. I don't mind saying, sir." She lifted her hands from the keys. "That large increase was highly unusual. We usually make increases gradually."

"Do you think I don't know what I'm doing?"

"No. No sir. Not at all. I was just saying…"

"Do you understand the concept of experimentation when first-prescribed dosages are inadequate?"

She looked up at him quickly, her eyes pleading. "I'm so sorry. I didn't mean to imply – "

"Never mind." He dropped an envelope on the desk. "Mail that immediately, please."

Proctor glanced over the address. "Dr. Johnathon Smith? Do we have a Dr. Smith on call?"

He ignored her question and strode away. "I will be back after I make my rounds."

Blanchard slipped a stethoscope into his jacket pocket as he exited the reception area. He looked very much the part of a true physician.

* * * * *

"Maisie," Nurse Caldwell said as she prepared to administer the injection.

"Yes?" She had finished telling Caldwell about the bird and the subsequent encounter with Blanchard. Nurse Caldwell's facial expression mirrored her own, brightening with the details of the bird's recovery, and falling into concern at hearing Blanchard's pronouncement of the end to a supposed evaluation.

"I don't want to have to give you this medication. I don't anymore think you should be here than the man in the moon. I know you're a praying woman, and so am I. So I intend to pray for Blanchard to come to his senses and release you."

"I don't blame you, Miss Caldwell. Don't get yourself in trouble on my behalf."

"Honey, if I thought getting in trouble would change what they do around here, I wouldn't hesitate. The past year, this place has been unlike any hospital I've ever worked in. And I don't mean better."

She moved closer with the needle. "Oh Lord," she whispered. "Take care of my little sister. Get her out of this place without harm, please." She slipped the needle into Maisie's arm. At the same time, a tear slipped from the nurse's eyes.

* * * * *

After completing medications, Nurse Caldwell returned to check on Maisie Slaughter. She had been concerned enough at the increased dosage of insulin to consider not giving her the injection at all. But on realizing that, even if she was fired for disobedience, that would not save Maisie from Blanchard's insistence on medicating her. On reaching the ward and turning toward Maisie's bed, what she saw held her speechless.

She stood at the foot of the bed, transfixed. A male orderly stood beside a bed across the aisle also watching.

The smile on Maisie's face was completely off the charts for someone who had been given the level of insulin administered. Though she appeared to be unconscious, she was not in any kind of induced coma other patients had been brought under. The fluid, graceful and even peaceful movements of her arms, almost as though she were swimming or worshiping, were completely unlike the jerky, uncertain mechanics of other patients undergoing far less treatment stress.

So engrossed was she that Caldwell did not hear Blanchard step up behind her. She jumped inwardly at his outburst.

"Can't you stop this?" Blanchard's question carried a tone of annoyance.

She turned to him. "Stop it?" Caldwell's own tone was almost incredulous.

He cut his eyes quickly to her. "Stop it! Stop it! Can you not hear clearly?" He spoke with a hard edge.

"No disrespect intended, Mister Blanchard, but why would we want to stop it?"

"What do you mean, 'Why would we want to stop it'"? He

glared at her mercilessly. She had referred to him as "Mister" before and watched him bristle, but she had no intention of playing to his delusion of being a medical doctor. The sharpness of his tone was intended to question her professionalism. "I should think it would be obvious to a professional why we would want to stop this, Miss Caldwell." His emphasis on "professional" came as demeaning to her.

Blanchard had never been particularly warm, but he had never spoken to her with such pointed mocking. The fact that he retaliated by calling her "Miss" when he knew she was a registered nurse and married woman, a mature married woman at that, carried the implication she was nothing more than a new hire, a minion in his staff. She had put up with a lot from this man. He who had ordered the abnormal boost to Maisie Slaughter's medication, and, as Proctor had suggested, intended to apply ECT, for no apparent reason.

"It is not as obvious to me – " Here she hesitated only a split second before continuing, "Mister Blanchard, as it may be to you. What I see is a patient who appears to be perfectly at peace despite the heavy, uncalled for medication you have foisted upon her."

Blanchard's face burned. He glanced around at the increased number of staffers, having stopped to see the unusual actions of the patient, now turning their attention to him and Caldwell. His eyes seethed. It may have been shock that kept him from retorting for several seconds.

"That is more than I want to hear from you, Miss Caldwell. Go immediately into my office and wait for me. You will want to gather your things from the locker, I'm sure."

"Fire me if you like. There was no good reason to place her on heavy insulin. And you have no right to conduct your electroshock experiments on her –"

"Electroconvulsive Therapy!" he corrected. "And it appears you have no restraints against overstepping your bounds."

"Nor do you. And furthermore, if you proceed with your hideous plan for electroshock against Miss Slaughter, or whatever you think will increase your prestige here, I will file a report against you with the State."

He spun toward her and leaned inches from her face. "I believe you have just been fired, Miss Caldwell. You and I have nothing more to say to each other. Please leave this facility now. Any back pay you may have coming will be handled without the need for you to ever darken the entrance to this hospital again!"

'The only darkness here, Sir, is your presence, and those of the demonic powers you serve."

Blanchard swelled up as though to explode upon her. The epithet he swore fell dully on her back as she stormed out of the ward between the parting columns of staff members and mobile patients who witnessed the exchange.

Blanchard glared at the gaggle of watchers until they dispersed. Then he marched out of the ward along the same path Caldwell had taken.

Behind him, a matron and a few patients stopped to watch the young woman who was the subject of the blow-up they witnessed.

Under a cone of lamplight illuminating the bed, the figure of the lovely young Maisie Slaughter, with long auburn hair draped across her pillow, lay in deep unconsciousness. Her eyes were closed, but behind the lids the movement was intent upon something unseen. Her arms, outside the sheets, waved conductor-like to an unheard melody, and likewise, the rest of her body seemed to be swaying to the same apparent music.

A close observer would note that tears seeped from underneath her eyelids.

And as strange as her behavior was, her smile was likely the only one in the entire hospital.

* * * * *

Maisie had never experienced the degree of closeness to the Savior that she was now experiencing. She felt as though she were swimming deep in a clear sea. How she got there, she did not know – only that she had no concern for being anywhere else.

She flowed with a current that came from behind her, not like waves, in surges, but in a gentle, steady movement in one inexorable direction, with Majesty just beyond reach. The sea was alight with a glow she had never seen, wherever she had been before being in the sea. Magnificent reefs grew far below her and crystal brilliance rippled above her in an undulating plane like a bed sheet flapping in the wind; this she took to be the surface of the sea. Her hair flowed behind her in tingly orchestration. The water did not seem wet or settle in her ears or assault her open eyes the way she had experienced somewhere before in a crystal clear pool with other people nearby. In fact, the only sense she had that she was in water was weightlessness and being moved completely by the flow of something strong and gentle.

Oddest of all was the music she heard and the unutterable song being sung by voices in the flow. She saw no one else. She likened this to being in the meadow of a farm, dancing and singing to the Lord, her Master. Only, she had an urge to feel the coolness of grass under her feet and a breeze, and she wanted to be more exuberant in her movements rather than flow along in this seemingly controlled movement. The flow seemed to be the music and song and she was merely carried along. Still, in the mystery of it all, she knew she was singing to Him, the great and mighty God, Creator of all things. It just seemed He was there, invisibly, before her.

On and on she swam. The movements of her hands and feet, though giving the appearance of being productive in the swim, were more the fluid movements of an orchestral conductor never tiring of the melody. Huge fish and sea creatures watched her pass, but they were merely incidental to her, relegated to the periphery of her awareness. She was in the song and the song was in her. She was in her Master and He was in her, an invisible charging of life and strength and joy.

Would she ever return from where the sea was taking her? The question barely registered in her mind, swallowed up in the peace and joy. All that really mattered was that she was here – and so was He.

Vernon Blanchard stormed from the hallway into the reception area, his face red and his eyes hard.

"Oh, Doc Blanchard," called Nurse Proctor, barely glancing above her work station. "Another man called enquiring about the Slaughter patient. I told him right off he could not visit her and that she was undergoing treatment."

The low swinging door separating her from the reception area slammed against the side of the counter. Proctor jumped and gave a startled cry as Blanchard pushed his way through toward his office door.

She managed to blurt a question: "Did you hear me?"

He stopped abruptly and said, "See that the Slaughter patient receives glucose to bring her out of coma, and prepare her for ECT immediately!"

He forged ahead without acknowledging her further, shoving his door open and slamming it shut behind him.

CHAPTER SEVENTEEN

The rain slacked off considerably, so that driving was a little less stressful for Adam. His thoughts were flying, and he was bothered by the phone calls he had made. The officer he spoke with at the Sheriff's office acted as though he knew nothing about the murder of Ray Lee Colbert or the fact that Adam was considered a suspect. Had that changed? Had Sheriff Mobley actually backtracked and absolved him as a suspect? Of course, he probably knew, anyway, that Riley was the guilty party, but would Mobley go so far as to turn on Riley? That did not seem logical unless what Maisie said to him had somehow hit home and caused him to reconsider everything.

And more disturbing was his brief conversation with the nurse at Mid-State Hospital. She said Maisie was undergoing treatment, that she could not have visitors. That did not sound at all as though she was only there for some evaluation. Had they evaluated her so quickly and decided she needed treatment. That was not logical either. Anyone could see she was far from anything that could be considered crazy. But his confidence in her did nothing to settle a growing sense of anxiety about what might have happened there.

He had decided not to bother calling Sheriff Mobley. Instead, he was determined to find out about Maisie himself. An attendant at the gas station where he filled up gave him directions to Mid-State Hospital and he would be there in less than forty-five minutes.

* * * * *

Captain Art Lowe was cursing himself for not getting more

details from Adam Woods earlier, until the telephone rang. Maybe that was Woods calling back now, he thought.

"Sheriff's Office, Captain Lowe speaking," he said, picking up the phone quickly.

"Captain Lowe, this is Sheriff Carson over in Settles County. Just need to confirm the APB information you gave our dispatcher this morning. You're looking for a black 1936 Chevrolet coupe?"

"Yes sir, being driven by a Caucasian male, approximately twenty-one or twenty-two years of age, name of Adam Woods."

"Well, one of my patrol officers just radioed in and I reminded him of that information. He said he'd just a few minutes before seen a car of that description headed toward Mooresville. Probably crossed the county line by now."

"Mooresville, uh?" Lowe calculated it to be an hour away from Odino, maybe two.

"Yessir, does your subject have people, that is, relatives, in the vicinity?"

"Not to my knowledge, Sheriff." He would call the law enforcement agencies in the Mooresville area to alert them. "Look, Sheriff, I sure do appreciate your calling me. I'll get with the folks over in Compton County to be on the lookout. Thanks for calling."

As he hung up, it occurred to him that Sheriff Mobley had driven the Slaughter woman to Mooresville, to the State Hospital. Maybe that was where he was headed. It could be that he was friends with her. The oppressive feelings he had encountered earlier suddenly vaporized. He was excited again.

* * * * *

Adam found a place to park in the broad circular drive in front of the three-story, red brick building. He had not anticipated the place was so big, and yet so uncluttered with vehicle or foot traffic. Hospitals were normally busy with visitors coming and going. Here was only a large linen delivery truck backed up to a small ante-building at the left end of the structure, half a dozen cars parked in what appeared to be an employee lot facing the left side of the main building, and no one walking around the grounds that stretched to his right beyond the long facade.

The windows on the top two floors of the main building sported heavy wire grillwork over double-sash windows, some of glass in which had been painted white. Another building about a block away, to the right side of the main structure, appeared to be a more recent addition, of two stories, and bearing the same kind of secured windows. No human activity and the brighter, newer appearance of the building suggested it might not yet be in use.

To the right of the massive double doors fronting the main building, a large, engraved bronze plaque identified the building as "Mid-State Hospital for the Insane, Administration Building."

He entered a black-and-white tile foyer with a large unmanned desk in the center, flanked by several gray steel doors. One door was directly behind the desk at a distance of about fifteen feet. A sign on it read, "East Wing Staff Only." To the left, in a wall perpendicular to the desk, another door was identified with large painted lettering: "North Wing Staff Only." He turned in the opposite direction and confirmed a third door led into the South Wing. A less imposing door to the right of it bore the sign, "Administration Office, Vernon Blanchard, Director. Visitor Sign In." He opened the door and entered.

Inside, the tile floors were polished and the walls appropriately clean and painted, but there was no hospital smell to the place.

"Hello," he called when he saw no one behind the counter to his right.

A woman in starched white nurse uniform stood and looked at him as though surprised to see someone come in.

"May I help you?" She asked with an officious air about her.

"I'm here to see a woman that came here for evaluation," said Adam, not sure how to begin tracking Maisie down.

"And who might that be?"

He walked nearer. "Maisie Slaughter. She came in for an evaluation."

"So you said," she answered. Adam thought she became even more aloof than before, if that was possible. "I'm afraid the Slaughter patient cannot have visitors."

"Patient?" Adam asserted. "She's not a patient. She's being –"

"Yes, you said that already. Evaluated." She stretched a thin, brief and unconvincing smile at him, and added, "But she is a patient and she cannot have visitors."

Adam stood still as the woman disappeared from view behind the counter. Anger rose in him and he struggled for something to say that might be a calm appeal to reason.

"Uh, Ma'am?"

The nurse stood again. "Yes?"

"Look, I've driven a long way to see her, and –"

The lady leveled her eyes at Adam and cut him off. "I'm sure you have, sir, but an officer of the law also drove a long way to bring her here for treatment, and that's exactly what we are providing. As you must surely realize, this is a hospital."

He glared at the dim, high ceiling for a moment, trying to compose himself.

"Look, I know what it is," he said. "You've locked up my friend and..."

She interrupted again. "We do not simply lock people up. We protect them from themselves and others."

He modified his voice to match her stern tone. "You've locked her up like one of your crazy people, and I came to take her home." He stared at the woman before continuing.

"Just tell me where she is, okay? I've heard stories about what you all do to people in places like this."

The woman took a deep breath, cleared her face of the signs of annoyance and flipped another stretched smile onto her face.

"Please have a seat," she said as she stood with papers in her hand and disappeared through a doorway behind her.

He decided he did not want to sit in one of the few uncomfortable-looking chairs against the left wall, so he stood.

More than five minutes later, the nurse returned, followed by a tall rail-thin man with meticulously combed and varnished graying brown hair. He stepped forward to the counter.

"Mr. –" He consulted a slip of paper in his hand and left the question hanging. "Are you a relative of the Slaughter patient?"

"Adam Woods. Maisie Slaughter's my friend."

"I'm afraid that won't – "

He stepped forward quickly, but not in a threatening way. "I want to see her."

"Sir, I'm the Administrator, Vernon Blanchard."

"Fine, Mister Blanchard. Will you take me to see my friend?" Adam forced a courteous smile. "Now?"

"Very well. Follow me." Blanchard turned and stalked off with Adam at his heels. Over his shoulder, he spoke to Proctor: "Hold glucose till I get back."

After a silent march along three hollow and dim corridors, silent except for the echo of their shoes against tile, and a hurried climb up a flight of stairs in a cold concrete stairwell, they arrived at double doors, marked "East Wing," which Blanchard pushed through without slowing.

Adam's eyes fell as he entered behind the administrator. A cacophony of groanings met their entrance as a backdrop for bed after bed of sheet-covered forms that showed only vague movement. The heads that turned toward the pair of men did so very slowly, and the eyes that tried to focus on them tracked too slowly to bring awareness.

Adam was still staring at unintrigued faces when Blanchard halted in front of him.

"You have five minutes. Enjoy your visit with your friend," said the man blandly, his hand gesturing palm-up to a lone bed in a dark alcove of the ward. Blanchard strode away as Adam moved slowly toward the figure in the bed. A stout young woman in white uniform who had been hovering near the bed backed away and drifted out of his sight.

The patient, whom he did not recognize quickly, lay face up with gaunt, ashen features, open mouth and closed eyelids. Matted auburn hair, with what appeared to be wet streaks, was bunched in wads against the pillow. Her skin glistened with wet streaks as though someone had hastily wiped her face with a too-damp cloth. Except for slight movement of the diaphragm underneath the sheet, the body might have been a corpse.

"Maisie?" he asked softly, leaning over her form.

He reached to her cautiously and nudged her shoulder. "Maisie?"

She did not move.

"She's medicated," said a voice behind him.

Adam turned to see the nurse who had been standing nearby moments earlier. She might have been in her late twenties or early thirties and looked frightened.

"I'm Lorene Mills. I've been watching after her. Are you a relative?" The softness of her voice did not seem to match the bulk of her figure.

"She's my friend. What –" He turned back to Maisie. "What's happened to her?"

"I've only been working on this wing today, so I don't know a lot about her case. They – we have to keep her medicated. It's for her own good," she added.

Adam knelt beside the bed and leaned closer.

"Maisie, can you hear me?"

"She hasn't been awake on my shift yet. I think she just had ECT a few hours ago."

"ECT? What's that?" he asked in apparent shock.

"Electroconvulsive therapy. It works wonders on some patients."

"Electro – " He halted. "I don't understand. There must be some mistake. She's not insane."

"She has a sweet, pretty smile. Like an angel."

"Why?" He asked. "Why is she medicated? What did she do?"

"I'm sorry, I don't really know."

"Aren't you a nurse? What do her records say?"

"No sir. I'm just a matron, an aide. I've only been here – "

"Yeah, just today. My God!" He shook his head. "I can't believe this is Maisie."

"How old is she?"

"Twenty-one. She only got here yesterday!"

The young girl stifled surprise poorly. She wiped her eyes quickly, lowering her hand to her mouth. When she spoke, her voice quavered.

"Yesterday? The therapy sometimes makes –" Her words hung unfinished.

"What?"

"It sometimes hurts their memory."

Adam looked sick. After a moment, he stood abruptly. "Where's the man that brought me in here?" His face was determined. "Blanchard."

"The young woman backed away slowly. "I – I'll go get him." She turned and hurried away.

Moments later when Blanchard appeared, Adam took the man's elbow and pulled him aside.

"What on God's earth have you done to Maisie?"

Blanchard pulled his elbow away. "Your friend is a very ill woman. She –"

"She's not ill!" Adam protested.

"I'm sure you know much more than we experts do, Mister Woods." Blanchard insisted. "She is delusional and schizophrenic. She has wild conversations with birds and invisible people. Surely, you can see she is a danger to herself without treatment."

"I don't see any such thing! Who says she's delusional and schizophrenic?"

"Well trained doctors, sir, that's who. Maybe we should go out into the lobby. Becoming emotional around the patients is not good for them."

"I want to talk to one of these doctors," he demanded.

"Let's just go out into the lobby, Mister Woods." Blanchard started away.

Adam stared after him. He looked back at Maisie briefly before turning and following the administrator out of the ward.

In the hallway, Adam saw Blanchard leaning toward a woman in a nurse's uniform. He was speaking quietly next to her ear. The woman hurried off and Blanchard, with a glance back at Adam, proceeded down the hall.

Blanchard seemed insistent upon a long march to the reception area, hurrying away by a route that was not the way they had come, down the stairwell and through another series of intervening halls. Adam followed at a slight distance.

As they entered the reception foyer, two large aides dressed in white pants and white tee-shirts moved aside to allow Blanchard to pass between them, which he did and quickly turned back to face him. The three stared menacingly at Adam. The nurse he had seen Blanchard talking to outside the ward stood against the wall behind them, and the reception nurse was nowhere to be seen.

"Now, Mister Woods, you may voice your objections and complaints as loudly and as obnoxiously as you wish. What were your demands?" A slight smile played on the man's face.

"I want to speak with the doctor who is treating my friend," he demanded, taking a step forward.

"The attending physician is not on the premises today, Mister Woods." Blanchard's coy smile behind the pair of guard dogs was brave.

"Get him here."

"I'm sorry, sir, but we're not in the habit of demanding that our physicians jump when we call. Perhaps you could come back at a more convenient time."

"You – " Adam took another step and the attendants met him forcefully. One punched him in the stomach and the other, as Adam doubled over, skillfully twisted his arm to an abrupt angle behind his back.

"Security has been called, Mister Woods, and they are on their way. Would you mind waiting here for a few minutes until they can escort you off the property?"

Blanchard patted one of the attendants on the back as he swept past him into the hall.

"Have a pleasant day, Mister Woods."

CHAPTER EIGHTEEN

R. Burson Munter, M.D., Ph.D, was not famous by any means, at least not as famous as Dr. Walter Freeman. However, he believed there was room at the top for a second leucotomy celebrity. He had performed Freeman's signature transorbital lobotomy flawlessly, if that could be said at all of the nature of swirling blades around in a patient's frontal lobe hoping to sever brain connections that – perhaps – were the cause of abnormal and schizophrenic behavior. He had said more than once he did not understand why the procedure worked, given the simplicity of its objectionable method and the lack of true skill required, but did he really have to understand it if the results were more satisfactory than previous and existing alternative treatments? No, his lack of knowledge and training in the field of electricity never stopped him from turning on a light bulb.

Munter's office was in his home, a sprawling brick ranch on the southern outskirts of Chattanooga, Tennessee. A grove of apple trees occupied the view through his office window, beyond an expanse of lawn. He sat at his desk, his sock feet propped on the corner, and reviewed notes he had written months earlier on observing Walter Freeman perform three transorbital lobotomies in less than an hour at a hospital in Ohio. He had been told that the man actually performed his earliest procedures with ice picks. Common, household ice picks! Presumably, he had sterilized them. Obviously, it became apparent to him that if he intended to impress the medical community, he at least had to use instruments more suitable to the true practice of medicine. So at some indefinite point, Freeman had switched to an orbitoclast, a long blade whose steel shaft expanded into a handle topped with a slightly curved "T" shaped heel to fit the hand and facilitate tapping the blade through the thin bony part of the skull behind the eyeballs.

Munter laid his notes aside and picked up the note his wife had written him earlier. The Administrator at Mid-State Hospital, down in Georgia, had called to inquire whether he might come down very soon and perform several lobotomies. In fact, the note had an asterisk that led to a side note: "TOMORROW!!" He had planned to play golf tomorrow. He reckoned the drive to Mid-State would take about four or five fours, or, if the money was enough, he could charter a small plane and be there in less than two.

Munter recalled meeting the Administrator, an irritating man with an ingratiating attitude about him. He could imagine nothing he would rather avoid than spending a day or two under the man's unsettling observance. Nevertheless, he would be paid handsomely and possibly receive some attention from the press. He would have to increase his fee a bit to see how serious the man was.

He scribbled a note for his wife: "Tell them $500 for the day, plus expenses, plus $100 per procedure." If they could afford that, he would definitely go to Mid-State for a day.

* * * * *

Adam was still gasping for breath as the two aides dragged him outside the reception area through a side door. They stood him up on a narrow concrete sidewalk under the canopy of massive oaks and straightened his shirt.

The bigger man bent down to let Adam see his face. "Look, I'm sorry we had to rough you up a little, Bud. Blanchard is a –" He stopped mid-sentence. "Well, he's difficult to work for. But when he says Security is on the way, he probably means the cops."

"He did mean the cops," echoed the other aide.

"Yeah, so you ought to go on and get in your car. Don't hang around here and get arrested. You understand?"

Holding his stomach, Adam straightened a bit without responding. He took a couple of unsteady steps before stopping to regain his equilibrium.

The man seemed reluctant to go. "You came to see the young girl from Odino?"

Adam pivoted his head.

"Yeah," he managed.

The taller, heavy man stepped closer. "That's what Miss Mills said." His tone had become almost friendly. "Hey, I'm not a doctor or anything, but I know when somebody don't need to be here."

Adam looked at him with interest.

"There's a nurse that got canned for objecting to the girl's treatment. Her name is Caldwell. She lives in town. Probably only one or two Caldwells in the phone book." He gave Adam a nod and added. "You might want to give her a call."

"What's her first name?"

The man shrugged. "I think she lives on a street named after a flower. That's all I know."

* * * * *

Sheriff Mobley had to hold the telephone away from his ear. Lieutenant Bascomb "Bosco" Slaughter's response was loud and vehement on learning his sister had been admitted to an insane asylum.

"Who did that?" he demanded. "How could anybody in their right mind...?"

He was still ranting when Mobley placed the receiver to his head again. "I hate to be the one to tell you..."

Slaughter railed non-stop.

"Lieutenant Slaughter, we need..."

After a moment, Bosco Slaughter halted with a demanding question: "Where is she?"

"She's at Mid-State Hospital down in Mooresville."

"Who put her in there?"

Mobley hesitated a beat too long. "A citizen complained she was a danger to herself, and...' He took a breath. "And I drove her over there for evaluation."

147

Slaughter's response actually hurt Mobley's ear. However, the real pain was in his conscience, and had been for two days.

"You!!"

"Yessir. It was supposed to be an evaluation, but I think something's gone wrong."

Before he finished speaking, Slaughter began loudly railing once more. Mobley waited for an opening.

"Can you get home?" asked the Sheriff. He winced as the tirade took another tangent. "Yessir, I know you're in Germany. I am the one who called you."

After a moment, Mobley found an opening. "Would it help if I call your commanding officer?" He listened as Slaughter gave him the officer's name and how to reach him, and then explained in a calmer tone why he expected the request to be denied. "I understand," said Mobley when Slaughter finished. "I'll do whatever I can to get her out, and I'll be in touch to let you know what's going on."

When he finally hung up the phone, Mobley sat back in his chair. Bosco Slaughter had explained his unit was in the midst of maneuvers, and as the Army chaplain he was committed to being there until maneuvers were completed. And no, he did not believe his C.O. would approve emergency leave.

Mobley sat in the darkened space of his home office with the shade pulled. He had not wanted to take the risk of coming home, now that he had broken with Riley, but he owed it to Katie, his wife, to begin making amends. His pistol lay on the desk in front of him. Mobley retrieved it, rose and walked to the window. He pulled the shade slightly away to get a view of the driveway and the county roadway beyond. He would not put it past Potter Riley to follow him to his house, and bring one or two of his hired help with him. He would have to get back to the office in town to keep his wife out of harm's way.

The smell of catfish frying reminded him that Katie was preparing supper. He would stay a little longer for her, to have dinner with her, and then he would go. He could not make the call to Slaughter's C. O. from the Department with Lowe sitting on the switchboard out front. The man was already too interested in finding some way to trip him up. Outwardly, he was polite enough, but something had gotten into him in recent months. Lowe would be off-duty in half an hour. That would give Mobley time to have dinner before leaving.

Of course, Katie would suspect he was meeting some other woman, but he would have to take her on a nice vacation somewhere after all this Riley trouble was over, and convince her he was a changed man. He planned to be, after all. Maybe he would even arrange a second honeymoon, renew their wedding vows, really show her how special she was. He smiled at the idea.

He picked up the note with the phone number Slaughter had given him and stuffed it into a pocket. Maybe he could convince the officer to grant an emergency leave under the circumstances. Slaughter had to get home fast before something happened to Gal that would haunt Mobley for the rest of his life. For once, he cared about what happened to people as a result of his actions, both on a personal and a professional level.

* * * * *

Charlotte Colbert's face was drained and pale. She had walked the floor unceasingly the night before. Ray Lee was dead. Bondurant was dead. And only God knew where Adam was. She had prayed till her throat was sore and she could not cry another tear. Now she sat on the metal glider on the front porch, the lights in the house all off and the blackness of night her only comfort. Mosquitoes buzzed around her ears and feasted on her bare arms, but she barely had the energy or motivation to swat at them. Worry consumed her.

Had she ever really loved Ray Lee? She thought she did, but when the news of Bonder's death came, she found that fact devastating. Why, she did not know and had no will to find out.

Adam's absence and the Sheriff's suggestion he might be a suspect in Ray Lee's death tore the remaining strands of her heart asunder. Adam was not a killer. Her boy, so shunned all his life, without a fair chance at life from the very beginning, was too tender-hearted underneath the recent tough-talking bravado that seemed to come from nowhere when Ray Lee entered her life. She had neglected Adam for so long, failed to give him the reassurance he must have needed. That was the well-head for most of her tears. She had known, deep inside, she was neglecting his feelings. She had acted like an immature teenager since Ray Lee had been around.

The burden of Adam's plight settled upon her, pressing the light from her soul. Though she could shed no more tears, her chest heaved and shuddered with the weight of her sorrow. How quickly had her world come crashing down! How desperately she needed to hold her son again, to know he was safe, to tell him how much she loved him!

* * * * *

After hanging up the telephone, Adam returned to his car and sat in the dark parking lot of a church a mile or so from town. He had needed a secluded spot to sort out his conversation with the cautious and cryptic Helen Caldwell, the fired nurse. She had been reluctant to talk with him at first, but gradually opened up. She verified Maisie was, for some unknown reason, being hurried toward drastic treatment that could damage her for life, and that by the administrator, who seemed to have something to prove. She was worried for Maisie's sake, and knew nothing about any evaluation she was given, only that her own estimate of Maisie's condition was that she did not belong in a mental institution. She described the medication and electroconvulsinve treatment she thought was planned for her, and was not surprised to learn the latter had already been scheduled.

On hearing her detailed description of ECT, Adam was angrier than when he saw Maisie unconscious. What they were doing to Maisie was criminal, yet he was in the position of being unable to contact police without winding up in jail. Maybe that was the only solution, though, he thought. If he could convince the police that she was misdiagnosed and being mistreated, they could pull her out of the hospital. But would they believe him if they thought he was a murder suspect? Would they even believe a disgruntled ex-employee of the hospital?

He could not count on cooperation from the police. Besides, there might not be time to get the help of police if he understood the Caldwell lady correctly. She said she was almost sure Blanchard was getting Maisie ready for something she called a leucotomy. Some sort of brain surgery. The way Caldwell described it sickened him to the point of nausea. Such a treatment was insane in itself. It pained him to even think of Maisie being subjected to brain surgery! Was this place really a hospital or some house of horrors being run by the insane?

No, he could not wait. He had to do something himself. When he suggested he had to get Maisie out of there right away, the nurse had balked and grown silent. She clearly was not going to be cooperative with any kind of activity that might lead to physically removing someone from a state institution. But she had dropped a piece of information before hanging up that he was sure was intended to be of assistance in doing what he needed to do.

He recalled her last words. She had said, "Don't you go near that ward to try to get that young woman out. I'll not be party to that kind of clandestine thing. It would be very foolish if that's what you have in mind, especially before midnight or after 5:00AM." After a moment, she added, "No, Mister Woods, I urge you not to try anything as foolish as trying to break in one of those doors." Then she hung up.

It would have been more helpful if she had told him how to get inside without being detected, but he would take her hint at the best timeframe to make an attempt.

He looked at his wristwatch by the reflected glow of a security light beside the church. Eighty forty. Almost three and a half hours before midnight. He had not eaten, nor could he, and he could not sleep. It was too dangerous to go back to the hospital to try to find a way inside. The only thing he could do was wait.

Actually, he realized, there was one other thing he could

do. He could pray for Maisie.

CHAPTER NINETEEN

Adam stood in the shadows of old oaks behind the asylum's main building. The perspiration on his face and neck was far heavier than the temperature and humidity would normally produce, and that, despite a pleasant breeze that brushed against his face. He had made up his mind what he would do to get Maisie out of the place. But he had also prayed for her. As soon as he had done the latter, he was overcome with uneasiness that he interpreted as fear. Determined not to be restrained by fear, he had returned to the grounds of Mid-State Hospital and waited for silhouettes in the lighted windows to cease movement, indicating staff members were settling down or leaving for the night. The building a block away, which he had seen earlier, was indeed completely dark inside and out, confirming his suspicion that it was not yet inhabited, and would thus not likely contain witnesses to someone walking between the two buildings. He had parked his car there.

The more cars left the front lot, and the more lights flicked off inside, the more Adam's uneasiness grew. A quick survey of the long front face of the building, with the partially lighted reception area almost exactly in the middle, revealed only a couple of lights still lighted on each of the three floors. He held his hand up to the dim glow reflected from a security light outside the nearest exit door. His hand shook visibly. That irritated him. He would not be a coward and abandon Maisie to what the people at this hospital might do to her. In fact, he decided, he would wait no longer. Now was as good a time as any to go inside.

As he stepped from behind a tree, the word "No!" seemed to rise up inside him. It startled him so much that he retreated quickly to the safety of darkness. He had to get control of his emotions, Adam realized. Nervousness could cause him to make a stupid mistake and blow the whole rescue. He took several deep breaths and exhaled slowly. After a few more moments, he tested the small flashlight in his hand to make sure the light was still strong and he pressed forward slowly.

The nearest exit door was no more than forty yards from where he had hidden himself. He moved quickly to it. Even though approaching the door meant exposing himself in the dome of light given off by the security lamp, he had to check the handle of the door in case it had been inadvertently left unlocked. He stepped quickly into the lighted area, grasped the steel handle and pulled gently. The door did not budge. Anticipating that, he moved quickly to his right, toward the back entrance where he had seen a second lighted exit. Again, daring to enter the circle of light there, he tugged on the handle and found it fast. He had been hoping one of them had not fully latched. The nurse had specifically said not to try to break into one of the doors. Was that a subtle hint to try a window? After all, the doors were steel and reinforced, and the very appearance said they would be virtually impossible to break through under normal circumstances.

He ducked into the darkness once more and moved around the corner to the back side of the building, which he had not seen in daylight. There the structure extended a hundred yards or so to the intersection of a perpendicular wing that was equally long and with the same number of floors. Noting where the sun had gone down, he assumed that would be the East Wing, where he had seen Maisie earlier, and where he stood now was the South Wing.

On the ground level, in the angle of that intersection was a small area enclosed in a tall chain link fence. It appeared to be some sort of secure recreation area, though in the darkness of the space he saw nothing shaped like anything he associated with recreation. The rest of the grounds dropped off gradually to what appeared to be a park stretching just beyond the end of the wing to a service road and probably a delivery area behind the wing.

On this side of the building, only six windows showed direct light inside, one on each of the three floors and on each of the intersecting wings, all very near the intersections, suggesting an office or station at the entrance to each ward. In fact, he recalled having passed a large counter as he entered the ward where he saw Maisie. But which floor and which wing had he entered? He did remember climbing stairs, but not two flights, so he concluded she must be on the second floor.

Since the height of the windows on the bottom floor was relatively low, he needed no additional height to check them. He eased along the length of the darkened South wing, gripping each window sash, then moved along the outside of the East Wing. A few seconds of pushing and pulling at each confirmed all the first-floor windows were fastened securely.

Standing well away from the lighted windows near the intersection with the East Wing, Adam was scanning the windows of the second floor when he noticed what might be a black space at the base of one. It was on the South Wing, two away from the lighted window. He stepped back, shielding his eyes against the nearby lights, and saw that the window appeared to be raised two or three inches. Maybe he could find a way to climb to the window, and with a screwdriver, remove the wire cover.

He returned to his car, retrieved a screwdriver from the glove compartment and surveyed the darkened side of the building for anything that might get him high enough off the ground to breach the window.

Though he had no idea how long he had spent in trying windows, the sky was still dark. He guessed he had another three hours before the onset of daylight would prevent further efforts. He moved toward the chain-link fence defining the supposed recreation area, stepping quietly due to the nearness of the lighted rooms at the intersection of the wings. Inside the approximately fifteen foot square space, he saw the silhouette of a long, low wooden bench. If it was not somehow fixed to the ground or bound to the fence itself, he might be able to get it over the fence.

The fence was not topped with additional security wire, so, using the steel poles of the fastened gate, he climbed over and dropped noisily to the ground. After waiting to make sure he had not been heard, he slipped to the bench and pulled on one end. It lifted readily. Within minutes, he had slid it over the top of the fence, lowered it on the other side until the back legs caught on the fence top, and scaled the fence again. Lifting the bench from the fence top, he leaned it with its supporting legs outward, against the top of the first-floor window. Then, climbing up the rough underside of the wooden seat, he pulled himself onto the top of the window and began unscrewing the screws holding the steel grillwork over the second-floor window. He would need to remove at least six or eight screws at and near the bottom of the cover in order to have enough space to pull himself through an opening.

Suddenly, he noticed movement in his peripheral vision. He froze and turned his head slightly. Someone stood at the lighted second-floor window just twenty feet away. Was the person looking at him? He could not tell since the form was silhouetted against a bright light. Adam held his breath. His feet ached as he struggled to maintain balance on the narrow ledge. Gingerly, he shifted some of his weight to the top of the the bench for a moment to prevent a cramp.

The figure in the window raised a hand to its face, possibly to shield the light. It was a man, gauging from the shoulders and arms. Seconds passed. The man remained fixed. Was he staring at the spectacle of someone breaking into a window, maybe astonished at what he was seeing? Adam's heart pounded. His foot slipped slightly on the ledge, and he caught himself with a grip on the window cover. He willed every muscle in his feet and legs to hold still.

Finally, the man turned and walked slowly away from the window. Adam noticed for the first time that the glass of the window appeared to be frosted. He breathed relief. Maybe the man had seen nothing after all. Nevertheless, he had to work fast and quietly.

Removing enough screws took more time than he anticipated, but when the last one he could reach fell away, he pulled the covering outward, bending the wire edge out of the way. The window slid upward quietly at his nudging and a pine scented odor of cleaning products drifted toward him. Maybe he had found a supply closet. He reached inside the window and gripped the back edge, then, scraping the toes of his shoes against the brick edges to find a toe-hold, he struggled upward and into the opening, wiggling his lower torso through as he hand-walked across the dirty wooden floor. Finally inside, he lay on the floor in pitch blackness and moved his hands carefully in arcs for whatever might give him a clue to his surroundings. His right hand touched wet strands of cloth, perhaps a mop. Ahead was a gray line of reflected light on the floor, obviously coming underneath a door. He gradually maneuvered himself to a crouch, then to standing position and inched cautiously in the direction of the door.

Adam reached forward to find a handle, but cringed as a bug crawled under his pant leg onto his shin, moving quickly upward, He slapped at the creature several times, failing to halt it. By impulse he grabbed his pants above his knee, where he sensed the creature, and squashed it in the fold of cloth. The slimy residue felt creepy against his leg, but he shook the fabric until the small sticky clump fell downward.

Regaining his composure, he found the doorknob and turned it slowly until the latch was free, then pulled the door open slightly. In the dim light ahead lay a patch of tiled hallway and, eight feet away, a wooden handrail mounted against the opposite wall. He heard a feint hum as from some semi-dormant electrical equipment, but no sound of human activity. Arcing the door inward a foot or two, he leaned out for a look. To his left about fifteen feet was a dark wall with double doors that appeared to be the entrance to the South Wing ward. A sign above the door was illegible in darkness. To the right, only four or five feet away, was another doorway with a pair of double doors, each with small window openings at about average eye-level. The light through the openings was indirect and perhaps from only a single light fixture, possibly emanating from the room in which he had seen the man silhouetted.

He held his position for a moment listening for any movement. Did he hear music in the distance? A very low melody, possibly from a radio, wafted from beyond the doors.

Assessing where he might be in relation to Maisie's ward, he assumed she would be beyond the doors, past the lighted room and down the wing to the right.

Across the hall from where he watched, and a few feet to

the left was a door marked EXIT. A stairwell. Maybe, for fire purposes, the building might have another such exit just outside the East Wing as well.

The first thing necessary was to make sure he was not mistaken as to which ward he had seen her in, so he decided it would be smart to check the ward to his left. Glancing at the double doors to make sure there was no movement visible, he left the door behind him open and tiptoed to them. Once there, he pressed his face to the near door's small window and stared into the darkness of the ward, hoping his eyes would adjust and give some clue as to the layout. Soon he was able to discern only the shapes of beds on either side of a center aisle. He closed his eyes and recalled approaching Maisie's bed. She had occupied a bed that was the first one on the right side of the ward he had entered. Slipping quietly through the swinging door into the ward, he moved slowly in the darkness.

Suddenly he heard movement in the bed nearest him on the right. Adam froze. In the pale blackness a white figure rose on the bed. The hair on his neck rustled involuntarily.

"Mama?"

The voice was of a young adult male, afraid but hopeful.

Adam's heart pounded like never before. He had to respond or risk a louder, even panicked question.

"No, go back to sleep," he whispered.

"Can you get me some water?"

He agonized for a full moment, feeling the tug on his emotions of such a question. Without trying, he imagined a hopelessly bound, misdiagnosed young man experiencing a brief episode of clarity from medications. He actually wanted to fulfill the request.

With a twinge of guilt, he said, "Yeah, sure. Lie down and I'll be back in a couple of minutes."

He hurriedly returned to the double doors, and exited.

If he could get past the lighted room, or aid station, and find Maisie, he could carry her down the stairwell that presumably was positioned near the entrance to the other wing and move quickly to an exit.

As he leaned close to a window at the next set of double doors, he saw a male aide coming out of the lighted station toward the door. He could do nothing but flatten himself against the wall behind him. He leapt backward as the nearest door swung open, obscuring him from the view of the aide, who looked straight ahead as he breezed through. The door swung back. Adam tiptoed quickly, following the door on its backswing without being seen. As he passed the open doorway to the aide station, he glanced in and saw another man working over a tray. The sight startled Adam since he had not expected two people on duty. He could do nothing but continue. Hurrying past the doorway and out of the splash of light in the hall, he hesitated in the shadows. He judged that this wing was accessible through two sets of double doors, as was the South Wing. And since one of the workers was in the South ward, he might be coming into the East ward next, possibly making routine checks.

He had no time to wait. He ducked past the first set of doors into the same kind of short hall that separated the two sets of swinging doors on the other wing. He was in luck. There on the left side of the hall was an exit, exactly as he had supposed. He hurried to the second pair of double swinging doors.

"Luther?" A voice called from behind him.

That was the aide still in the nurses' station. Adam's pulse quickened. He eased the near door open and slipped quickly through. What he did not expect to see was a door on the right wall, light emanating underneath it. This must be the room in which he saw the man silhouetted, he thought. Either someone was still in there, or the aide who had passed by him moments ago, had left the room to go to the other ward, in which case, he might be returning quickly.

In the opposite direction, exactly where it should be, was the exit door he expected. He began inching forward to the shape of the first bed on the right.

CHAPTER TWENTY

A faded blue pickup truck with no bed slowed along a county road outside Odino. As it veered off the road onto the low, grassy shoulder, its headlights died and the motor cut off. The truck coasted between a pair of pine trees into the cover of a dense thicket until it came to a brakeless stop against a decomposing tree trunk on the ground. The driver opened his door slowly, but was unable to avoid the creaking squall that came from rusty hinges. The short, muscular man shined a flashlight at the package on the floor next to the gear shifter - a clock taped to a pair of thin red cylinders. It showed four o'clock. More than two hours before dawn. Mobley would be sound asleep.

His associate, a tall, skinny man with stooped shoulders, got out of the other side of the truck, leaving his door open as they had agreed. The dome light did not work anyway, and leaving the doors open would help them get away faster.

"Come on, Man, set the alarm and connect the wires. We need to get out of here."

"Shut up! We'll get it done!" The driver lifted a brown bottle and drained the last of his beer before tossing the empty into the darkness.

"Don't throw it out there, stupid! You've got your fingerprints all over it," the taller man groused.

The driver waved the complaint away and gingerly picked up the clock as his partner began searching for the bottle.

"...they catch you, they'll get me, too..." The partner was muttering as he kicked around in the dark.

"Quit your worryin', Harris. Riley said the new Sheriff was on his payroll. Didn't you hear that?"

"You trust Riley?" The man stooped for his quarry and returned to the truck, pushing the bottle under the seat.

"Who said I trust him? I'm leaving as soon as he pays us

the rest of the money."

"Where're you goin'?"

The driver laughed. "Think I'd tell you? I don't trust you any more'n I do him!"

"That's all right, Kell. I'm leavin', too."

Kell fastened the clock wires. "Was the red wire supposed to connect to the blue wire?"

The taller man straightened instantly. "You don't know!" he exclaimed.

Kell broke out in restrained laughter. "Kiddin', man!"

Harris cursed violently.

"All set! Let's go!" The driver set out at a fast walk, dodging low limbs and cradling his package in both hands. His partner caught up with him, maintaining a constant whispered chatter. A three minute walk brought them to the edge of a broad and deep lawn.

"There it is," the driver nodded toward a sizable brick ranch flanked by tall oak trees on either end. "The master bedroom is at the front corner. Take this and set it up against the house on this end."

"Me? I don't want to handle that thing!"

The shorter man grabbed his partner by the collar and jerked him around. "Take it or I'll kill you right here!"

Without another word, the man accepted the explosive and crept slowly from the trees onto the lawn.

"Hurry up!" the driver demanded in an angry whisper.

The man increased his stride until he reached the house. He bent slowly and placed the item gently on the ground before he turned, racing back.

The driver did not wait. He was already in the truck, fumbling with the ignition switch when his associate jumped in panting. The engine came to life and the truck lurched in reverse as both doors closed. With his free arm on the back of the seat, the driver wove his way out of the woods and onto the grassy shoulder once more, whipping the truck in a wide circle, then jamming the gear shifter forward and tearing up dirt toward the roadway in the direction from which they had traveled.

Once on pavement the engine roared and headlights came

on. The truck sped off and the two men whooped far too loudly for discretion.

The alarm had been set for 4:20AM.

*****

A loud sound startled Ott Mobley awake, at least, awake enough to realize he had finally fallen asleep after tossing and turning for hours. The room was almost pitch black, so it took a moment for him to realize he had fallen asleep on the sofa in his downtown office. Then his ears recognized the sound he had heard: a fire siren. The thought of a possible home or business in danger made him realize why he had decided to stay downtown. He had parked his car right in front of the office so that anyone watching his movements would know where he was. And he had made sure the overnight dispatcher in the outer office knew he was staying. He could rest easier knowing Katie was safer with him away. That meant a lot to him.

The call to Slaughter's Commanding Officer had been unsuccessful, which meant it was up to him alone to do something about Gal. He had decided to head over to Mooresville as soon as Lowe and the day shift came in.

Mobley turned on a lamp beside the sofa and glanced at the clock on the far wall. Four twenty seven. He could get another couple hours sleep in before he had to wake Katie. Maybe he would let her sleep late and bring her a ham biscuit and coffee from the diner. She loved diner breakfasts.

Before he could turn the lamp off again, a loud, urgent knock came against the office door. Instinctively, he reached for his weapon.

The door burst open and the overnight dispatcher stood there, his eyes wide and frightened.

*****

Bonder Woods woke from his dream, a persistent dream that replayed the awful night of Flynn Riley's death. This time, however, instead of feeling the desperate helplessness and horror of the tragedy that usually filled his gut for hours after each dream, he felt excitement. He immediately sat up and pronounced two names: "Harper Slatt and Melvin Conway."

He had no idea whether these names had ever been known to him before; he only recalled referring to them as "Bud" or "friend" or some other term that sufficed in place of an actual name. Yet, he was sure these were the names of the two men in the card game that stormy night. When the new Sheriff, Mobley, had questioned him after his capture about the witnesses, he described them but could not come up with names. He had no one to turn to for help locating them; Potter Riley saw to that. Even Mobley seemed reluctant to search for them, taking Riley's side that there was no card game, just a robbery attack by Bonder Woods against a defenseless young Flynn Riley. The so-called defense attorney assigned to him took it for granted that the witnesses were non-existent.

But now Warden Ingles was probing, looking for answers to questions no one had ever posed on Bonder's behalf. The man was looking for the truth. Whether he intended to help him obtain a retrial or parole, there was no way of knowing. Bonder could not quite allow himself to trust men in authoritative positions. He had seen too many that had been corrupted.

But how odd it was to have forgotten – if indeed he had ever known – the names of the two men, and then suddenly to have them come clearly to his mind!

He tried to sit up, but the pain was too much. Nevertheless, there would be no more sleep for his eyes this night. God had certainly given him the names of these men. Why, at this time, after years of sitting in solitary confinement, would he suddenly remember them, or know them, if not for the very power and grace of God Himself! Maybe the time had not been right before. Maybe things were changing now somehow. Maybe God was moving in his behalf, to alter his external circumstances as He had Bonder's internal condition.

That would be the subject of his fervent prayer. What better way to spend the next few hours while all around him was quiet and content!

How he hoped Warden Ingles would stop in for a visit today! But he had said he would be back in a couple of weeks. Maybe he could convince someone to make a phone call to Ingles. Not likely, but he would ask anyway. Now that a tiny ray of hope had entered the picture, time seemed to be more of an enemy than it had been in these many years. Minutes suddenly loomed as large as the years had previously seemed.

CHAPTER TWENTY-ONE

Adam tiptoed into the deeper darkness of the ward, away from the small, dim pool of light in front of the double swinging doors. The moans and occasional snorts of the patients throughout the ward were creepy to him, but only motivated him to hurry in his task. The shape of the first bed became clearer as he neared. The occupant made little bulk underneath the sheet, suggesting Maisie was indeed there.

He stopped, drawing in breath at the sight that confirmed it was Maisie. Her face was peaceful, even joyful as she slept. A soft smile lay on her face. He might have stumbled upon her sleeping in her farmhouse, for all he could discern. She looked nothing like the gaunt, lifeless form he had seen the day before.

He was so encouraged that he leaned down and took her hand, which lay restfully against her pillow.

"Maisie!" he whispered.

Instantly, her eyes opened and focused on him. She smiled.

"Adam! How sweet of you to come for me."

Stunned, he could only blink in amazement at her. She knew he had come to take her home.

"Would you please give me a hug, Adam? I feel so unwanted here."

Tears came to his eyes. Rather than let her see them, he quickly leaned down and hugged her, cradling her head in his right elbow. He wanted to kiss her on the cheek, but hesitated, letting her hair wipe the tears from his eyes, instead. In that moment, she kissed his cheek and her arms tightened around his neck. His heart swelled. Was it his imagination, or had she really kissed him? She had, he was certain. Her lips were warm and soft against his skin. He wanted more than anything to tell her he loved her, but could not. To do that when the great need was to get her out of this place was, to him, selfishness.

"Maisie, are you ready to go home?"

"Do you remember what I told you before leaving the farmhouse?"

"Maisie, we've got to go before somebody comes in."

"He said that you belong to *Him.*"

"I'm going to get you up, now, okay?" He pulled the sheet under her legs, effectively wrapping her in it, and lifted her body.

"He said, you will swim where your father waded, and you will find footing where he drowned. Do not be afraid of the river."

"I remember, Maisie," he continued in a whisper. "But you've got to be quiet, okay? He straightened, adjusting the loose ends of the dragging sheet into his grasp, and moved to the doors with his back against the farther wall to enable him to see part of the station through the glass of the next doors.

"Are we really – ?" She began, but he quickly cut her off.

"Hush, Maisie, please. We've got to get past two aides out there."

Through the window he saw something odd. The other set of double doors was partly open. Had they seen him? He was suddenly nervous. Searching the short hallway between the two sets of doors, he saw nothing else that suggested the aides were aware of his presence. Still, he had to wait. The light through the windows of the other doors was consistent and unbroken. If he could even see a shadow or flicker of light through those windows, it would confirm someone was on the other side instead of waiting somewhere along the short hall for him to come out.

Maisie shifted slightly and he looked down at her. She had rested her head on his shoulder and was sound asleep.

Just as well, he thought. He needed her cooperation with silence.

When he returned his attention to the hallway, the door underneath the exit sign opened and the aide that had been inside the station when he passed came out and moved directly to and through the swinging doors toward the nurses' station. Adam breathed relief, thankful he had waited. That might explain why the doors were open; the aide had gone out for a moment.

He decided to act quickly. Easing through the near door, careful to not wake Maisie by bumping her against it, he glided to the exit door. He had to bend down to grasp the doorknob, but in a moment he was in the open, dark stairwell easing the door back to the jamb. He found a handrail against the wall side of the staircase and, pressing his hip against it, used it to guide himself downward. At the bottom of the stairs, he groped for the doorknob until he succeeded in opening the door.

Here again, Adam was faced with a set of swinging doors to his right and to his left. Right, he knew, was the entrance to the main wing, and there, he had checked two doors from the outside, one on the very end and one near the main entrance. The door at the end of the wing seemed to be the most logical choice for him to use, since it obviously led through another ward, while the middle of the building was likely to have more foot traffic.

Low light seeped under the doors and through the glass. The aide station at the juncture of wings here might be unoccupied if the level of light meant anything. Since he had not seen any activity when he tried the first-floor windows, he felt comfortable proceeding. Leaving the stairwell cautiously, he headed for the double doors at the aide station. Through the glass, he saw no movement whatsoever and noted that he heard no radio – both positive indications. He pushed through and tiptoed to the counter, peeking around the corner. The room appeared to be vacant. A low-wattage lamp gave minimal light from the top of a desk. He hurried past, bore left toward the last ward and eased through both sets of double doors.

Even through the darkness of the ward, he clearly saw the exit door at the end, as it was indicated by a red light and EXIT sign. It was there, as he took note of the direct pathway to freedom, that he realized he had been wrong. That door would absolutely be locked to keep patients from leaving the building. How stupid, he thought. Now he would have to go to the other door, through the most likely occupied area. He mentally chastised himself for not considering that, but he had no choice except to press onward. Hurrying back to the intersection of the two wings, he slipped past the vacant aide station once again to what would be the last set of double doors. Bright light shone through these, suggesting more employees might be there.

Once he reached the doors he eased near for a peek through the window. On the other side was a well lighted hallway with doors interspersed on both sides – offices or storage rooms – instead of a ward. Not more than thirty feet on the left was an EXIT sign posted on the wall beside an alcove. That should be the other door he had tried, on the front side of the building.

The hallway was empty. At the other end of the hall was a single door without a window in it. He was surprised. No apparent activity.

Emboldened, he pushed through the doors with his hip, gently swinging Maisie clear of them and ran to the alcove. He quickly ducked into the open space before the last barricade. He studied the door latch. It was a horizontal bar with a smaller release bar in its middle, made to be easily opened in a fire or some other emergency. Still, he had no idea if the way would be clear outside. He could not just burst through, though every impulse urged him toward that. Again, using his hip, he pressed the bar and pushed the door slowly open. The bright outside light obscured the trees beyond, but from what he could see – which did not include the vast area behind the door – his way was clear. He had come this far and he had no better options.

Shoving the door wide open he stepped out and hurried away from the light to the safety of darkness. Once there, he turned to make sure he had not missed something, like a party of security officers leering behind him. Nothing. A few raindrops streaked through the glow of the security light. Dawn was very near.

He took a deep breath, readjusted Maisie in his arms, and

rushed away in the direction of the unoccupied new building.

* * * * *

Red flashes from several vehicles streaked across the lawn and lit nearby pine trees in eerie intervals.

An off-duty fireman standing near the hook-and-ladder unit said for the third time to anyone who would listen, "I'm serious. It nearly knocked my beer off the counter at the County Line Bar. Man, that was some explosion! I jumped in my car and – "

"Look, Larson, would you just shut up?" A fireman rolling up a hose dropped it and came at the man in a threatening way. He stopped short. "Ain't you got any sense of decency at all? Sheriff Mobley's right over there." He pointed to the Fire Chief's sedan, its emergency light dormant and a lone silhouette immobile in the back seat.

The drunk was unperturbed. "To heck with Mobley! Everybody knows – "

The other fireman wasted no time diving at the man and jerking him straight by the collar, swearing through gritted teeth.

"I told you to shut up! The man lost his wife. If you say one more word, I'll knock you back to County Line." He pushed the man backward, "Now get out of here or I'll have a deputy haul you in for obstruction."

Larson looked ready to accept the challenge when another fireman stepped between them. He put his gloved hand on the man's shoulder and spoke firmly. "Go on home, Larson. It's not worth losing your job over. Go sleep it off."

After a moment of staring, Larson turned and stalked unsteadily away.

The eastern sky was transitioning from navy to gray. The coroner was finishing up in front of the steaming shell of the house, making notes on a clipboard. A pair of deputies stood talking behind Mobley's patrol car, its headlights trained on the blackened front door.

Raindrops began tapping against the fire trucks and, illuminated by the emergency lights, fell like red comets in waves against the scene.

CHAPTER TWENTY-TWO

Adam reached the car before the rain increased and opened the passenger door to place Maisie on the seat. Suddenly, a beam of light illuminated him from the direction of the new building a few yards away. He lurched and almost dropped Maisie onto the seat.

"Don't move, Mister Woods, not a muscle!"

Adam closed his eyes. His heart sank. His first thought was, "Maisie! What will happen to her?"

Footsteps crunched on gravel as two silhouettes , backlit by headlights from a car, approached him. He could do nothing. Before they reached him a second vehicle swung into the parking area and stopped behind his car with headlights trained on him and Maisie.

"I'm Tom Nolan, Compton County Sheriff, Mister Woods. You are under arrest for kidnapping and suspicion of murder. My deputy will take charge of the patient, and as soon as he does, I want to see your hands high in the air. Understand?"

Cold fear settled in Adam's gut. Murder? He had hoped that lie would go away when Sheriff Mobley had time to think over the words from God. And kidnapping. Was this what it meant to swim where his father waded? His mother would be humiliated, broken. And worse, Maisie would be at the mercy of the quack, Blanchard! He had failed her.

A deputy probably in his mid-fifties moved between him and the car and took Maisie, still sleeping soundly, from his arms. He glanced at the deputy, who paid no attention to Adam, concerning himself with carefully taking Maisie from his arms. Strangely, Adam appreciated the deputy's care. He released her weight to him and raised his arms in the air. The

Sheriff grabbed his hands and pulled them roughly down to his lower back and cuffed them tightly, the metal biting hard against his wrists.

"Did you lose a glove, Mister Woods? One glove wouldn't do much good in keeping fingerprints off doors and windows."

Why bother explaining, Adam thought. "Can I explain why I had to get her out of there?"

"Save it for the judge, friend. If I was your lawyer, I'd tell you not to say a thing right now."

The Sheriff pulled Adam's wrists to check the handcuffs.

"So, Mister Woods?" Another man behind him spoke. Adam instantly recognized the voice of Blanchard, the hospital administrator. Adam felt the man's gloating tone already.

"I'm not surprised to see you don't take advice very well. Looks like you might just wind up with a felony charge for your stupidity."

A third voice broke in, possibly the aide he had encountered the evening before as he was escorted from the building. "Yeah, we could've called the law while you were in the building, but Mister Blanchard, here, figured you were so hardheaded you probably needed a kidnapping charge."

"Okay, that's enough," interjected the Sheriff. "Do you have a gurney waiting?"

"Sure, sure," answered the aide. "At the main entrance."

"My deputy will take the young lady there and help you get her back inside. Roland?"

"Got it, Sheriff," said the deputy. "I'll carry her over and make sure these boneheads take good care of her."

* * * * *

The ride to jail had been excruciating, not so much for the discomfort in his body, but for the agony in his mind. Not only had he fulfilled the prophetic words his mother had always warned him with – he had grown up to be like his father – but he ached because of Maisie's circumstance. He had been so close to freeing her; at least he thought so. Why did it have to happen that way? Couldn't he have made it to his car and got away before the Sheriff showed up? Couldn't Mobley have had a change of heart and come back for Maisie? Where had God been in all of this? He was supposed to be taking care of Maisie since she was His child!

And now, he had messed up everything by letting himself get caught. Not only could he not save Maisie from the doctors at that hospital, no one else was on her side. If he could get out on bail, he would go back to the hospital and take her away by force if necessary. But he was stuck. He had no attorney, nor any money to pay one.

He had heard the police would allow you one phone call from jail. Maybe he could call his mother and see if she had some solution that could get him out. Better yet, he would call Sheriff Mobley and convince him to get Maisie out of the hospital. But why would Mobley do it? He had no incentive to go out of his way for Adam or Maisie.

An incentive! The idea came to Adam in a flash of realization. He would be the incentive; he would agree to whatever charges they wanted to file against him, in exchange for bringing Maisie home to her farm. That would work! Mobley would have a solution to the murder of Ray Lee Colbert; there would be no need for a trial, because he would confess to everything. His mother would be safe because Riley would be off the hook for murder. And Maisie would be safely back at her farm.

He would call Mobley as soon as they let him use a telephone. He had no choice but to wait.

Later, he sat on a metal bench they called a bunk in the smelly, damp cell. A bare yellow bulb above the door to the rest of the jail kept several moths entertained and provided enough light to see there was a book on the floor next to him. It was a Bible. He stared at it off and on for the next few minutes, refusing to pick it up because he was disappointed in its Author. Why hadn't He kept Maisie away from that place? She was so confident He would take care of her, and, yet, what had He done? Forgotten about her.

He reached for the book, but stopped before touching it, as he recalled the conversation with Maisie in her garden. She had said something that stuck in his mind: that she knows Jesus. That she talks with Him and hears Him talking to her. That she had turned to Him when she had no one else to turn to. When he had said he didn't know it was possible to know Jesus or God, she had said, "It's not only possible; it's necessary."

Beside her truck, in front of the farm supply store, she had said something else. She had said that God wanted to be a friend to him. A friend! That seemed like the most impossible of all things she had said to him. Yet, she obviously believed what she was saying. Had he ever met anyone with the kind of character she had? No, he had not. She was the most credible person he knew – at least, for the short period of time he had with her.

"Start by talking to Him," she had said. "Most act as though He's dead. But He's more real than anybody I know."

He touched his cheek, wondering if she had really kissed him or if he had imagined it because it was what he wanted to believe happened. No, he would not have made that up. She really kissed him. But more than likely it was because she had been in some dream state and not fully conscious of what she was doing. Still, he recalled the tenderness of it, the thrill it gave him. Even if it was not born of a special feeling for him, it was real and valuable to him. Maisie was more real than anybody Adam knew. But that was probably because he admired and – yes – loved her. She was so wonderful that he wanted to spend the rest of his life getting to know her, even as just a friend.

No doubt, that had been what motivated her to know God. She admired and loved Him and believed He was wonderful.

Trouble was, Adam had to admit, he felt none of those things toward God or Jesus. He had heard many things in the few times he visited church, but they seemed more like a fairy tale than real life.

The question arose in Adam's mind: "Have you ever made an effort to know God?"

No, he had not.

But now, he had no one else to turn to.

He reached down and picked up the book from the floor.

He wiped dirt from the cover and opened it. In the weak light he saw at the top of the page, "The Gospel of John." He would have to sit on the floor at the opposite side of the cell, where the light was somewhat stronger, if he was going to be able to read anything. Adam took the book to the patch of light and lowered himself to the hard, cold concrete floor.

"This is for you, Maisie," he whispered.

The first words he read struck him as ironic. Here he was in what appeared to be the ending of all he had hoped for, and the first words were, "In the beginning..."

CHAPTER TWENTY-THREE

Dr. Munter decided to drive down to Mid-State Hospital instead of chartering a plane. Weather reports had predicted a beautiful, clear day, perfect for a drive in his '49 Buick Roadmaster convertible. The tan leather seats were immaculate, as was the brown convertible top. He loved the way people turned their heads to gawk at the cream dream as he drove through small towns and stopped at diners. He could easily afford a Caddy, but somehow this Roadmaster far outclassed its more expensive cousin. Driving this machine was worth taking an extra three or so hours rather than flying on such a beautiful day.

Highway 41 was virtually deserted as he crossed the line into Georgia. He punched the accelerator and thrilled at the power of this car, watching the speedometer needle quickly arc to 70 miles per hour. The sun had been up for an hour, and Munter intended to get past Atlanta as fast as he could. If he could get to Mooresville by lunchtime, he could get at least six or eight lobotomies done today, and with a line-up of patients ready and waiting, he could do two or three times that many. That is, if Blanchard was as organized and professional as he pretended.

He flipped the radio on and found a station playing music. Steering with his left hand, Munter lifted his right hand above the windshield and let the force of wind limber up his wrist as he moved it, conductor-like, to the strains of Nat King Cole singing "Mona Lisa." If he was lucky, he might be able to put a Mona Lisa smile on someone's face today. Even though the procedure was a crap shoot, it produced decent results in some patients. Then he recalled the Mona Lisa eyes. No, they were too piercing. That would not be a very likely outcome for this day's work. The piercing would be all on his part.

* * * * *

Captain Art Lowe stared at the flip-fold calendar hanging on the wall above his desk. He had actually reached forward to make a note of the funeral time before his mind snapped back to the way it used to be, before he became a bitter, hard-faced cop. The act of writing that note on the calendar would represent what he had become, an automaton of some kind with no human empathy. The fact that he had involuntarily stopped himself opened his eyes to the existence of something inside, a long ignored part of himself, revealing itself in a spark of recognition as if to say, No, no more; this has to stop! His hand holding the pencil still hovered before the calendar date as he processed the realization. He knew he was waking from some self-induced stupor, seeing himself as though for the first time in years.

Sheriff Mobley had been in his office since sunup, a beaten man, gravely troubled, unlike anything Lowe had seen in the man, ever. His wife had been murdered, but the man was not outraged, storming, vowing revenge, plotting retaliation. His eyes were red when he had walked softly, ghost-like past the dispatch desk, opened his office door and closed it silently behind him.

The image that had startled Lowe out of his stupor was the idea that Mobley would walk out of his office, see a cold, callous note on the calendar – Funeral: 11AM – and the impersonality of it would be the straw that broke his fragile facade, that pushed him over the edge into oblivion. Suddenly, Lowe could not stand the thought of that happening. He fought a swelling in his throat and moisture trying to break from his eyes. Who, after all, deserved to experience what his one-time friend, Ott Mobley, must be at this moment going through? No one.

And he, Art Lowe, had almost been party to the murder.

Complicit, at least, in the detached and culpable way he shook hands with the devil, Potter Riley. How had he let bitterness and envy get such a hold on him as to turn his back not only on his co-worker, but on his moral mind and sensibility?

He felt as though he had been unconscious for months.

He had said nothing to Ott, had not even offered a pathetic "I'm sorry," or a hand on the shoulder. He had watched that zombie pass by, without an iota of care that he had lost his wonderful wife, the friendly, outgoing lady who had made him, Art Lowe, sandwiches and remembered to bring him coffee when she brought it to Ott on long case-weary nights, who had invited him to supper so many nights before he met his own wife-to-be.

Not a doubt lay in his mind as to who the murderer was. Potter Riley was the embodiment of evil, even considering all the low-life thieves and killers Lowe had seen over his fourteen or so years in law enforcement.

All this swept through him in a moment before he withdrew his pencil.

Something had to be done. He could not let Ott Mobley go through this alone. Though no one could say anything that would help, he had to say or do something to try to ease the hurt in the troubled soul beyond that door. Suddenly he knew the one thing he needed most to do, would not help Ott heal. It would help Lowe heal.

He picked up the telephone and dialed. When the gruff voice came on the line, Lowe was resolute and angry.

"You murdering son of a _____!" he said in a low growl.

"He was a bad man, Captain Lowe."

The admission startled Lowe. But it also made him realize Riley did not know the Sheriff had not been killed in the blast. He was completely unaware of who was killed.

"I will get you for what you've done, Riley. Count on it!"

"So, your backbone's turned to jelly, uh?"

"You'll find out what my backbone's made of."

"Oh? Well, maybe you'd better keep an eye on your backbone."

"That a threat?"

"Count on it."

The line clicked off.

* * * * *

Maisie awoke to a stirring about her bed. The ward was still dark, with only the hall lights illuminating the front area. Two male aides, one on each side of her, were tucking her bed linens underneath her. A gurney waited to her left, presumably to take her somewhere. The young matron, Lorene Mills, stood at the foot of the bed staring at a clipboard.

"What are they doing?" asked Maisie.

Mills looked up. She appeared more timid than usual.

"Preparing to take you to, uh, another room." She feigned an optimistic look. "My guess is you'll be dismissed in a day or two."

"What other room?"

"Just an examination room." The young aide looked away, then turned her attention again to the clipboard. In an offhand way, she added, "I have something to help you remain calm."

"You have to forgive your father, you know."

Mills reacted as though she had been slapped. As she stared at Maisie, her face and her eyes turned crimson. Her lower lip quivered. The other aides, having completed their task, moved to the gurney and waited for something from the matron.

"It's too late for him, but you can still be saved," Maisie said softly.

Without speaking to Maisie or acknowledging the aides, Mills whirled and hurried away. The aides shrugged at each other and moved to a bench against the wall beside the swinging doors and sat.

Maisie closed her eyes and focused her attention on something that had been on her mind before waking, something about Adam. She had dreamed that he had been there the night before, and that he had come to take her home. It seemed so real. He had asked her to be quiet as he lifted her from her bed. In the dream, she had been at once surprised and, somehow, not surprised he had come for her. And something else. She had kissed him on the cheek. She knew he was rescuing her because of something more than friendship or loyalty, and she felt very drawn to him for the risk he was taking. His coming to her was the most heroic and sacrificial act she could imagine other than what Jesus had done for the world. If Adam were only a believer! She could imagine herself loving someone with that kind of determination and character. She wondered then whether he might, in reality, have considered coming for her.

Instantly, she knew. Her eyes opened wide at the realization of what the Holy Spirit was revealing to her.

Adam had come for her. It was not a dream.

She had kissed him.

Then, as quickly, she realized he had been caught, for his attempt had not succeeded.

She had to do something.

She struggled to free herself from the tightly wrapped linens, propping herself on her elbows for leverage.

At that same moment, a nurse appeared beside her bed with a metal tray, which she placed on a bedside stand.

"Here, Dear. Be still." She knelt beside the bed and took a syringe from the tray, needle up, tapped the side and plunged a small amount of liquid out." When Maisie resisted, the nurse persisted in a more insistent manner than Caldwell or Mills had used. "It's just a mild dose of insulin, Honey. Don't worry." Lifting the sheet, she slipped the syringe underneath. Maisie felt a slight sting.

The nurse muttered to Maisie, "That wasn't too hard. Don't know why that Mills girl couldn't do it. You're a good patient, Dear."

Maisie sighed as she dropped prone again. Frustration rose in her. She wanted to do something, to forcefully change the circumstances – hers and Adam's alike. Ordinarily, she was content to watch God surprise her, but lately she had experienced more surprises than she could handle. Still, she knew that God could – and would – do far more than she could ever hope to do. Most of life's battles were spiritual, after all, totally immune to natural remedy – in fact, often only complicated by them. She had learned that lesson too many times to succumb to the deception that her meager fleshly will could bring satisfaction.

Maisie cast the frustration away, asking the Lord to take it. She began praying silently, more for Adam than herself. It was imperative for God to touch him, to open his spiritual eyes. She reminded herself not to have selfish motivation, but to desire God's perfect will for her friend. Whether Adam realized it or not, he so desperately needed to know the Living God.

Tears rose to her eyes and she wept softly. He had endangered himself for her. She could read his sincere desire for friendship when they first met in town. She had sensed he would make a very good friend; he had just never had the chance. Now, she was overwhelmed at the extent of his care for her.

The medication began to pull her from her surroundings, into a different realm. She had to maintain some awareness, especially of God's presence.

"Oh, Father. Take my hand. I will not leave You. I will not succumb to the demands of darkness. Keep me by Your side."

She could not see His smile, but sensed somewhere in her being that He was pleased with her insistence. In that, she rested. He was pleased.

CHAPTER TWENTY-FOUR

He had said something that stopped Adam, this Jesus had. He told a man that he must be born again. Adam set the Bible, still open, on the metal surface of the bunk and sat beside it. Jesus had not been speaking of just the one man, though. He had said – what was it He said? Adam picked the book up again and held it under a dim shaft of light.

"Except a man be born again, he cannot see the kingdom of God."

A man. Any man.

What could that possibly mean? The person He said it to was just as perplexed. He had responded, "How can a man be born when he is old? Can he enter the second time into his mother's womb, and be born?"

Good question.

Whatever it meant, it was so important that apparently nobody was getting into heaven without that happening. He set the book down once more and let the puzzle stew in his mind. Born again. And Jesus had said "of water and of the Spirit." He knew of people being baptized, but that didn't appear to make them newly born. Of course, he had never seen them baptized. He had only heard his mother say that so-and-so had got baptized, or was going to.

Maisie would know what it meant. If anybody had got born again, she had. Thinking of her again brought fear into his mid-section. He would not have a second chance to break her out of that hell hole.

He had prayed earlier, but without knowing whether God heard him. He knew he had better do it again.

"God, I read where Jesus turned water into wine. The

people at that hospital seem determined to do something bad to Maisie. The medicine they're giving her – God, it sounds dangerous. Please do something to it so it won't hurt her. Maybe turn it into water or something safe. You and I both know there's nothing wrong with her. Just some bull-headed guy wants to make a name for himself. God, she is the most harmless, sweetest person I know. Can you work it so that I can call the Sheriff in Odino? Lord, I tried and failed to get her out. But if I can talk to the Sheriff I might be able to do it this time."

Adam did not know whether he was praying the right way, but Maisie had said, "Just talk to Him."

"You talking to yourself, son?"

Adam startled and turned to the voice. A man in uniform stood at the cell door staring at him through the bars.

"I thought you were trying to get somebody out of that place, not escaping, yourself."

Ignoring his comment, Adam stood. "Can you let me use the telephone?"

"No attorney I know will answer a phone before ten A.M."

"I want to call a cop."

"What? We don't have enough cops around here, you got to call another one?"

Again, he ignored the humor. "Can I use the phone?"

"I'll check." He turned to walk away, and spoke over his shoulder. "Sorry to interrupt your conversation. Proceed."

* * * * *

Rain had settled over Mooresville around daybreak, a steady shower under a gray blanketed sky. Nurse Proctor opened the side entrance door with her key and stepped inside, shaking her umbrella over the step outside before closing it and stowing it in a black metal cylinder inside the door. She hung her raincoat on a coat rack in the corner and flipped on the office lights. She normally came in early, to get her day organized and to make a pot of coffee for Doc

Blanchard. This morning she decided she would make enough for herself as well.

Fetching the coffee pot from the shelf behind the reception desk, she opened Blanchard's office door and headed for his private bathroom, where she often filled the pot with water at his sink.

Halfway across the room, she bent to pick up a slip of paper on the floor, and glanced at it before tossing it onto his desk. The paper was a check stub, and the name and amount on it stopped her.

"Dr. Johnathon Smith? One thousand dollars?"

Her stomach sank with instant dread. Of course, she remembered the envelope Blanchard told her to mail. But the thing that caused her anxiety was something the Slaughter girl had said the night she was admitted. She had blurted something about twenty thousand dollars being stolen. It had sounded bizarre when the girl said it, and Proctor had attributed it to the strange and often disassociated things some patients tended to say.

Surely, Blanchard was not – She could not complete the thought. It was too far-fetched, too terrible to consider. Nevertheless, she knew nothing of a Doctor Johnathon Smith, and she had been around the hospital a lot longer than Blanchard had. She almost tossed the paper onto his desk and walked away, but held back. Instead, she folded the stub lightly and slipped it into the pocket of her cardigan, without knowing quite why. If he mentioned it, she would consider it unsuspicious and produce the stub, saying she found it somewhere in the reception area, to avoid the impression she had been snooping in his office. If he did not mention the stub, maybe he had something to hide. After all, documentation for a check that large would be important to keep on file, and if he was not openly concerned about its absence, she would – well, she would wait and see how she would react.

Suddenly, she did not want coffee. She needed to think. If Blanchard insisted on having coffee, she would make it, but for now, she had no desire to cater to his whims. She took the coffee pot back to its place on the shelf and closed Blanchard's office door.

This promised to be a dreary day in more ways than one.

* * * * *

As a throwback from his military days, Sonny Ingles habitually ran five miles every morning before sunup, rain or cloudless skies, snow or oppressive humidity, the conditions mattered little to him. Today, as the sky was shifting to a pale gray and rain pelted him in the face and made a rapid tapping noise against his yellow rubberized canvas slicker, his thoughts were on the inmate, Bondurant Woods. The man had held his peace when asked to identify or guess who his attacker had been. He knew who was behind it, but refused to implicate another inmate, who had probably just been acting for money.

Maybe Ingles was being too soft, as most everyone over him believed, but he could not help but accept Woods' story about the fight that got him into prison. The man had certainly lived a sordid life – the marks on his body and personality revealed that – but something had apparently happened to him in prison to change him. No, his did not appear to be a typical case of jailhouse religion. The man was unusual. No deep-seated bitterness, no con-man gratuitous pleasantry, no superficiality of mind and expression. Woods had a realness about him that belied his big house record and the fact that somebody had gone to a lot of trouble to try and kill him.

Ingles almost wished he could get back over to the medium-security facility sooner than promised. But Woods was still in rough shape. Pushing him to remember more details would just hinder his recuperation. The man needed rest.

And now that he was thinking about the whole scenario, he realized he could not keep the story out there much longer about an inmate being killed. Reporters had already been calling, and some of his staff had been grousing about covering for an injured inmate, wanting to know what the special treatment was all about. No, he had to resolve this thing quickly, get Woods returned to Mooresville or transferred permanently elsewhere and clear up the story about him being killed. As it was, the Board would be furious with him for such a preposterous ruse.

Woods had spoken of the Sheriff over in Ocmulgee County, a man named Mobley. Ingles had not heard of him, and needed to find out if he was still Sheriff there, but without saying it outright, Woods had suggested the man was prone to favoritism, particularly when the favor went to the father of the deceased, Riley. While Woods was recuperating, maybe it would prove beneficial to make a call to see where Mobley was these days. A little fact-checking would help support his belief in Woods' story. He had passing acquaintance with the District Attorney, Staples, and decided he would be a good source of information. Staples might even remember the murder trial of Bonder Woods. But, from what he knew of Staples, he was not much of a conversationalist, and very opinionated. If he was to get the information he needed, Ingles would need to choose his words carefully, not to suggest Woods' trial had been a mockery of justice, though such a thing was possible in some districts.

Ingles did not slow his pace as he approached his driveway. He was a man that ran hard to the finish. Splashing through the shallow puddles lining the sidewalk and overlapping low spots in his front lawn, he ran all the way into his open carport, and slowed to a cool-down loop around his prized '49 Ford pickup truck. He made up his mind. He would call Staples right away and try to get basic information. If it was not forthcoming, he would take a little drive over to Odino. Time was important if he was going to be able to justify his attention to the Woods case. And he would need to provide some answers to his Board and staff right away.

CHAPTER TWENTY-FIVE

The radio announcer stated the time was 12:40PM when Dr. Munter steered his Buick into the parking lot of Mid-State Hospital. The rain he encountered south of Atlanta had abated to a drizzle, though the sky was still grey with low-hanging clouds. With the top up, driving had been much less fun than he had anticipated. Nevertheless, he had made good time through Atlanta. Now he had to get to work quickly, complete as many lobotomies as he could, and hope he could get them all done by 5:00 or 5:30. He would stay in a decent motel, if Mooresville even had one, and head back to Chattanooga first thing the next morning.

Everything depended on the preparations made by Blanchard. Munter made up his mind not to assume the worst or the best, but to prepare himself for local incompetency. That meant being ready to make loud demands to get people hopping if things were not as he expected them to be. He had asked his wife to make clear to Blanchard, or whoever she spoke with, that he expected to have patients scheduled in thirty-minute intervals and they were to receive insulin injections and a muscle relaxant no earlier than fifteen minutes prior and ECT five minutes prior. It would not be pleasant if patients began coming out of the electro-shock induced stupor during the procedure.

Munter took his valise, which held his new stainless steel orbitoclasts in their smart black case, and slipped his umbrella from behind the seat. He checked his watch. 12:44. Glancing in the rearview mirror to make sure his tie was straight and his mustache neatly trimmed, Munter jutted out his chin and flashed his teeth. He thought his resemblance to Clark Gable was striking. Remembering a photo session he had been the subject of in Ohio, he chastised himself for not asking his wife to have Blanchard notify the Atlanta and Macon newspapers of his visit today. He made a mental note to not let that kind of mistake happen in the future.

Exiting the Buick under a large black umbrella, Munter strode toward the hospital entrance with the cadence of a military commander. He could almost hear a John Phillip Sousa march strike up in his mind. Just let someone dare not meet his expectations! Such a one would have a blistering earful today if things did not go according to clockwork.

* * * * *

Ingles hung up the phone after talking with District Attorney Warren Staples. Staples remembered the Woods case and, while seeming a bit guarded with Ingles, admitted that he had suspected at the time that he was not getting all the information from the Sheriff's department, but that he had no evidence of obstruction and no investigative staff of his own. He had his personal opinions of the devious machinations Potter Riley was capable of on a normal basis, not to mention a situation in which he had reason, in his own mind, to seek vengeance. Woods had made claims of witnesses, but none was ever named or located. Could Riley have tampered with such witnesses? Yes, Staples felt sure he could have, but, again, he had no evidence. Yes, Mobley was still Sheriff, but he was in no condition to engage in a discussion about the details of a trial – his wife had just been violently murdered, and the Sheriff was taking it very hard. He had offered no motive, suspects or details concerning the murder of the Sheriff's wife, and Ingles had not pressed.

In the end, Ingles was at a standstill, unless he could go around the Sheriff and talk directly with Potter Riley. As warden of a prison, however, he had no status as an investigator and no legal authority to even go about asking questions of witnesses in an old, closed case. And to impose on a grieving man, whether culpable or not in the conviction of Bonder Woods, was something Sonny Ingles was not willing to do. At least, not right away.

The one disturbing thing he learned from his brief conversation with Staples was about Bonder Woods' son. The young man was being sought for questioning on suspicion of murder. Not the murder of the Sheriff's wife, but of the younger Woods' step-father. Not only was Ingles shocked to find the small town was a hotbed for violence, but he was distraught at the idea that Bonder Woods' son might have learned violence from his father. The old saw, that the apple doesn't fall far from the tree, might prove to be too true in this instance. Not only would that be bad news for Bonder, but it would pull the rug out from under all Ingles' justification for trying to help the elder Woods. That kind of information would make the assumption of Bonder Woods' guilt by members of the Board difficult to overcome.

He ran a hand over his short, wet hair. He needed a shower. And he needed to think. Had he overstepped common sense on behalf of Bonder Woods? Had he gotten himself in a predicament he could not justify to those he answered to? It was beginning to look as though he had.

The truth was crucial, but he had made decisions based on the assumption Woods was being truthful. Perhaps he had not been smart to trust Woods. He had felt a sort of compassion for him, a desire to rescue him, and had, perhaps, let that blind him to the possibility Woods was not innocent. And to everyone from the governor down, he would be seen as meddling in something that was none of his affair. Protecting a prisoner from the threat of murder was one thing, but fabricating his death, withholding information from the newspapers and trying to gather information toward seeking a re-trial for a convicted murderer was another.

Well, thought Ingles, he had enjoyed his position as warden. If he lost that post for doing what he believed was right and good, he would get over it. The question was, what could he do now to resolve all these issues?

Captain Art Lowe settled down at his desk after a busy and harrowing morning. Not only had the Sheriff's wife been murdered, and most of the department had been working on some aspect of that case since dawn, but nothing about law enforcement as usual had slowed to allow him to focus on building a case against the killer, who, everyone knew, was Potter Riley or someone who worked for him.

At least, routine duties were working well. At that moment, one of his deputies was booking a pair of drunks caught speeding away from the County Line Bar. Sheriff Nolan in Compton County left a message with the night dispatcher that Adam Woods was in custody and ready for pickup. And a woman living a mile from Sheriff Mobley's home had called saying she was coming in from milking her cow early this morning when she saw what appeared to be an old truck speed past her place only minutes before the explosion. She had not thought anything about it until she heard about the explosion on the radio. Lowe had offered to come right out to talk with her but she said she had to come into town anyway and would be right in.

Sheriff Mobley was too much in shock and grief to hear news, even good news, but once the funeral was over, maybe he would be glad to hear what had been done. And who knew – by that time, they could have suspects in his wife's murder in jail!

As he was finalizing his report of the possible witness's call, the telephone rang.

"Sheriff's Office, Captain Lowe speaking."

"Captain Lowe, this is Adam Woods. I've got to speak with Sheriff Mobley."

"Well, morning, Mister Woods," he said confidently, leaning back in his chair. "I understand you're taking a little siesta in the Compton County jail."

"Is Sheriff Mobley there? It's real important that I speak with him."

"He's unavailable at the moment. How can I help you? You

ready to come back and face the music in the murder of Ray Colbert?"

"I ...um... I'm ready to make a deal with the Sheriff."

"Oh yeah? What kind of deal?" Lowe leaned farther back, jiggling a pencil lazily between two fingers.

"That's not something I want to talk about over the phone. But I need his help in trying to get my friend out of the hospital in Mooresville."

"Oh, you'd rather not, eh? Well, I'm sure we'll get the opportunity to talk real soon."

"Can you ask the Sheriff to speak with me?"

"He's unavailable. Someone will be picking you up in the next twenty-four hours, so you'll have the opportunity to speak with him soon enough."

"You don't understand, sir. My friend is in danger – "

"I understand clearly, Mister Woods. Have a pleasant trip down here. We look forward to talking with you."

Lowe hung up the phone. He had no doubt that Woods had witnessed Potter Riley, or one of his henchmen, kill Ray Colbert. But in the absence of corroborating evidence, it would come down to Woods' word against Riley's, or whoever pulled the trigger. And without that supporting evidence a jury might be convinced Adam Woods accused Riley to divert attention from himself and to get back at the old man for allegedly paying off or getting rid of witnesses in his father's trial. So there would still be a lot of work to get an indictment against Riley.

* * * * *

Potter Riley let the screen door slam behind him and loafed to the telephone ringing in the kitchen. He picked it up and spoke.

"Yeah?"

"Riley. I've got some information for you."

Riley drew himself up and dropped his fist onto the kitchen counter like a sledge hammer. "What the hell do you mean calling me?" he demanded.

"Settle down, Fat Man. Me and the dingbat you gave me to work with are in jail."

"Jail?" Riley thundered.

"Relax, it's just a DUI and speeding charge. After you paid us, we had a drink or two on the way out. You've got to get us out."

"Get you out?"

"That's right. Pay the bail and we'll both disappear. Don't pay the bail and we both talk."

"You low-life – !"

"Easy, Mister Big. Just pay the bail and you'll be fine. And here's a news flash: when they were booking us in, guess who called the dispatcher? The Woods guy. And from what I made of the conversation, he must have told the cop something about a deal in Colbert's murder. So you'd better make yourself disappear, too."

Riley fumed, gripping the receiver as though to crush it. Yet he remained silent.

"You still there, Riley?"

"What did you hear them saying about the explosion?"

"Not a thing! Tighter than a drum! They don't have a clue who was involved."

"Keep your mouth shut and you will live to see another day."

"You are going to go bail for us, right?"

"You'll be out in an hour. But if you say one word about me, you will not be able to get far enough away to hide from me."

"I hear you, Big'un! Much obliged for the bail."

CHAPTER TWENTY-SIX

Adam was on his knees beside the metal bunk, fighting the urge to yell and cry. He had never felt more urgency to do something desperate, nor more helpless to do anything at all. His only chance had been the Sheriff in Odino, and he had used his one telephone call to get his help. That had been a total bust.

He heard a voice.

"Get up."

Startled, he looked up and toward the cell door. No one was there. Goose bumps rose on his arms and a shiver started up his back. He did not move.

"Get up, Son."

He swung around. A man's dark face was pressed against the bars of the opposite cell.

"Whatever you're facing, if you ain't going' to pray you might as well get up."

Breathing a sigh of relief that the voice was human, Adam pivoted about to a sitting position, with his back against the cold metal edge of his bunk. He rubbed his eyes.

"I've been praying."

"If you're going to pray, don't worry. And if you're going to worry, don't pray. Can't do both."

"It's just stuff I can't do anything about."

"Tell me something new! That's how come you're in jail, Bub."

"What do you mean?"

"God's got you here to open your eyes. Jail is God's mercy; don't you know that?"

"How would you know what God's doing? You're in jail,

too."

"That don't mean I can't tell you the truth."

"Yeah, but – "

"Ain't no but about it. Gospel truth is you got to be born again if you want God's full help."

Adam sat up straighter. "You know what that means?"

"I got born again in the big house, doin' seven to ten for bad checks. Did six and they let me out."

"So what are you doing back in?"

"Haven't left yet. Transferred from prison to th' local jail till they finalize the papers. I'll be out tomorrow."

"So how did you get born again?"

"Asked Him. You believe Jesus died for your sins, don't you?"

"Yeah."

"Believe He rose from the dead?"

"Yeah."

"Know you're a sinner, don't you?"

"Yeah. Somebody told me about being born in sin."

"Then ask Jesus to forgive you and come into your heart. If you mean it, He'll do it."

"Well, when do you get born again?"

"When the Holy Spirit comes in. He can't come into a sinner, and once Jesus forgives you, and you truly believe in Him, the Holy Spirit will come in your heart and start working in you."

"That's it?"

"Well, you got to be serious, of course."

Adam stared blankly, trying to process what he had heard.

"What you waitin' for?"

"I can do it now?"

"You have a better time in mind?"

Adam shrugged. He turned back around and leaned his arms and head on the bunk. Before praying he swiveled his head.

"Who do I ask, God or Jesus?"

"Are you pulling my leg? You're trying to make this too hard, man."

Adam shrugged. He could not help thinking of Maisie as

he prayed. She said he would have to give his life to Jesus. That was exactly what he was doing. And he knew it was what he had needed to do all along.

* * * * *

"Nurse Proctor?"

"Yes," said Proctor into the telephone at the reception desk. The woman caller's voice sounded familiar. "How can I help you?"

"Before you hang up, I have to tell you two things."

"Caldwell? Is that you?"

"The first thing is that if you let Blanchard go through with lobotomizing the young woman, Maisie Slaughter, you will be committing the worst error of your career – maybe even a crime."

"I appreciate your concern, but what those in charge do is of no concern to me. They make the decisions; I don't."

"That young woman could be permanently damaged. Her mind could be destroyed, and if you sit back – "

"I told you, it's not up to me."

"You can stop it."

"I cannot."

"The second thing is, I have reason to believe Mister Blanchard is embezzling funds from the hospital."

Proctor drew in a breath sharply.

"Did you hear me?" asked Caldwell when Proctor did not respond.

"What makes you say a thing like that?" Her voice had dropped to just above a whisper.

"Have you seen his new Cadillac?"

"A new car is no reason to make that kind of charge."

"I heard him on the phone with someone about two weeks ago, saying he could pay for something when his father's estate is settled. The 'something' cost five thousand dollars."

"And just what is suspicious about that?"

"I knew his father. He was poor as a church mouse, and

died an alcoholic owing everybody in the county."

"Still, that – "

"The next day I saw Hendricks, the bookkeeper give Blanchard a thick envelope."

"Miss Caldwell," Proctor began.

"I saw him take money out of the envelope and count it."

Proctor tried to muster conviction in her words. "That is a very serious charge. I advise you to keep such things to yourself if you have nothing more than suspicion, Miss Caldwell."

'It's 'Nurse' Caldwell. And don't say I didn't warn you on both counts. If I read in the paper that my fears have been realized in either case, I'll be talking to the authorities and they might just consider you an accessory."

The line went dead, and Nurse Proctor went limp. Fear crept into her gut and her hand was shaking as she hung up the receiver.

Despite her response to Caldwell, Proctor knew she was right about both circumstances. Maisie Slaughter was being rushed into treatment for which she had absolutely no need. She knew it, but had ignored it. And she had tried to explain away the check stub, hoping against hope that it meant nothing. She had tried to please Doc Blanchard by explicit compliance, and she had rationalized his peculiarity of affecting the image of a physician as a desire for professionalism. But the truth appeared to be that he was a crook.

"Nurse Proctor!"

She started at his shout. Looking around, she saw Blanchard storming into the reception area from the hall.

"Why aren't you assisting with preparations?" he demanded. "We have patients waiting for ECT who have not received injections. Do I have to show you everything to do?"

"N-No sir," she answered. "I, uh – "

"Then go! Go! Don't stand around stammering! Doctor Munter has completed two procedures already!" He wheeled about and hurried out again, muttering.

At that moment a violent scream issued from the Prep room. Blanchard broke into a run.

At a loss for what else to do, Proctor raced after him through the prep room and into the treatment room where Munter stood, holding bloody leucotomes high as if to protect them. A few feet away an aide was struggling with a male patient on a gurney. From the man's eye sockets, blood streamed and splattered onto his cheeks, ears, the gurney and the floor as he thrashed about. Blanchard stopped short of the bloody scene and stood entranced., Proctor pulled up behind him and shrieked.

"You didn't anesthetize him properly," Munter accused, looking at Blanchard.

Blanchard only stammered.

Proctor turned back to the Prep room. Two gurneys with fidgety patients on them rocked dangerously as frantic nurses tried to calm them enough to receive injections. No one was connected to the ECT unit against the right wall. And beyond the opposite door waited a line of four more gurneys. Looking for Maisie Slaughter, she hurried toward the line of gurneys. Maisie lay calmly on the one nearest the door. She was third in line for an injection.

Proctor stepped beside her and touched the young woman's shoulder. Her eyes jerked open, revealing a hint of worry. She was obviously trying desperately to remain peaceful amid the chaos.

Proctor leaned down to her. "I'm taking you out," she said as she unlocked the wheels and began steering the device toward double doors leading into the South ward, where the least aware, least ambulatory and most vocal patients resided. Pressing the gurney ahead of her, she pushed it through the swinging doors into the noisy ward, and wheeled right, toward the intersection of the aide station and the main hall. With no time to plan, the only way she knew to save the woman from the procedure was to get her to the nearest exit and put her into her car.

As she reached the relative quiet of the hall, two aides stepped in front of the gurney and stopped her.

"No you don't!" one said.

Immediately, Blanchard appeared from behind her, his face red and contorted.

"What is the meaning of this? What do you think you're doing?"

"This patient was in line to receive leucotomy, Mister Blanchard," Proctor said. "It was obviously an error. As you know, she was taken in for evaluation."

"I know very well what her status is, Nurse! And so do you! How dare you take it upon yourself to reverse my orders!"

He moved past the gurney to tower over her, staring into her face.

"You were purposely sabotaging this woman's treatment, were you not?"

"I – I didn't want you to make a mistake that could damage her, and your career, that's all!"

Blanchard turned to the aides. "Get the patient back to the Prep room. Put her at the head of the line!"

He whirled back to Proctor. "As for you, either get back in there and get busy assisting or gather your things and get out!"

"But – !"

"You heard me! Make your choice now."

Proctor, fuming, pushed past him and headed to the reception area.

* * * * *

Blanchard returned to the Treatment room and assured Munter that preparations would be handled properly. In the Prep room, he pressed the pair of nurses to make up for lost time. Then he positioned himself beside Maisie's gurney, with his fists on his hips, as if to guard her from any further intrusions. One of the nurses clumsily grabbed a hypodermic needle and pressed it into Maisie's hip. Allowing virtually no time for the insulin to have its effect, aides wheeled her to the ECT machine and began strapping her securely to the gurney while another, younger nurse prepared to position the electrodes. Hesitating, the young nurse turned toward Blanchard.

"Mister Blanchard," she called across the room. "This

patient has not yet responded to the insulin. She's still conscious."

Maisie had turned her head to look at Blanchard as well.

The Administrator, who had observed their preparations, locked eyes with Maisie.

"Proceed!" he said.

"But sir, she could fracture or dislocate a bone in convulsion if she's not sufficiently relaxed."

He cursed, still glaring at Maisie. "Place the band on her, nurse. I take full responsibility."

Reluctantly, the woman returned to her task. She placed the electrode band around Maisie's skull and strapped it across her forehead. From a side table, she retrieved a thick rubber tube and placed it between Maisie's teeth while positioning her head face up. An aide placed one hand under her jaw and the other on the crown of her head, pressing her jaw against the rubber tube.

Doctor Munter appeared at the doorway. "What's the hold-up?"

The young nurse turned to him. "This patient has just been given a relaxant, and it hasn't taken effect yet. Are we to administer ECT without waiting?"

"I told her to go ahead, Doctor Munter," Blanchard asserted.

Munter looked from the nurse to Blanchard and back again. "Give her another half dose of relaxant," he told her. With a frustrated but determined look, the young woman stared at him. Quickly, an older nurse stepped forward and prepared the injection.

Once the sedative was given, Munter pointed to the nearest male aide. "Now you, go hold the patient down while she convulses. She's likely to be more animated than most."

Releasing Maisie's head, the young nurse spoke again. "I – I respectfully decline to do this."

Blanchard rushed forward. "Get out! Get out!" he shouted at her. The nurse jumped backward, staring, horrified at Blanchard, who acted as though he intended to administer the electric shock himself.

"Mister Blanchard!" Munter barked, taking a step toward

the man. "I'll handle this, if you don't mind."

Blanchard halted and shot an angry glare at the young nurse, who was walking toward the hallway, keeping guard over her shoulder lest Blanchard start at her again.

Munter nodded to the older nurse. "Take her place, Nurse. The dial is already set at the proper charge. All you will need to do is flip the power toggle. Leave it on for five seconds, then turn it off again. It's very simple."

Munter then turned an impatient look on Blanchard. "And now if I may, I will return to my work. Do you think you can handle this from here?"

Without waiting for a response, the physician wheeled and strode back to the operating room. Blanchard motioned for the young nurse to leave the room, which she immediately did.

As the replacement nurse reached for the power switch, Blanchard spoke again.

"Turn the power on!"

The nurse stopped her hand, held it above the switch and faced him with narrowed eyes. The two aides also faced him with impatient looks. "Mister Blanchard," said the nurse. "If you want to do this yourself, I will gladly follow my young protégé out of the room. Otherwise, please allow me to do what I've been told."

Blanchard, red-faced and angry, clenched his jaw. He appeared ready to react, but held his peace and took a step back. "Go ahead," he said finally.

Waiting a second longer before giving her attention once again to the task, she grasped the switch and snapped it. Instantly, Maisie arched her back in a violent movement and shook under the constraints, her neck flexing and forcing her head back at a sharp angle until she appeared to be supported only by her head and heels. A muffled moan rose from deep in her throat. The gurney rattled and the nurse cried out. Her hand darted toward the switch.

"No!" screamed Blanchard.

For a split second, the nurse hesitated, but without turning to see him, she slapped the switch off. Instantly, Maisie's form dropped again, and twitched at nearly every extremity.

"That was only three seconds," complained Blanchard.

The nurse rose on her heels with her shoulders squared. Her eyes and face spoke more loudly than anything she could say. With her jaw set and brow furrowed, she spoke in measured monotone.

"It was five!"

Both aides released the patient and stood erect, agreeing with her in slow, perturbed nods.

Maisie's quivering body seemed to deflate. The severed end of the rubber tube dropped from between her clinched teeth and bounced to the floor.

Blanchard watched as the aides unlocked the gurney's wheels and steered it to the operating room.

Munter, having completed a procedure, was across the room. He dipped the blood-smeared leucotomes into a vial of alcohol and swished them around several times, removed them and wiped them carefully with a cloth. His attendant nurse re-entered one door as the aides wheeled in Maisie's gurney through the other, with her limp, unconscious form.

He nodded to the spot where he wanted the gurney, and the aides complied. They locked the wheels again and returned to the preparation and treatment room.

Glancing through the open doorway, Munter saw Blanchard watching.

"Perhaps you'd like to come in and watch, Mister Blanchard. You seem to have some special interest in seeing this patient —" He hesitated a moment, then continued, "— restored to productive life."

Blanchard stepped forward and into the room. "Thank you, Doctor," he said. "This one will be our crowning achievement. She will be proof that success is eminently achievable in the field."

"No doubt," he muttered without looking at the man. "But whose?"

At that, Munter lifted Maisie's right eyelid and slipped one of his leucotomes underneath. As he did, Maisie's left eye snapped open and locked with Munter's eyes.

The man gasped audibly.

CHAPTER TWENTY-SEVEN

Adam lay on the cold steel bunk, his eyes open, but without seeing his surroundings. He was completely absorbed in the knowledge that God, in the Person of the Holy Spirit, had entered his life.

It had seemed so impossible, he thought. Yet, he could not disbelieve that something had occurred deep inside him. Adam Woods, a marked nobody with no pedigree or special characteristics that would recommend him to anyone, much less to the holy Creator of every living thing! Something had certainly happened to him, something he could not quite describe. His senses felt normal, but his awareness and will seemed to have been awakened from a long sleep.

He communed silently.

Maisie said You talk to her. The thought was directed upward, to exactly where, he was not sure, but he continued. Please take care of her. And tell her I tried.

He waited. A minute. Two. Maisie had not said exactly how God spoke to her, but Adam heard nothing.

Can you hear me? Should I talk out loud or is it okay to just think? Am I supposed to kneel? I will if you want.

Adam waited again. Maybe he was asking too many questions.

Suddenly he heard his name. Startled, he sat up.

A silhouetted figure stood in the open doorway by which he had been brought to the cell the night before. Adam blinked. The figure moved his way along the narrow aisle between cells.

"You awake, Woods?"

"Yes!" he called.

"You got a visitor."

* * * * *

Sonny Ingles had made the call to Sheriff Mobley's office and had spoken with the dispatcher, intrigued to learn Bonder's son was in jail in the next county. He had not been charged, but had been caught taking a patient from Mid-State Hospital, of all things. He was due to be relocated to Odino later in the day or next morning. Probably the young Woods had heard news of his father's death, but Ingles had decided not to mention anything about Bonder Woods being alive if he could avoid it. After all, he had only one purpose in making the visit: to get a read on the son's attitude. Was he a killer or a con man? Was he bitter and cold or was he genuinely innocent? If Ingles had been fooled by Bonder Woods, he certainly stood a chance of being fooled by his son as well, but he had his guard up. He would not be taken in easily.

Ingles followed the guard into the dimly lighted cell area, where the deputy stopped at the second cell on the right. A tall, slim young man stood and moved to the cell door and grasped the bars of the door. He was a young version of Bonder Woods. From his frame, height, serious face and earnest eyes, the resemblance was remarkable, thought Ingles. He thought it was odd that Woods was wearing a single glove. When he looked too long at it, the young man dropped his hands.

"I'll be back in ten minutes, Warden," said the deputy politely. He left Ingles facing the cell.

"Hi, Son. I'm Sonny Ingles, Warden at Jameston Prison."

Adam studied his face without speaking. He seemed neither worried nor angry to Ingles, but if he had to describe him, he would have to say the young Woods was peaceful.

"I – uh – knew your Daddy."

"Really?" Adam's face opened a bit, showing interest.

Ingles nodded. "I always wanted to, well, prove he was innocent of murder."

"You thought I would have some kind of proof?"

"No, no, I learned you were in jail here, and I was just – I mean, I just thought I'd stop by and say I'm sorry about your Daddy."

"Sorry? For what?"

"Oh, then you don't about the attack?" He studied the young man a moment for any sign of ambivalence or lack of concern. "He was stabbed." Ingles looked away to avoid saying anything further.

"That's how he died?" Adam's face registered somberness, but not grief or sadness.

Ingles nodded. "Yes, I'm sorry to -"

"I didn't know how -" Adam broke off his response.

Ingles waited a moment before pressing on.

"I'm told you might be a material witness or suspect in the death of your step-father."

Adam held his peace.

"You know anything about a man named Potter Riley?"

Adam nodded. "I do."

"I have reason to believe he might have been behind the attack on your father."

Again Adam hesitated before speaking, wondering whether the man was talking about his real father or his step-father. He leaned a bit closer to the cell door, his eyes fixed on the warden's eyes.

"Ray Lee?"

Ingles halted a second before nodding.

"What do you know about a man named Jesus Christ?" Adam asked.

Ingles looked startled. "Well, not nearly all I want to. But I know He's the Son of God, raised from the dead for you and me."

Adam seemed to release a breath and relax somewhat.

"Then I can trust you. Potter Riley murdered my step-father and tried to kill me when I drove up on the scene. He might be the devil himself."

"You witnessed the murder?"

"I heard the shotgun blast as I drove up to meet my step-daddy. When I turned the car toward them, Ray Lee was lying on the ground, twitching, and Riley was reloading for a shot at me."

"You're sure it was Riley?"

"No question about it."

"What's this deal about you trying to kidnap a patient from Mid-State Hospital?"

Adam grabbed the bars again with tight fists. "They're trying to kill my – my friend. The Sheriff took her down to Mid-State for an evaluation – said people had complained she was a danger to herself and others. But all she was doing was dancing and singing to the Lord! I went to see her and they had her all doped up and were planning to operate on her. I've got to get her out of there before they hurt her."

"Take it easy, Son. Which Sheriff?"

"Ott Mobley. He acted like he didn't really want to take her, but he didn't come back to get her like he said he would. I tried to reach him by phone a little while ago, but I couldn't talk to him."

"Mobley? Well, he won't be going back to Mid-State soon. Somebody murdered his wife."

"What?"

Ingle nodded. "Blew up their house. The Sheriff happened to be at his office. I hear he's grieving himself half to death."

"Riley," Adam muttered.

"You think Riley's behind that, too?"

"Something must have gone haywire between the two of them. It's common knowledge Mobley fended for Riley for years. Riley's the only person around who'd do something like that."

Ingles stood in thought. Mobley's grief, no doubt, was real. If what young Woods said was true, Mobley would be well aware of who ordered the blast. It stood to reason that as soon as Mobley recovered sufficiently from shock, he would go after Riley, assuming he was at odds with the man. Time suddenly seemed to be of the essence. If anyone had information that would exonerate Bonder Woods of murder, it would be Riley. Ingles would have to press on in what he had begun, and do it quickly if all he had heard was true.

Ingles had been holding his hat. He placed it on his head. "I think I'll go over to Odino and see what I can turn up."

"Can you help my friend?" Adam asked.

Ingles halted. Something about the young man's plea communicated sincerity and selflessness. The tone convinced Ingles instantly it came from an innocent man. Encouraged, he wanted to say yes, but needed to know more about the situation.

"I can't promise anything, but I'll try." He smiled a friendly smile at Adam. "Take it easy, Son. Put it in the Lord's hands. They're a whole lot bigger than mine and yours."

He hurried out of the cell block.

* * * * *

The keys jangled, pulling Kell away from his daydream of fishing on the Mexican side of the Gulf of California. That, to him, was the perfect place to get away from the law. Isolated, sparsely populated and cheap. He could live off of five thousand dollars a long time down there. And if he could somehow get Harris's share of the money, well, he might just stay there forever.

"Up and out, Pardner! Somebody paid your bail." A jailer stood at the cell door, fitting a key into the lock. "Your friend's already up front. If you hurry you might be able to catch him." The lock opened with a loud snap and the door swung open.

"Mighty kind of you, Sir," said Kell getting to his feet. "My sweet Aunt Sadie had to mortgage her estate to go my bail."

"Sure, sure! Let's go up front and you can collect your personal effects."

* * * * *

Late in the day, well into the second shift, Ott Mobley rose from the sofa in his office. He had wept, cursed, prayed, paced, fallen into sleep, and awoke completely drained. Grief had wracked him. His beautiful and sweet wife, to whom he owed so much, including his changed life and words of repentance and affection, was gone. He could do nothing about it. But he could wipe Potter Riley off the face of the earth. He washed his face and picked his revolver from the desk and his holster from the drawer.

Art Lowe, seated at the dispatcher's desk, held a Coca-Cola bottle in one hand and had just lifted a ham sandwich to his mouth when the Sheriff's office door opened and Ott Mobley marched out. His eyes were red and his face resolute. He looked straight ahead, made no eye contact with Lowe.

"I've got to pay a visit to someone," he said as he breezed by Lowe.

"Sheriff – "

"I'll be at Riley's place."

Lowe started to his feet, but the glass door to the street was opening and the Sheriff was outside before he could object. The fact did not escape Lowe that the Sheriff had a holster and revolver strapped on, something he almost never did. He hurried to the door. Sheriff Mobley was already in his patrol car.

"Oh my God!" he exclaimed to himself as the car left the curb.

"What's up?" called a jailer across the room.

"Take the dispatch desk, Will. Hurry! I need to catch up with Sheriff Mobley."

The jailer continued dealing with a prisoner he was releasing. "Just a minute, Art."

"Now, Will! I'm gone. Call me on the radio in as soon as you get to the desk." Lowe tossed his sandwich in the garbage can and rushed out the front.

* * * * *

Harris had not waited around for Kell's release, which was fine with Kell. He wanted nothing to do with that halfwit; he had "clumsy" written all over him. Until the last few moments, Kell had been anxious to leave, considering the fact they had booked him on a DUI charge instead of felony murder. But now, he had been shocked to see the Sheriff alive, and he heard the Sheriff say he was on the way to Riley's place. That meant there would be no murder charge, since apparently no one was killed in the blast. But it could mean that the Sheriff suspected Riley of arranging the attempt on his life. Attempted murder was still a felony.

Kell had two choices: he could high-tail it to Mexico and hope Riley kept his mouth shut, or he could go straight to Riley's place and make sure the Sheriff died this time. If things worked out, maybe Riley would pony up with another thousand or two.

CHAPTER TWENTY-EIGHT

Maisie Slaughter awoke from the procedure, her un-bandaged eyes swollen and bruised. Dark, greenish arcs underlay both eyes. She lay flat on her back in a lone bed in the middle of a sizeable white room. The walls were bare except for a framed certificate of some sort to the left of a closed door. A single cabinet clinging to the wall in front of her held several squatty brown bottles and a small cardboard box. She studied the portion of room she could see through her left eye, but a dull pain prevented her from turning her head.

"My head hurts," she said softly, her words slurred and drawn out. No one stepped into her view. She tried to move her hands. They were restrained.

"Why am I here?" she asked louder, though still weak. She was shocked to hear her words coming out slowly, nearly individually. What was wrong with her ability to speak?

After several minutes, a door opened not far away and the air above her face stirred. She forced her head slowly to the right against the pain and saw a shadow move on the right wall.

"Hello?" she said. Her voice broke with the attempt at increased volume.

A woman in white moved into her vision and leaned forward. The familiar face bore a curious expression. When she spoke, it was with surprise in her voice. "You're okay?"

"My head." She moved her head slowly back and forth. "It hurts."

The woman moved nearer the foot of the bed, enabling Maisie to see without straining.

"Do you remember me? Lorene Mills?"

"I think so."

"How long have you been awake?"

"I don't know. What happened?" Why was she speaking so slowly?

"I, uh, let me get the doctor." The woman moved quickly out of view.

Moments later, a man in casual clothing strolled into the room and stood before her. The long sleeves of his white shirt were rolled to the elbow and he held a hand towel in both hands as if he had been interrupted while drying them. He squinted over wire-rimmed glasses and observed Maisie.

"My head hurts," she said, with effort enunciating the words. "What happened to me?"

The man's eyes widened slightly and he glanced at the matron to his left, who kept her gaze on Maisie. Then he stepped closer, moving alongside the bed to peer into Maisie's eyes.

"Why does my head hurt?" she asked, dragging her words.

Finally, the man spoke, pronouncing slowly to match her speech. "You've just undergone a procedure known as transorbital leucotomy."

"Trans – ." She halted. "You scrambled my brain?"

The doctor's mouth opened briefly, moved in apparent confusion, and closed, as his eyes resorted to blinking. The silence expanded.

"Yes," she answered herself sadly.

Maisie closed her eyes. Tears with traces of blood escaped and ran down her cheek.

"Wipe my eyes?" she asked softly.

The matron's own eyes reddened as she fumbled to find a tissue. The doctor stared for a long time, the hand towel immobile before him. He began slowly to shake his head.

"Why were you here?" he asked only little above a whisper, his throat constricted.

"I don't know," she answered groggily. "A man – Mister, uh, somebody – was going to e-e-eval – "

"I understand she was here for evaluation," offered Mills.

"An evaluation?" He seemed dumbfounded. "How long has she been here?"

"I don't know," Maisie said.

The young matron spoke. "Two or three days."

"Two or three days? Are you serious?" He yelled, flinging the hand towel at a nearby chair. "Blanchard is a maniac!" He wheeled on the aide, who had retreated toward the door, perhaps out of embarrassment. "He's an absolute idiot! Where does he get off bringing this patient in for --?" He halted, muttering to himself. "I might have – " Breaking off his brief tirade, he stormed from the room.

"May I have water?"

Loud male voices in confrontation echoed through adjacent rooms, making words difficult to discern. Mills brought a small cup and lifted Maisie's head gently to help her drink. She turned her head several times toward the door through which the sounds of argument came, possibly expecting the men to come into the room. She squinted, thinking.

"A visitor?" Maisie asked.

Mills, disturbed and distracted, took a moment to reply. "Uh, yes, Honey. A young man, uh, he visited."

"How do I look?"

Again she held back. After moving to the door and looking into the next room, she came closer to Maisie and whispered. "You have to leave here. Mister Blanchard intends to show you to the newspapers tomorrow, and tell them you were seriously disturbed before the procedure. He wants reporters to see you alert and clear-thinking."

"The young man? Where -- ?"

"Maisie, do you hear what I'm saying? He wants to use you wrongly to make himself look good."

"Leave?"

"Listen carefully. My shift ends in an hour. Tonight, don't take the medicine they give you. Wait until all the lights are off except in the halls. Then slip out of bed. I'll leave a long coat under your bed. Put it on and find your way downstairs and outside. I'll be in my uncle's car, looking for you."

Maisie looked earnestly into the young matron's face.

"You love Jesus?"

The matron wept. She nodded.

"A sister!" Maisie exclaimed, bloody tears brimming under her eyes. She tried unsuccessfully to raise her head.

"Sh-h! Listen! Can you remember what I said?"

"To leave."

"I mean, about the coat and slipping outside. Can you do it?"

"Take my hand."

Mills knelt beside the low bed and took Maisie's strapped left hand in both of hers. The matron's hand responded to Maisie's grip by turning dark red at the extremities.

Maisie closed the one unswollen eye. Her lips moved without sound.

Mills tried to extract her hand. When she succeeded, she shook circulation back into it.

"I have to go. I will be in a gray sedan. I'll pass slowly in front of the building until I see you. Got it?"

Maisie's eye opened. "Got it."

"Do you remember what you said to me?"

"Your father?"

She nodded. "I forgave him."

Maisie smiled.

Mills hurried out the door.

* * * * *

When he braked, Ott Mobley's patrol car virtually slid to a stop in the grassless front yard of Potter Riley's house. As he opened the car door, he unholstered his .38 caliber Chief's Special revolver, flipped open the cylinder to ensure it was fully loaded and snapped it briskly shut. He was approximately twenty feet from the wooden porch steps when Riley's voice came loud from one of the two front windows.

"Don't take another step, Ott, or I'll cut you down."

Ott saw the slightest glint of metal in the raised window to the right of the porch. Without aiming, he jerked the .38 up and fired twice through the billowing curtains.

"You fool!" shouted Riley. "My wife's in here!"

"Let her come out the front door," called Mobley, standing stock still in the wide open yard, his pistol still trained on the window. "You're not that big a coward, are you? To hide behind a woman?"

A barrel appeared in the space between the curtains. Before it leveled on him, Mobley ran toward the porch. He hit the first step as a blast tore up the ground behind him. Without slowing, he bounded onto the porch, jerked open the screen door and darted into the dark hallway. At the sound of boots on the hall floor, another blast obliterated much of the upper half of the wooden door to his right, sending splinters across a tight radius in front of him. Riley had to be using his double-barrel shotgun, thought Mobley. The only pump he had was a smaller gage. He ducked under the holes in the door and posted himself on the opposite side of the door.

He had been in the house many times. The room Riley was in connected with another room parallel with the hallway. He also knew that any movement by Riley, who weighed well over two-hundred-fifty pounds, would be announced by the creaky floors of the old house.

"Let your wife go, Riley. Be a man and come out with your hands up. You'd rather die in prison than for me to spill your guts all over the floor, wouldn't you?"

Mobley stepped quickly backward two paces. Instantly, another blast knocked plaster off the wall where he had been standing. Mobley calculated it had taken Riley about fifteen seconds to re-load the shotgun.

He moved quietly back to the position he had held before, staying close to the wall to avoid creaks, himself.

"All right, then. You're a dead man, as far as I'm concerned, Riley. You deserve to die like a rattler, murdering my wife the way you did. I'll be only too happy to – "

Another blast ripped into the wall sending debris and splinters into his leg. He had waited too long before trying to dodge the next blast. His left leg was bleeding, but not fast, indicating it was a flesh wound. He figured he had ten seconds before Riley was reloaded. Mobley stepped back and put his shoulder in to the door with the full force of his weight. The door burst open and Riley stood behind his stoic, angry wife, one arm around her shoulders and the other cradling the opened shotgun. The old man had a shotgun shell squeezed between his teeth; the brass butt of another one shone from the open breech.

"Drop it, Riley. Let her go."

Riley snapped the shotgun closed and let the shell fall from his mouth.

"Back away, Ott," he warned. "I only need one shot."

"Sheriff, this old man of mine ain't got the nerve to shoot me. He hires others to do his killing."

"Shut up, Esther!" growled Riley. He raised the shotgun until it pointed at the Sheriff.

"You shut up!" The old woman retorted, shoving the shotgun barrel aside.

"You killed Ray Lee Colbert, didn't you Riley?"

Riley grinned. "It was an accident." He retrained the weapon's barrel on Mobley.

"And you killed my wife."

"Your wife?" Riley sounded surprised.

"She was in my home when you had it blown up."

"That was for you, Ott. I can't help it if she happened to be – "

"Mrs. Riley, move away from him." Mobley stretched his pistol toward Riley's head and pulled the hammer back with his thumb.

"You!" The woman shouted at someone to Mobley's left. A shot rang out before Mobley could turn. Across the room, a window shattered as the shot went wide.

Mobley whirled and fired, hitting the man in the side. The man, Kell, dropped his pistol as he instinctively grasped the wound and howled in pain. At the same instant, Mrs. Riley jerked away from her husband, stepped in front of him and grabbed the barrel of the weapon, hefting it high. Mobley swung back around, unable to shoot with Mrs. Riley in the way.

"That's enough!" She bellowed at Riley. "You're not agonna kill the Sheriff."

"Esther! Don't make me hurt you."

"Nothing you could do would top the last twenty years of

hurt!"

"Drop your gun, Sheriff," called Riley, training the shotgun in his direction with some difficulty around his wife.

Mobley held fast. His pant leg was saturated now and blood trickled onto the floor.

"Ain't you satisfied you shot him in the leg?" the woman yelled. "And you!" She pointed at Kell, who had raised himself to one knee and was reaching for the pistol. "You leave that gun be!" The man halted without looking around. From the tone of her voice, she might have held a gun herself.

"Come on, Riley!" shouted Kell through gritted teeth. "I'm shot but I ain't dying. Let's get out of here before more cops show up."

"If you shoot the Sheriff, Potter, you'd better shoot me, too." His wife held out her arms.

Riley swung his free arm around his wife again and pulled her toward the door where Kell now stood. "We're leaving, Mobley. Take his gun, Kell."

Kell picked the pistol from the floor and aimed it at Mobley's head as he rushed. He jerked the revolver out of the Sheriff's hand, shoved it under his belt, drew back the other, and smashed it against the left side of Mobley's head, knocking him to the floor.

The instant Mobley hit the floor, Riley shoved his wife away and raised the shotgun toward the Sheriff.

"No!" shouted his wife and jumped in the line of fire as the blast went off.

The old woman dropped to the floor.

Riley cursed. "You couldn't leave things alone, Esther!"

The wail of a nearing siren broke through the open window.

Kell ran. Riley grabbed the shotgun shell from the floor and hurried after Kell.

CHAPTER TWENTY-NINE

A woman of about sixty years entered the Sheriff's office, closing the door behind her. She took one look at the deputy behind the desk. She was dressed in a pair of old overalls and wore a threadbare lavender cardigan sweater, even though the day was warm.

"Are you Officer Lowe?"

He swung his feet off the desk and gave her an important look. "No Ma'am. I'm Deputy Willoughby. What can I do for you?"

"I think I might have seen the murderers who blew up the Sheriff's house."

Willoughby straightened and gave her his full attention. "Is that a fact? Come on over and have a seat, Mrs. _____"

She made her way to the chair Willoughby indicated as he grabbed a legal pad and pen. "Martin. Eva Martin and I live down the road from – from the Sheriff's place."

"What did you see, Mrs. Martin?" He held his pen over the paper as he stared at her.

"It was a truck, came speeding by my house as I came out of the barn."

"What kind of truck, Ma'am?"

"I couldn't tell what make, but it didn't have a bed on the back. It appeared to be old, and had two people inside."

Willoughby wrote intently until realization came to him. "No bed on the back?"

"No sir. It had no bed on the back."

He slapped the pen onto the desk, jumped to the radio and slapped his fist onto the microphone key.

"Dispatch to Unit two, Captain Lowe! Come in, Lowe!"

* * * * *

Lowe slid his patrol car alongside the Sheriff's vehicle and jumped out. He ran in a low crouch, shotgun at the ready. Taking the steps in two bounds, he took cover beside the screen door. Through the wire he could see the hall was dark except for the light of a window in the back of the house. The door to the first room on the right was open, the wall to the left of it riddled with holes and wood splinters scattered across the floor. Drops of fresh blood trailed from the left side of the door to inside the room.

Another door on the right side of the hall was closed. He darted to the opposite side of the screen door for a look at the rest of the hall. Nothing moved. No sound came from inside. He eased the door open and stepped inside moving slowly forward. Once he was directly across from the open door, he saw the feet of two bodies, a man and a woman. He recognized Sheriff Mobley's boots.

Still moving cautiously, he advanced to the shattered wall and peered inside the room. Neither body moved. The woman was bloody; the Sheriff's left pant leg and boot showed blood. His hat lay five feet beyond. Sweeping the room with his shotgun, he moved quickly to the Sheriff and placed a palm against his neck. He had a pulse. He touched the woman's neck; she was dead.

In an open doorway to his left, several drops of blood lay on the floor. He crept to the door and saw more blood drops leading to a third room and beyond.

Suddenly a motor roared to life out back, revved in escape.

He ran through the next doorway, into a kitchen and to an open back door. He rushed onto the back porch as, a hundred yards away, a truck sped off behind a cloud of dust. Instinctively, he raised the shotgun before realizing the truck was well out of range. Through the dust, he could not discern the make of the truck, only that it appeared to have no bed.

Kell winced with every bump in the dirt road. He checked the wound in his side. Though he had bled a lot and the pain was significant, the damage seemed to be relatively minor. The bullet had gone in and out the fleshy part of his side, below his ribs, apparently shallow enough that it missed all organs.

Because he kept his right hand pressed tight against the wound, releasing it only long enough to shift gears, while steering with his left hand, the truck swerved and fishtailed in the road.

"Can't you keep this heap on the road?" yelled Riley over the roar of the old truck. He was turned sideways on the seat, watching out the back window. "I don't see the deputy yet, but he'll be coming after us."

"If you don't like my driving, get out and walk!"

Riley shot him an angry look. "There's a fork in the road ahead." Riley turned and pointed. "Take the right fork. But slow down until you get over that little rise to keep the dust down."

As Riley swung his attention back to the road behind, Kell braked hard, almost throwing the old man into the floor. Before he could react, the truck hit something and bounced wildly.

"What the – !"

"A dumb dog!" shouted Kell, slowing only slightly onto the right fork.

Riley looked back and saw a black and tan beagle lying motionless in the road. Still, no patrol car was visible. The truck topped the small rise and the road behind them was obscured, allowing Riley to relax his vigilance.

"See that old sharecropper house ahead?" Riley pointed to a dilapidated cabin sitting amid overgrown weeds and flanked by thick woods. "Turn off just past it, but do it slow. I don't want to leave a trail of dust. This used to be my property and it goes back nearly a mile to a paved road, where we can double back, cross the river and head toward the Alabama line."

"Riley, I rescued you from that cop 'cause I need some more money!"

"Rescued me? You nearly got us both killed."

"You're in my truck, ain't you? If you want to go any farther with me, give me another five thousand dollars, Riley."

"Five thousand! Your truck ain't even worth two hundred dollars."

"That ain't the point! I came back for you and now I'm driving you away from a guaranteed murder charge."

Kell slowed the truck and steered off the roadway and onto a narrow, rutted lane that wound past the old cabin into a virtual forest of tall pine trees.

"I'll give you five hundred, and you take me to Alabama."

"I'm headed west, Riley. I ain't got time to drive you all over the country."

"That is west!"

"Two thousand dollars, or I'm dumping you first chance I get. I came back to help and now I got a bullet hole that needs doctoring."

"All right, all right!" Riley shouted. He pointed to a side trail on the right. "It goes that way. Turn here."

"Show me the money, Riley."

"You saw how I left! Did you see me take the time to get cash out of my dresser? I've got ways of getting cash, but you'll have to wait till we get out of town."

"Don't mess with me, Riley. I'll dump you right here in these woods."

"Fine! I know where we are, and you don't even know which way is west. But if you want money, you've got to get me where I can get some."

Kell shook his head and held his peace. He kept the truck in second gear. The going was slow, but it was not as bumpy as barreling down the dirt road had been.

The sun was low in the sky, and the trees blocked much of the available light. Kell reached for the headlamp switch on the dash.

"Leave 'em off, Moron!" barked Riley. "You want to let everybody within a mile know we're out here?"

Kell fumed, but kept his thoughts to himself. He could put

up with the old devil a little while longer if it meant getting more money from him. But if he kept up the demanding attitude and insults, he would kick him out and find his own way to the highway. After all, the five thousand he had in his satchel behind the seat was more than enough to buy him a life of partying in Mexico.

* * * * *

The ward lights were off and Maisie replayed in her mind the things she had heard Lorene Mills say: "coat under the bed, go outside, gray sedan." She listened for sounds from beyond the double doors. All was quiet. Faint light shone through the small windows in the doors. She rose from the bed, trying to ignore the ache that had spread from her swollen eyes throughout her body. She knelt, moving her hand back and forth underneath the metal frame. Touching fabric, she grasped it and drew it into the little swatch of light beside her. It was a coat of thick, wool-like material, long and appearing to be pink in color. She stood with difficulty and slipped her pain-wracked arms into the sleeves, pulling the oversized garment around her and forcing her fingers to fasten the large black buttons.

"Where are you going?" The voice was wispy, birdlike.

Maisie stopped and focused her open eye into the darkness of the ward. Although she could not see who spoke, she recognized the voice: the young woman in the wheelchair. The name came to her.

"Sarah?" She dared not speak very loud.

"Can I know Him?"

Maisie tiptoed toward the sound of Sarah's voice, her every muscle crying out in discomfort. Entering the dark area across the ward from her own bed, her vision began to adjust. She made out two beds; something moved in one, a woman? The woman appeared to be standing on her bed. As Maisie neared, she held her hand out to Sarah.

Astonished, she said, "I thought you couldn't walk."

"Is He still alive?"

Smiling, Maisie tugged at Sarah's hand until the woman sat on the bed. Maisie sat beside her.

"Yes," Maisie whispered.

"Somebody said a crazy person – " Sarah's words came measured and singular. " – cannot know Him."

"Do you want to?"

"Yes."

Tears rolled down Maisie's cheek.

"Then you're not crazy."

Maisie could feel the presence of the Lord. Gingerly, she placed her hands on the sides of Sarah's face. Her thumbs moved slowly to the cheekbones under the eyes. They were wet.

In the blackness, Maisie closed her eye and looked upward, trying to see the brightness of His presence through her spirit. His warmth and compassion filled her immediately.

"Father," she whispered. Struggling to find words, she quickly realized they were unnecessary. "Thank You."

Sarah moaned. Tears literally cascaded over Maisie's thumbs. The sounds of her weeping were soft, yet loud in Maisie's heart. Sarah trembled slightly, then shook with sobs that filled Maisie's being. She knew God was performing work in Sarah.

Moments passed and Sarah gingerly raised her hands into the air. She whispered the name, "Jesus." She repeated it. Once more.

Masie kissed Sarah's cheek and stood. Smoothing Sarah's hair as the woman continued to weep, she leaned over and spoke softly into her ear.

"I will see you again."

The stiffness in her body had abated somewhat. She made her way to the double door, and, seeing no one through the small window, slipped between the swinging doors and out the stairwell door by the dim light of the exit sign.

CHAPTER THIRTY

Proctor unlocked the side door to the Administration area. Darkness had not yet fully lifted, as the first graying of day barely showed in the east. Though she was arriving at work under what a casual observer might call normal circumstances, she felt a heaviness pervading her person as well as the building itself. That heaviness did not go away with the opening of the door and turning on lights. According to the clock against the back wall, she had arrived at her normal time, 6:45.

She felt sadness and a sense of loss. Would this be her last day here? She had pretty much destroyed her working relationship with Blanchard. She had been caught trying to sneak a patient out of the hospital; Blanchard had yelled at her and threatened to fire her. Never, in her years of loyal service at Mid-State Hospital, had she ever resisted authority or been yelled at on her job. But she had been right, she insisted to herself, right to try to get the young Slaughter woman out of harm's way. It had been wrong to submit her to such treatment. Caldwell had warned her about allowing that to happen, and in fact, had confirmed her suspicion that something was terribly wrong with Blanchard's financial management.

Would she do again what she had done yesterday? Yes, she decided, she would. It had been the very thing she would hope others would do in the face of injustice. She had failed in getting Maisie Slaughter out of the hospital, but she had tried. Suddenly, she realized the young man who had been arrested for supposedly kidnapping her two nights previously had been no more criminal in his intent than she had. He had come to visit, had seen the danger and had tried his best to get her out of the place.

As she placed her purse and sweater on the reception desk, she saw a note on her typewriter. She picked it up.

"Nurse Proctor, first thing in the morning, call the local newspaper and radio station and inform them I plan to hold a news conference promptly at noon. Mention only that the subject of it will be exciting news of recent breakthroughs at M-SH. Blanchard."

Suddenly, Proctor had a sense of revulsion, understanding what was behind Blanchard's push to get Maisie Slaughter, a perfectly healthy young woman, under Dr. Munter's knife. He wanted notoriety and had planned to portray the young woman as a seriously disturbed schizophrenic patient who had been given reprieve by lobotomy. Anger rose in her breast. The apparent fraudulent handling of money was clear, as well. Blanchard was grasping for all he could take in his temporary position, using it to catapult himself to a higher position.

How she had been duped! She had assumed his pretensions at being a doctor – carrying a stethoscope in the pocket of a lab jacket, making patient rounds, prescribing treatment – was simply enthusiasm for his job and concerned interest in the patients.

In that moment, Nurse Proctor's job loyalty and desire for employment security vanished. This was a defining moment for her. She would not look back on this time of her life with regret that she had passively acquiesced to the designs of an egomaniac. Instead, she would lose her job.

* * * * *

Adam slept peacefully and awoke at the sound of keys rattling.

"Woods? Up and at 'em! You're being extradited to another jurisdiction."

He opened his eyes and saw the silhouette of a jailer fumbling with the lock. How could he have slept so soundly with all the concerns he had? Adam silently chastised himself for sleeping instead of planning. He would push hard today to meet with Sheriff Mobley, even threatening to divulge certain information he had heard about the Sheriff's questionable activities if he did not do something to help Maisie. Adrenaline coursed through him as the urgency to act on her behalf took hold of him.

Adam had nothing to carry out of the cell except his single glove, which he tugged onto his right hand.

* * * * *

The sound of glass bottles clinking together rang through the street as a milk truck rattled past the front of the Sheriff's Department. Art Lowe sat with Deputy Willoughby on the front steps watching the night dissolve as the first rays of light broke over the buildings of downtown Odino. Each man held a paper cup of black liquid that had been steaming hot coffee an hour earlier.

They had discussed every strange and distressing detail of the events of the past few days, at least all they could sort out. The murders of Ray Lee Colbert, Mrs. Mobley, and now Mrs. Riley. The virtually inarguable fact that Potter Riley was behind them all and whether his confession to Sheriff Mobley was shakable, given the possibility a slick lawyer would suggest that Mobley was blinded by grief and a misplaced desire for revenge against his wife's unidentified killer. The fact they had held two prime murder suspects in their jail on DUI charges and released them both. The escape of Riley and one of the suspects to parts unknown. The Sheriff's leg wound and possible concussion from his run-in with Riley and the other suspect. The possibility of a lawsuit by the angry brother of the young woman Mobley took to Mid-State. And the apparent necessity of reversing the extradition of Adam Woods, and returning him to Mooresville to face kidnapping charges. As for the latter, they could not do anything with Woods until the DA reviewed all the evidence.

Things had become highly complicated in tiny Odino, Georgia. The men stared at the sidewalk below them as if the solutions to everything lay there.

"What I don't understand," mused Lowe, "is how Riley and Kell got away in that old beat-up truck, when I was only a couple of minutes behind them after checking on Ott."

"I sent out the APB as soon as you radioed me," answered Willoughby.

Lowe nodded.

"We even had the tag number of the truck," the deputy added. "But he could have taken a side road or rabbit trail. All that land out there is or was his."

Lowe looked up suddenly and emptied his cup onto the grass. "I'll bet you're right! He might not have ever left. Maybe he hid on his own property while we chased all around the county looking for him." He stood and crumpled the cup in his fist.

"Let's go inside and look at the map to see where he might have turned off."

The two went to the wall behind the dispatcher's desk and turned the area light on.

"There's his place, right there," said Willoughby placing his finger at a space between two roads. He moved his hand in a broad circle around the spot. "And most all of this land is his." He pointed again, "There's an old sharecropper house here and thick woods back behind it. I don't suppose he could've cut back through those woods to get to the highway over there."

"Maybe he could, but we had units on all the roads around there in just a few minutes. He would have had to be flying through those woods to get to the highway before us. That's what makes me think he never left."

Lowe threw his cup into the trash can. "I'm going out there. Maybe I'll see tire tracks. Stand by the radio and have backup ready nearby." He grabbed his hat and rushed out the door.

* * * * *

Vernon Blanchard breezed into the reception area as though nothing had happened the day before. He actually seemed to be lighthearted.

"Good morning, Nurse Proctor," he said in an impersonal, business-like tone. He already wore a sparkling white clinical jacket with a stethoscope draped from one pocket as he floated past her desk to his office. He halted at the door as if suddenly remembering something important. "Have you contacted the media yet?"

Without looking up from her typing, Proctor replied in as normal a tone as possible, "I have the phone numbers. I'll call as soon as their offices open for business."

"Very good. Let me know as soon as you reach them." He closed the door. A second later, he re-opened it. "Oh, and ask the staff on the East Wing to get the Slaughter patient cleaned up and dressed to attend the noon news conference. If they need to put makeup on her face to cover bruising, they must do that. I want to see how she looks no later than eleven fifteen."

The door closed again abruptly.

Her eyes fixed on a typewriter page, her fingers poised over the keyboard, Proctor muttered, "Oh, I don't think they'll be that interested in the patient. But they might have a lot of questions for you."

The page was filled, single-spaced. At the head was the day's date and a headline reading, "Testimony of What I Have Witnessed at Mid-State Hospital."

CHAPTER THIRTY-ONE

All lights in the department's suite of offices were on now and, outside, Odino was showing signs of waking. The sun was fully up and a newspaper boy opened the glass door, tossed a rolled-up paper inside and let the door close itself.

At the other end of the office, a Compton County deputy entered a door from the back parking lot, leading a tall young man wearing handcuffs and a single black glove.

Willoughby rose and strode over to the counter where the other deputy was completing a processing form. "Hey," he said to the other deputy, extending his hand. "I'm Don Willoughby. You're Stewart, right?"

Stewart shook his hand. "Yeah, call me Steve."

"This is Mister Woods, I presume?" Willoughby asked, nodding toward Adam.

"That's him."

"Step over here a minute, Steve. I want to mention a couple of things in private. Have a seat there, Mister Woods," he said, pointing to a folding chair with its back against a wooden rail dividing the processing area from the rest of the office.

Adam Woods sat down, and watched over his shoulder with sleepy eyes.

The deputy followed Willoughby to the dispatcher's desk.

"We might be dropping charges against Woods today," he said in a low voice. "That might mean you'll need to come back over and pick him up. We won't know until the Sheriff comes in and talks with the DA."

"Figures," said Stewart. "What? You don't have enough evidence?"

"Got a confession from the real killer."

"Oh, so maybe the guy's legit when he says he was trying to rescue the girl from Mid-State?"

"He's a loner, but no record over here. I heard something about that deal over there, but I don't have any relevant details." He leaned against the wall. "So what did he do?"

"Broke into the hospital sometime after midnight the other night – "

"Which took a lot of nerve!" said Willoughby. "I don't think I'd want to go in there even in broad daylight."

Stewart chuckled. "I know what you mean. The place gives me the willies."

"So he got the girl out before getting caught?"

"Yeah, the staff had already called Sheriff Nolan and told him what was up."

"How'd they know and still let him get outside with the patient?"

"A setup. The weird guy who's the temporary director over there seemed to know Woods would be back after being tossed out earlier in the day. Some of the staff knew to let him get by them inside. I guess they wanted to set him up for a federal charge instead of B & E."

'Nice guys." Willoughby gestured toward Adam. "Don't mention anything to him about what I just told you. Things change, you know."

Stewart nodded and headed toward the back door.

"I hope everything works out for you, Woods. Take it easy."

Adam stood as Willoughby approached him. "I'm sorry to hear about Sheriff Mobley's wife. Is he expected in today? I'm trying to get my friend out of Mid-State before they hurt her."

"Don't know yet, man. He took a nasty lick in an arrest attempt. We'll see. Let's go."

Adam rose and followed the deputy through a locked steel door into the cell block.

* * * * *

Lowe had been surprised at how quickly he saw tracks after turning off the dirt road behind Riley's house. He followed them for almost a mile through dense pine woods before spotting the old truck, its doors standing wide open. Lowe exited the patrol car and unholstered his revolver. Moving slowly and scanning the spaces between trees to both sides of the trail, he approached the truck. Before he reached the bare rear chassis, he spotted something troubling. Blood was spattered against the inside frame of the driver's side door.

Closer, he saw blood on weeds underneath the door and striations on the ground, suggesting a body had been dragged away. The cab was empty. As he moved to the front of the truck, the smell struck him. He had smelled death enough to know what he was about to find.

* * * * *

According to the clock against the reception area wall, the time was 10:58. Nurse Proctor answered a phone call from the nurses' station on East Ward. A woman's voice, sounding radically pinched and stressed, said it was urgent that she speak with Doc Blanchard. Wanting desperately to know what great drama prompted the urgency, Proctor nevertheless, stifled her curiosity and put her through. Moments later, despite the thickness of the office door, she heard Blanchard's panicked voice cry, "You cannot be serious!"

At 10:59, Vernon Blanchard opened his office door and, with skin pale and eyes wide, stood transfixed in the doorway, staring at open space.

Proctor, even in her secret anticipation, could not contain her curiosity.

"What on earth has happened?" she asked.

"The Slaughter patient," he answered without bringing his focus to her. "She's disappeared."

"Disappeared?"

He did not answer. A moment later, the sound of frantic movement in the hall erupted into a limited cacophony of voices as five staff members crowded through the door into the reception area virtually simultaneously. Three nurses and two male aides were in a heated discussion that gave no clue as to who was talking with whom.

"Stop it!" he demanded in rage. The five silenced and turned their frightened eyes toward him.

"The woman cannot be missing," Blanchard said evenly, as though he had regained total control of his faculties, reasoned the situation out thoroughly and concluded the staff members present were wrong.

"But – !" A large aide named Phillip was the one who spoke. Blanchard let him go no further.

"No!" He slammed his open palm on the reception counter. "It is eleven oh two. Go back up there and find her. Look under every bed, in every bed, in laundry and supply rooms, in the staff restrooms. It may be that she has mistakenly got into another patient's bed. It may be that she has sleepwalked to another Ward. Check them all. Make sure the window that was breached two nights ago is still nailed shut. In fact, check all windows and doors for tampering. Be back here no later than eleven twenty." The irises of his eyes were tinted red. "With her!"

"But -- !"

Blanchard's enraged glare snapped to the nurse's eyes. He fumed, daring the one to continue. The nurse wilted.

"Eleven twenty." Blanchard spun on his heel and marched back into the office, slamming the door. The five dispersed instantly and ran into the hall.

Proctor was dazed. Had Maisie connected somehow with what she tried to do by wheeling her gurney out of the preparation room? Had she taken the act as not only permission to escape, but the inspiration and impetus to do it? Had she, indeed, been able to evade all notice and simply walk out? Or had the Woods man escaped jail and returned for her successfully?

This, she thought, will be a very interesting news conference. She walked calmly to her desk, reached into a bottom drawer and retrieved ten copies of the letter she had mimeographed earlier. She plucked her sweater and purse from the coat rack behind the desk and, without announcing to her employer where she was going, left to run a few errands.

* * * * *

Adam Woods lay atop a bunk virtually identical to the one he had occupied mere hours before, studying a large room cramped with small cells – a twin to the one he had recently departed – reflecting on the thought that he had experienced movement but no progress. He was in the very guts of the office with which he had so diligently tried to communicate, without success, and was no further along in his efforts to free Maisie.

He had prayed. And he had prayed. He was frustrated.

Yet, for some reason, he could not seem to muster up the kind of worry that he felt Maisie deserved from him. He was perplexed because he was certain his desire to free her had not abated. His desire for her safety had not flagged. Something in his head or elsewhere was sure that she was going to be okay. It made no sense.

He thought of his mother, and how worried she probably was about him, but neither did that cause him the anxiety he should have felt. And he thought about the murder charge and kidnapping charge that would likely materialize, and the trial or trials, the potential long jail sentences, the wasting of his youth in a harsh and evil prison environment, the shame of ending up like his father, the prospect of never enjoying friends, a wife and family, a career. Any of these looming concerns ought to be cause for immeasurable misery. But they weighed almost less than nothing in his mind.

He did not understand. And he decided not to resist the experience. Maybe this was one of the results of giving one's life to Jesus Christ. When he ran out of solutions, maybe he was supposed to simply trust that God would take care of it.

Willoughby had just moments ago answered Captain Lowe's radio call. He had located a corpse in the woods behind Potter Riley's place, and requested that he call the county coroner. Willoughby had just reached Nelda Smart, the assistant to the Coroner, when an elderly man walked in off the street and stood beside the dispatch desk.

"Hey, Deputy, I need to file a report."

Willoughby held up his hand to silence the man.

"It's Willoughby, Nelda, at the Sheriff's Department. Is the Coroner available right now?" As he waited, he made the mistake of raising his eyes to the old man.

"Yeah, I want to file a report, Deputy." The man pressed closer to the desk.

Willoughby covered the telephone receiver with his hand.

"Sir, if you don't mind, I'm on an important phone call. Please have a seat over there until I'm done." He pointed to a trio of chairs along the wall inside the front entrance.

"Well, if you can give me a form or something, I can start filling out my report."

"Excuse me, Nelda –" Willoughby was irritated. "Sir, I just told you I'm on a call. If you'll have a seat, I'll get with you – "

The old man stood abruptly, cursed and stomped out of the building.

Willoughby shook his head and returned to his call. What a bunch of jerks! They must be coming out of the woodwork today, he thought.

CHAPTER THIRTY-TWO

Blanchard was fuming. The Slaughter patient was missing. He had commissioned a dozen staffers to search every cubbyhole, closet, bed and storage space in the entire building. They had come up empty-handed. Proctor had now disappeared without a word. And a strange young man wearing a tie and who called himself a reporter was sitting in the reception area even though the press conference was fifteen minutes away. He got up from his desk and opened his office door a crack to peek out. The young man was still sitting out there, reading. A woman had joined him and was pacing back and forth in front of the reception counter as if she were concerned about something. And Proctor was still not at her desk.

He took a deep breath and opened the door quickly, hurried out with a clipboard in his hand to give the impression he was on a mission. Before he reached the counter in front of Proctor's desk, the duo had simultaneously sprung into action, coming for him.

"Are you Mister Blanchard?" they both asked, crowding his path of escape.

He held up his hand and put on a quick though stretched smile. "Sorry, but the news conference will be delayed a little. I have an important task to – "

The woman interrupted. "Mister Blanchard, is it true you have leuco-, leuco- -- excuse me." She consulted a sheet of paper she held in her hand, all the while backing up in Blanchard's path as he tried to brush past her. Before she could pronounce the word correctly, Blanchard broke in.

"As I said, I have some very important issues to attend to."

He pushed past the woman as she stopped at the hall doorway. The young reporter continued past her as well.

"Come back here, Luther. You can't go in that area," she called and reached for his sleeve.

"Who says?" he challenged her.

"The sign." She pointed above the door. He leaned back in to read it.

"It says 'Authorized Personnel Only,'" she said.

He sauntered back into the room. "Well, I was here first, Corrie. When he comes back, I've got first shot at him."

"All's fair in love and war," she parroted and returned to pacing.

"Well this is neither," he corrected. "You need to use professional courtesy."

The exterior entrance door opened and a middle-aged man with well oiled hair stepped inside. Seeing the two, he nodded to them and smiled broadly.

"What are you doing here, Baker?" asked the young man. "This isn't about entertainment; it's about news."

"Hey, Bobby," the woman said, paying him little attention, keeping her focus on the paper she held, instead.

"News is entertainment, Luther, or didn't you know?" Looking around the office, he pulled a folded sheet of paper from his jacket pocket and asked, "Where's the suspect?"

"Just hurried out to some important task."

"I saw the DA and Sheriff Nolan getting out of their cars a few seconds ago."

"Looks like it could be big. I've got my camera." The young man headed toward a chair and picked up his camera.

The door opened again and in walked the Sheriff and a tall man in an expensive suit, both holding typed pages. They only nodded at the other three.

"Gentlemen," said Bobby Baker . "What do you make of this?"

The District Attorney sat down and smiled. "We just came to listen and see what's going on, Mister Baker. Just listen and see. That's all."

Using a telephone at the nurses' station, Blanchard called Proctor's home and a restaurant she was known to frequent for lunch, both without success. He had pressed the aides and nurses once more to search for Slaughter, which they went through the motions of doing and returned within minutes. Blanchard had stalled as long as he could. Every effort at finding the patient had failed. He would have to cancel the press conference. He returned to the administration office.

Entering the reception area once more, he was surprised to see seven or eight people waiting, one of whom appeared to be the local Sheriff. He advanced no more than two steps into the room and was surrounded by reporters asking questions.

He raised both hands to halt the confusion.

"I want to offer my apologies," Blanchard said in a loud voice. "But I am forced to cancel the press conference. One of my patients is, uh, unfortunately indisposed. I'd like to reschedule in a few days, as soon as circumstances permit. Again, I'm very sorry if I have inconvenienced you."

One of the reporters pressed forward holding a sheet of paper. "You are Vernon Blanchard, aren't you?"

"Yes, but – "

"Who is this Nurse Corry Proctor that is making these charges against you?"

"Charges?" Blanchard paled, his face registering complete confusion. "What are you talking about?"

A tall man in a suit stepped forward, holding a paper.

"Mister Blanchard, I'm District Attorney Warren Staples, and according to this document, you have a couple of confessions you want to make, based on some pretty serious criminal charges. Are you aware of this testimony by a staff member of yours?"

Blanchard moved his head slowly, side to side. "I – I don't know what – What charges? Proctor? I was just preparing for the – "

"Mister Blanchard," said Staples as the Sheriff stepped beside him. "This Nurse Proctor has accused you of embezzling funds from the hospital..."

What?" he yelled.

"...and of performing a dangerous surgical procedure on a person who was never admitted as a patient, but only here for evaluation."

"I – I – don't know anything about – " Blanchard's body began shaking, his eyes darting from Staples to the Sheriff and back.

"I'm not here to have you arrested, Mister Blanchard, but I advise you to secure the services of a competent attorney. We will investigate these charges quickly and thoroughly and will be in contact with you. In the meantime," he gestured to the reporters standing by. "I would advise you to refrain from answering questions from anyone until you have legal counsel."

The Sheriff turned to the reporters as a group. "Time to go, folks. The show's over. For now, at least."

When the Sheriff had herded everyone outside, Blanchard staggered slowly toward his office. Before he opened the door, he saw a dozen or more nurses and aides gathered in the hall doorway, staring at him and whispering among themselves. He was speechless. Hurriedly, he opened his office door and closed it behind himself.

* * * * *

Ott Mobley entered the Sheriff's office with apparent difficulty. Leaning on a wooden crutch under his left armpit, Mobley guided his bandaged leg through the doorway while holding the door open with his right hand. Gripped in his right hand was a small brown bag. His left eye was black and swollen nearly closed.

"Sheriff, you shouldn't – " said Lowe, hurrying to help his boss through the door.

"I'm okay." Mobley nodded him away as he eased the door closed. "Got a few minutes?"

"Sure, sure. You want to go in your office?"

Mobley nodded. "Can you get me a glass of water?" He held the bag up. "Pain medicine."

"Be right back," said Lowe, hurrying away.

When Lowe returned, Mobley had settled on the sofa in his office with his left leg elevated on a pillow. He took the cup Lowe offered, extracted a couple of pills from a bottle in the bag and swallowed them with the water. Lowe sat opposite him in a vinyl upholstered chair.

"Can you bring me up to date, Captain Lowe?'

"Are you sure you're up to it, Sheriff? You've had – "

"Thank you, Wayne. I appreciate the concern, but I need to get my mind off my troubles and connect with my job again."

"All right."

"How bad did I screw things up by running off to Riley's place in a rage?"

Lowe smiled. "You didn't do anything. Riley's had murder in him for nearly twenty years. We know he killed his wife and the man who was with him."

Mobley shook his head sadly. "She tried to protect me before I got cold-cocked. I wonder if she died trying. Riley didn't deserve her."

Lowe nodded. "The man who hit you was named Kell. Apparently, Riley killed him and left his truck in the woods nearby. I think Riley doubled back to his place and used his wife's car to escape. We don't have a description of it yet."

"It's a black '46 Ford. I.D. the license plates through the county."

"We've got somebody looking up the records now," Lowe nodded. "We believe Riley headed west, since the nearest paved road goes east into town or west toward Alabama. Another man, named Wylie Harris, was arrested with Kell yesterday morning and released just before he was. We think it was Kell and Harris who – "

"Who killed my wife."

Lowe was silent for a moment, watching his boss. Assured the man was okay, he proceeded. "Based on what you told me yesterday, we relayed to the DA details suggesting that Riley was the likely killer of Ray Lee Colbert, and he approved returning Adam Woods to Compton County to face the kidnapping charge."

Mobley held up his hand. "See what we can do to intervene on Woods' behalf with the Compton Sheriff."

"On his behalf? Why?"

"A couple of reasons. I agree with him that the Slaughter girl may be in danger at Mid-State. I got a creepy feeling from the so-called Administrator there. I think he qualifies as a prospective patient more than Maisie Slaughter does."

"Well, about her, we got word from the Compton Sheriff a little while ago that she has apparently either escaped or has been taken out of the hospital. And there might be charges coming up against that administrator."

"She's gone?"

He nodded in the affirmative.

"And they have no idea where she went?"

"None. She was there last night and not there this morning. The danger you're talking about? It might have become reality. Sheriff Nolan over there says she was one of six or eight patients who received some kind of brain surgery yesterday."

Mobley leaned forward. "Brain surgery? You're not serious!"

Lowe shrugged. "That's what he said."

"Maisie Slaughter is harmless, and saner than most people I know." He closed his eyes. "It's my fault she was there. I should have refused to take her. But this preacher came in here claiming she was a danger to herself and the community."

Lowe was silent for a moment, then, "Her brother called several times this morning. He's worried about her and wants to talk with you."

Sheriff Mobley shifted his leg off the pillow and slid forward. "I've got to get over to Mid-State, to help find her."

"Ott, you're in no shape to go over there. Let me take care of that."

"You drive." He paused in thought. "Hey, and while we're at it, let's take Adam Woods."

"Woods? He just got here."

Mobley nodded. "He's had one thing on his mind: getting

her out of there and back home. Risked a jail sentence trying to rescue her from that hell hole. I'm not going to mention that she's missing until we get to Mid-State. No need in causing him more agony than he's had."

"Well, what'll we tell him when he wants to know why he's going back over there?"

"Say we want to talk with the Sheriff about the charge against him. That's true."

"You want him in cuffs?"

"No, the guy's as harmless as she is. If I'd been him, and cared for Maisie Slaughter the way he seems to, I would've tried to break her out of that place, myself."

"Shouldn't we get an okay from the DA before we do that, or at least talk to Sheriff Nolan in Compton County?"

"Nope. If they don't like it, well, maybe you'll wind up being the interim Sheriff. At this point, I think it's the right thing to do, and that's enough for me. Besides, we'll stop by and talk to the Sheriff over there after we leave Mid-State."

"You're not feeling a little guilty, are you? For taking her up there?"

"Probably. I've got to do something to help make up for it."

Lowe put a hand on Ott's shoulder as he tried to stand.

"Ott, I just want to say one thing. You're a good man, and I will stand with you come what may."

"Thanks, Wayne. I really appreciate that."

"And Ott." Mobley made it to his feet and turned to Lowe. "I'm awful sorry about – " Lowe choked up, unable to speak her name.

Mobley's eyes reddened and brimmed over. He nodded. "We'll get Riley."

CHAPTER THIRTY-THREE

The rifle was one he had kept in the carport where his wife's Ford generally was parked. He had killed a dog with it once and let Ray Lee take it for some little extortion thing he was working. Otherwise, it was merely a scarred-up British bolt-action Enfield his uncle had picked up for twenty dollars after the German armistice, along with a single box of 30.06 cartridges. Riley had six of those cartridges in his pants pockets. He figured he would only need one.

He was still breathing heavily after the hike up the hill from the little creek where he parked the car. From the ridge, he had a nearly perfect view of the Sheriff's office building sixty yards down the eastern slope. With the afternoon sun behind him and trees surrounding him, he had clear, well lit view of the back and side of the building. His primary target was Adam Woods, the only witness to Ray Lee's murder. The scope mounted atop the receiver gave a decent view through a window in the cell block. His secondary target, should he fail to have an opening on Woods, was Sheriff Ott Mobley, who had cost Riley everything that remained of his broken life: his home, his secure position in business and, of course, his wife.

Through the scope, he had seen someone pacing in a cell, but had been unable to see the face clearly. Now that the sun was providing light at a better angle, he propped a piece of pine limb under the forearm rest to steady his aim, fixed the crosshairs in the center of the window and timed the appearance of the head in the targeted space. He counted through several appearances of the person in the window and saw some predictability. Four seconds after passing out of view on the right side of the window, he reappeared in the window;

six seconds after moving away from the left side of the space, he reappeared.

He chose to fire on Woods' return from the right side of the window space. The head appeared, moved to the left; he counted six seconds; the head reappeared and disappeared. He counted: as he gradually squeezed the trigger, he counted, "one, two, three –" the head reappeared. Too quickly. Something was off. He counted to six. The head did not reappear.

Riley snorted, and cursed under his breath.

He waited. Ten seconds. Thirty seconds.

Angry, he cursed again. He lay the rifle aside and slapped an ant on his neck. He pulled a pint bottle out of his back pocket, unscrewed the cap and took a long drink, downing the few remaining ounces, and tossed the bottle down the hill.

He repositioned the rifle and scope on the window and waited. No one moved inside.

The back door of the building opened and Art Lowe stepped out and headed to a patrol car, a 1950 Ford, painted in typical police fashion with black fenders, hood and trunk, and white doors and roof. Out of sheer frustration, Riley was tempted to shoot him as he reached for the driver side door and opened it. Lowe got in, cranked the car and backed it closer to the building. He left it running and got out, returning into the building. Suddenly Riley realized he was picking someone up – in all likelihood, the injured Ott Mobley. He moved the rifle to sight in on the exit door. Before he was set, the door opened and Mobley hobbled out. Quickly, Riley moved the barrel to match his movement while getting the scope fixed on him.

Just as Riley was ready to pull the trigger, the exit opened again and Lowe hurried out guiding Adam Woods with his hand on an elbow. Here was the primary target. Before Riley could fix site on Woods, Lowe had whisked him into the back seat and closed the door. Lowe was climbing into the driver's seat next to Mobley when Riley finally settled the crosshairs on the shape in the back seat. He squeezed the trigger just as the car lurched forward. The rifle bucked with the explosion and the muzzle blast scattered the leaves and pine needles underneath the barrel as the window of the patrol car shattered.

Riley let the rifle drop, pushed himself to his knees and crawled out from under the low limbs. He struggled to his feet and dashed down the opposite side of the hill wildly. He fell with a loud grunt and slid a couple of feet, picked himself up again and ran as fast as his weight would allow toward the car.

* * * * *

"Good afternoon, friends and neighbors of Compton and surrounding counties," gushed Bobby Baker in uncommonly bright and eager voice. "Do I have a show for you today!"

Bobby Baker lifted a couple of legal pad sheets onto which he had scribbled notes, "Whew! I don't know when we've had such goings on in our area, and most of this happened since I spoke with you all yesterday morning."

He lifted a paper cup steaming with coffee, blew on it and decided to draw out the suspense. "Oh boy, this coffee is hot." Leaning off mike while smiling to himself, he called, "Hey can somebody bring me some cold milk to pour in my coffee. You know I can't drink it boiling like this!" Of course, he was completely alone in the studio.

Leaning to the microphone again, he continued the ruse. "Ah, thanks, that's a lot better." He hesitated. "Ahh! Now, to the news I was referring to. There's been some strange goings-on over at MSH the last few days. Of course, those of you who've lived here know that MSH stands for Mid-State Hospital, the state hospital for the insane. And you know there's always strange things going on there, but these are stranger than normal.

"I happened to be chatting with our good Sheriff, and the well known District Attorney, Mister Warren Staples, yesterday, and learned about some possible intrigue at MSH. The kind of intrigue that has a certain hospital administrator in hot water over two very big crimes – or I should say possible crimes! I cannot give you a lot of specifics, folks; after all, these are just charges. No one's been convicted yet. But let me just say this: a young patient who was brought in for evaluation recently was kidnapped from the hospital a couple of nights ago. A suspect is in custody and the young woman was returned safely. However, afterward, she MAY have had brain surgery performed on her – WITHOUT any real evaluation at all by a qualified physician!"

Baker grinned and picked up his coffee cup once more. He leaned aside and called, "Hey, can somebody bring me one of those cinnamon buns from the break room?" This he did, knowing full well that some of his listeners were wont to bring in sweets for him if he merely hinted. "What? We're out?"

He straightened at the microphone again, rustling his notes. "Oh well, I need to get back to this news anyway.

"There's going to be some kind of unraveling to do to get to the bottom of how this happened to a poor young woman who was just in for evaluation. ...AND the other thing is that SUPPOSEDLY someone at MSH – I'm not naming any names – has embezzled a large amount of hospital money. Oh! Oh!"

Baker reached across the counter to a turntable, switched it on and placed a 45RPM record on the spinning disc with practiced ease, He held the needle poised above the edge of the record.

"I've just been informed we need to take a commercial break. But please, please, please don't go anywhere, because I've got to tell you the biggest piece of news as soon as we come back." He set the needle on the first groove of the record, and immediately popular music took the place of his voice in the monitors.

Lifting a typed page from the counter, he began reading a script for an advertiser.

As hoped, the station's telephone lines were busy the entire day, as the Afternoon Show remained on air far later than its normally scheduled hours. Bobby related all the details available and some that were not. People in the listening area were shocked and appalled and demanded that the state investigate the goings-on. The mystery of the missing patient – Bobby's *coup de grace* – when finally measured out in suspenseful morsels, set people in motion. They got in their cars and began driving around the MSH grounds and surrounding residential areas in search of the mysterious woman.

* * * * *

The Settles County Hospital was the nearest medical facility to Odino. The drive in the patrol car, a distance of sixteen miles, took thirteen minutes. With Mobley in the back seat attending to the victim, Lowe radioed ahead, and emergency personnel were waiting at the emergency entrance when they arrived. Adam Woods was placed on a gurney and rushed inside.

Immediately after the attack on Woods, Mobley had taken control, ordering Lowe to forget the shooter and to drive with siren and lights activated while he did what he could for Woods. Lowe contacted Willoughby at the dispatcher's desk and had him send patrols from both directions to the trail that followed the creek. And he ordered an APB for the Ford Riley was probably driving, since it was obvious he was the most likely suspect.

With the patient transferred, Mobley got on the radio.

"Give me an update, Willoughby."

"Units are on the scene and have found where the car was parked. No sign of the perpetrator. They're combing the area now."

"Any sign of Riley's car elsewhere?"

"Nothing yet, Sheriff."

"Keep me posted."

Mobley limped to the emergency area with Lowe at his side. "Can you find me a telephone to use?" he asked.

"Sure," Lowe said and hurried inside.

When Mobley entered, Lowe directed him to an office a few feet down a hall. Mobley sat at the desk and dialed the Compton County Sheriff's office.

When the Sheriff came on the line, Mobley said, "Tom, this is Ott Mobley. Your prisoner's been shot."

He gave him details of the attack and the basics of what he knew about the suspect and probable motive.

"Look, Tom," he continued. "I know this is going to sound crazy, but I want your cooperation in convincing the D.A. to drop charges against Woods." He listened for a moment. "Yes, assuming he pulls through this surgery. If you've got a few minutes, I'd like to sit down with you and explain why I'm asking this favor." He waited as Nolan spoke with someone nearby before coming back on line. "Okay, I can be there in fifteen minutes. Thanks," Mobley said.

* * * * *

Late Friday afternoon, Sonny Ingles stepped inside the Ocmulgee County Sheriff's office to find a chaotic scene. Three deputies talked animatedly on separate phones around the room, one was jotting notes as he listened to a man across a desk. When he tried to get the attention of a dispatcher, the man waved him to a chair and told him to please have a seat. He sat next to an elderly man in overalls who had a dark scowl on his face. He nodded to the man as he took a seat.

The man snarled a greeting unintelligibly. Ingles responded, "Has it been this way all afternoon?"

The old man cursed, "It's my second time in here in two days."

Ingles shook his head and turned his attention away, but the man continued.

"That _____ Riley runs over my dog and I can't get anybody here to do anything about it. Paid fifty dollars for that dog."

The mention of Riley regained Ingles' attention.

"You mean Potter Riley?"

He nodded and hit the heel of his fist against the chair arm. "Been covering for that _____ for years, and what did it get me? Him and his hired help didn't even stop. Just run over 'im and kept right on going."

The old man was about the right age. Ingles decided to

take a wild guess.

"You talking about the Bonder Woods trial?"

He did not miss a beat. "I took Riley's side and kept my mouth shut."

Ingles turned slightly toward him. "Say, it doesn't look like they're going to get to us today. I'm going to go get a cup of coffee. Why don't I buy you one? I'd like to hear more about that trial."

"Suits me. I ain't got nothing better to do." He jammed his hat onto his head and pushed himself to his feet.

Ingles stood with him and offered his hand. "Sonny Ingles."

The old man took his hand. "Melvin Conway," he said.

CHAPTER THIRTY-FOUR

Night descended on Odino, Georgia, clear and with a warm wind from the southwest. Maisie Slaughter lay on her back on the grass, weeping, unable to speak.

Her body ached. The contortions of her face brought her discomfort. Even the act of lightly wiping tears from her eyes was painful. But none of that mattered.

She was home. Lying face-up in her pasture, seeing the stars as though for the very first time, she was filled to overflowing with joy. She could not stop the tears.

How she wished she could dance and worship before God, to let her bruised spirit attempt to express her wonder at His goodness and grace, though she knew that her feeble attempts in the past had all been so inadequate to the purpose, and would always be until heaven.

Do you forgive?

The thought came to her through her spirit, she knew.

"Yes, yes! I do!" she cried. "Anything! Everything!"

She raised her hands to heaven.

"I don't understand. But I forgive!"

The pasture was to be the first place Maisie came when Lorene Mills brought her home, but a sprinkle of rain delayed her return there for a day. The drive had been a blur for Maisie. Mills had helped her into the back seat, covered her with a blanket and, after getting from Maisie that she lived in Odino, drove away. The next moment Maisie was aware, Mills was shaking her awake and offering her a sip of coffee. The car was parked in the well-lighted lot of a restaurant. She took a sip and promptly exclaimed, "Yuck!" It was not how she remembered coffee tasting, and declined more.

From there, Mills got more specific directions. In the end, Maisie could not identify her property in the dark, though she knew she was near, and asked to be let out along the roadway. Mills, reluctant to drop her off in a place with no house in sight and only woods, agreed only after Maisie saw her mailbox on a post beside her long unpaved drive. Maisie thanked her profusely. With every step she took toward her home, she grew stronger and more elated.

She went inside the farmhouse as the shower commenced. Before sleeping, she took a pencil and sheet of paper and sat at the kitchen table. With the purpose of inventorying and exercising her brain, wrote down every scrap of information she could remember, labeling facts as belonging to recent events or the time prior to being in the hospital; anything indeterminable was identified with a question mark.

Scripture portions; her brother; her friend, Adam; his last name; the model of her truck; what she had planted in the garden, and when she had planted it; the name of the Sheriff; her parents' names and birthdays; the names of people at Mid-State Hospital; which day and what time she arrived at the hospital; the name of the aide who brought her home; the name of the clerk at the farm supply store. And, the details of a specific request she had made of Lorene Mills before getting out of her car.

Maisie wrote for nearly two hours, pausing only to force herself to spell correctly and write neatly. She went into the bathroom to study her face, but after a few seconds, turned out the light and decided not to look at herself in a mirror for a week. To remind herself to keep that commitment, she hung a towel over the mirror. Seeing herself this way was too much a reminder of the hurt and anxiety she suffered. She willed herself to forget the image in the mirror, and rely fully on God's precious declaration that, by the stripes on Jesus' back she had been healed.

Sometime in the early hours before dawn, Maisie fell exhausted into bed and slept virtually all day Friday, rising only at sundown. Without thought for food or any other thing, she bathed and, walking stiffly, took a blanket outside again as darkness settled. And here she had remained. In and out of prayer. In and out of sleep.

The moon rose and dimmed the stars with its fullness. A deer wandered past, grazing peacefully as though the blanket-bundled form were not there. A dove called. And the moon slowly slipped toward the horizon.

As the sky brightened to lavender and a breeze drifted over her, Maisie awoke, alert and refreshed. She had much to do, today, foremost among things was finding out where Adam was and how she could go to him. For that, she would need a meal and time to sort through how to go about seeing Adam.

As the rest of the world was waking up, she would have breakfast. A real breakfast of eggs from the henhouse and toasted bread of whatever kind she might still have in the house. She would brew a pot of coffee and sit on the porch sipping it. She would relish her home. And then she would set her mind to reading the Bible. She needed the strength that would come from that. For in that way, she would wash her soul of everything unpleasant and purge her mind of fears and any hidden bitterness she might uncover.

She had been in a wilderness, a wasteland of evil and dryness, and she set her heart to returning fully to peace and joy only attainable in the presence of the Holy Spirit.

* * * * *

"What are you saying?" asked Bonder Woods, struggling to lift himself onto his elbows in the bed.

Sonny Ingles' smile was broad, his eyes wide. "I'm saying I found one of the witnesses who were in that shed the night Flynn Riley died. His name is Conway."

"Melvin Conway," said Bonder, his eyes watering. "He admitted it was an accident?"

Ingles nodded. The sight of Bonder Wood's tears provoked Ingles' eyes to moisten. "He said it was Flynn who started the fight and tried to take your winnings."

"Oh, thank God!" Bonder could not restrain his emotion. He wept openly. "Thank you, God!"

Ingles waited a moment until Bonder wiped his eyes and looked up at him, before continuing.

"I told Conway that Riley was a suspect in at least four murders, to make sure he held no more allegiance to the man. Then I asked if he would mind walking over to the DA's office with me. He was mad enough at Riley for running over his dog that he didn't hesitate. We walked across the square to the DA's office and he told the same story to Warren Staples.

"Four murders?"

Ingles explained the circumstances as they had been described to him. He mentioned nothing of Adam Woods having been shot, even though the first report indicated the wound was not life-threatening.

"Do you think – ?" Bonder stopped himself, afraid to ask.

"A retrial? It's almost a certainty," he answered in anticipation of the question. "I don't know how long it will take, but Conway didn't back off one bit. He even said he had felt bad for years about not coming forward to testify. But Riley had threatened to kill him."

Bonder Woods reached over to Ingles' hand and grasped it. He squeezed it with all his might. His eyes, though tightly shut against more tears, could not hold them back, His body shook as he wept, and he covered his eyes with his free arm.

"Thank you, God," he whispered.

* * * * *

Maisie washed her face in cold well water on the back porch, a habit she had developed as a child, before the family had running water. She stretched her legs, arms and back against the morning sun and dried her face. She was opening the screen door when the long unused telephone rang. Immediately, her thoughts went to Lorene Mills. She followed the sound into the kitchen and found the handset underneath a bread box where, she recalled, she had placed it months before.

"Hello."

Lorene's voice came on. "How are you, Maisie?"

"I am – absolutely wonderful!" She still formed words slowly. "And getting better every day." She noted the strength of her voice, which she had not heard except when praying aloud over the past couple of days.

"I contacted the police, like you asked me, Maisie."

"And what did they say?" Her eagerness was very apparent.

"The officer I spoke with would not tell me anything."

"What?"

"Nothing. He said he knew nothing about anyone by that name, and had no record of an attempted kidnapping."

Puzzled, Maisie frowned, processing the unexpected report.

"Actually," Lorene corrected, "he said they had no charges against anyone by that name. Wasn't that a strange way to phrase it?"

After a couple of seconds Maisie realized what this turn of events likely meant. She smiled.

"He's been released!"

"Released?"

"That's got to be it!"

"Seriously? You think they would – ?"

"That has to be the answer! Yes, I'm sure that's what he was trying to say. Maybe he felt he could not give out details at this point."

"You think so?"

"Yes," Maisie answered confidently. "I'm not worried now. He will come to see me."

Lorene hesitated in responding. "Well, if you think so. Are you sure you're okay, I mean – how about your memory?"

"It's coming together."

"Really?" The girl seemed astonished.

"Definitely! You are Lorene Mills. You drove me home in your uncle's car – let's see – about 31 or 32 hours ago. I spent five days in a virtual torture chamber in a corner of Hades called Mid-State Hospital. And you rescued me!"

"You amaze me!"

"God is faithful! He's the amazing One!"

They spoke little more, with Lorene reporting the arrest of Vernon Blanchard and the appointment of a new interim director. Maisie asked the young aide to come and spend a few days with her, she, answering that she would try when she got her next free day. Then Maisie hung up the phone and managed to move, in a semblance of dancing, into the living room where she danced before the Lord as she hummed a song already echoing in her heart.

* * * * *

Sheriff Ott Mobley strode with a limp into the office.

"Morning, Art," he said, nodding to Lowe who sat at the dispatcher's desk drinking coffee. "Anything new on Riley?"

"No leads."

"He seems to have disappeared."

"Ott," Lowe said, setting his cup down and rising. "Got a minute in your office?"

"Sure, come on in." He left the door open behind him as he made his way to his desk. Lowe followed and closed the door behind him.

"I need to talk to you."

Mobley sat at his desk and looked down at his hands. "Art, actually, I've been wanting to talk with you."

Lowe took a seat.

"When all this comes out, with Riley and all, I guess you know you'll be made interim Sheriff."

"Let's not think about all that right now, Ott."

"I've got to be thinking about it. I'm guilty of a lot. And frankly, I'm ready to get all that stuff off my conscience. I played with fire. I had a contract with the devil." He shook his head. "I must have been stupid. I aided and abetted Potter Riley's rise to power. God help me! I deserve whatever happens to me."

Ott buried his face in his hands. "But Katie didn't deserve –!" His voice broke.

Lowe gave his friend a few moments before speaking.

"Look, Ott. I won't be made Sheriff."

Mobley looked up slowly.

"I was tempted," said Lowe pressing on. "Riley offered to make me Sheriff when you cut ties with him. He offered me lots of money, and I told him I'd work with him."

Mobley was stunned.

"But when – " Lowe halted, struggling. "When Katie –" He shook his head. "I called him and swore to kill him."

Mobley nodded at Lowe, his face registering understanding.

"I swear, I never helped him do anything. I was crazy for even considering working for him."

"You don't have to say anymore, Art. I understand." He looked down. "Don't worry about it anymore. We'll catch him, and if I know anything about him, he will not be taken alive."

"And you don't have to worry about anything, either, Ott."

Mobley smiled at his friend. "No, I'll leave my part in the hands of Warren Staples. I'm going to meet with him tomorrow and tell him everything. Then I'll resign as Sheriff."

"You don't have to do that, Ott."

"You'll make a fine Sheriff, Art." Mobley gave him a sympathetic smile.

"Want me to check on Woods, see how he's doing?"

"Yeah. And see if Nolan has talked with the DA about dropping charges. I want to see something good come out of all this. And if you're up to it, let's go out to the Slaughter place to see if maybe Gal made her way back there."

CHAPTER THIRTY-FIVE

The bullet had struck Adam in the left hip and lodged in the fleshy muscles surrounding the back side of his hip bone. A couple dozen tiny shards of glass had been the source of most of the bleeding, but they had all been extracted with patience. He had endured excruciating pain during the ride to the hospital, but the Sheriff himself had sat in the back seat with him and kept him talking while holding a compress against his hip.

He awoke from the surgery late in the afternoon on Friday and spent an hour regaining awareness of where he was and why. He learned from a nurse that a deputy was posted outside his room. When Sheriff Mobley and the deputy who drove the patrol car came by to see how he was doing, Mobley told him that Maisie was no longer at Mid-State, but had left on her own sometime Thursday night or Friday morning. Adam sensed the Sheriff was soft-pedaling her disappearance, and he asked if he knew where she had gone. He did not. No one seemed to know.

When the Sheriff told him the likelihood all charges would be dropped against him, Adam felt himself begin to gain strength emotionally. He spent the rest of the day thinking about what he could do to find Maisie.

Saturday morning, after a sound night's sleep, he awoke with a rudimentary plan and an urge to get out of the hospital as soon as possible. Wound or no wound, he was going to Maisie's farm.

With the aid of the pain medication, he steadied himself with a hand against the wall, dragged himself out of bed and hobbled down the hallway to find a doctor.

"Mister Woods!"

The alarmed voice was a nurse behind him.

"What are you doing out of bed?" She hurried to him and tried to steer him back to his room.

"I need to talk with a doctor about going home."

She nudged him into a reversal of his course. "Oh, you won't be going home today. I can tell you that much."

"I don't feel bad."

"That's medication talking, Mister Woods. You'll feel it for certain when that wears off."

"You haven't run out, have you?"

She looked puzzled.

"I mean, you've got more pain medication, don't you?"

"Of course!"

"Then just give me some more."

"No you don't! It's not that simple, young fella! You've got to be careful moving around or you'll break a stitch and start bleeding."

"Okay, I'll be careful after I leave. Can you get that doctor for me?"

She stopped, and glared at him. "Don't you think I know you were in custody of the law when you came in here?"

"I was told they were dropping all charges."

"Well, I haven't been told that, so get yourself back in there before I call the Sheriff." She gave him a gentle shove at the doorway.

"Will you please get the doctor to come by here?"

She glared harder.

"Please," he repeated. "It's very important."

She appeared to soften somewhat. "We'll see! But only if you get back in bed now."

"I'm as good as there, Ma'am!"

* * * * *

Potter Riley was spooked. He had barely slept. Every snap or creak of the old barn convinced him armed deputies were sneaking up on him. Every moan of the wind became a voice, sometimes that of Ray Lee Colbert and others, of Esther. He tried to calm himself, to think rationally. Of course the noises were mice. The voices were just the wind playing with his imagination, or they came from an owl in the trees nearby. Still, he could not deny the clear voice of Esther. "Why-y-y?" she asked him over and over until he pulled at his hair and gnashed his teeth.

Harper Slatt found the hiding place for him, guaranteeing he would be safe there. It held his car, just like Slatt had said it would. But the old man didn't say anything about the place being haunted. Slatt brought him a gallon of moonshine, a pistol and a bucket of white house paint with a brush. He mocked when Riley told him to find a new hiding place where there were no voices.

"There ain't anyplace you won't hear the voices of them you killed," he had replied, smirking. He nodded toward the jug. "Drink till they go away."

Riley had taken that advice, but they had not gone away. He slept in the back seat of Esther's car with the windows rolled up and the doors locked. When he woke to the sounds and voices, he drank. And when they got louder he cursed them and threatened them with his pistol.

Today, after a maddening night, the wind was low, a mere whisper. With one of the doors slightly opened he had enough light to paint his car. Riley used the brush on the car's roof and hood, occasionally looking through the cracks between the boards in the barn door to make sure no one was sneaking up on him.

As he slapped the paint on, he muttered to God and Satan, alternately accusing them of trying to kill him.

"You can't scare me. I know what you're doing." He set the brush down and lifted the jug of liquor, swallowing hard.

Riley wiped his mouth on his sleeve. "Esther's dead."

Even without wind, he seemed to hear a taunting denial. *You're a fool. You think I'm that easy to kill?*

"Shut up!" he demanded over his shoulder. "You're nothing! Nothing! I'll kill you all over again if I need to."

You can't find me. I'll suffocate you while you sleep.

"Shut up, I said!" He whirled around violently, swinging the big brush as if to hit someone behind him. Paint spattered against the car's windshield and the barn wall in a long arc.

"I will get out of here!" he shouted. "Soon as I finish with this car, I'm leaving and you'll never find me."

You can't hide.

Riley gritted his teeth and seethed. He tossed the dripping brush onto the hood of the car and pulled the revolver from his pants waist. He stared into the dark spaces at the back of the barn, swept his eyes across the hay loft above him.

"Show your ugly face!"

You didn't think I was ugly when I married you.

"Shut up or I'll kill you!" he growled.

Now the voice of Ray Lee spoke up. *You can't kill us.*

Riley cocked the pistol's hammer and aimed at the emptiness, his hand shaking wildly. "Show your face!" he shouted into the shadows.

Now the voices went silent. The barn creaked with the heat of the sun moving toward noon, and a gust of wind whistled.

He waited until he was sure they were gone before uncocking the pistol and stowing it under his belt again.

He retrieved the paint brush. A split-second later, a field mouse scampered out of the darkness toward the partially open door. Riley yelped in fright. He whorled and threw the brush in the direction of the movement he had seen from the corner of his eye. The brush banged against the door and dropped to the dirt, leaving a splash of white running in streams down the boards.

Every part of Riley's body shook. As he stared at the white splatter, it seemed to turn red before his eyes.

"No!" shouted Riley and turned away. He grabbed the jug from the ground and held it to his chest as he staggered to the back door of the car and opened it. He took a long swallow from the jug and set it on the floor of the car before climbing in and falling headlong on to the back seat.

* * * * *

Adam explained, calmly at first, why he wanted to leave the hospital. The physician patiently explained why it was dangerous for him to do that. Adam questioned if there was any legal reason requiring him to stay. The doctor admitted there was not; the Sheriff had confirmed no charges were pending. He pressed Adam to find out why he felt so strongly about leaving. Adam related the news of Maisie's disappearance. The doctor assumed he was talking about a patient who had escaped from Mid-State. Adam, frustrated with the resistance and useless explanations, finally ended the discussion.

"Thanks for your concern, but just give me whatever release I need to sign, and enough pain medication to last me a couple of days. I'm leaving."

The physician stalked out of the room, and within moments the nurse came in with Adam's clothes.

"You're being hard-headed, you know," she said.

"I know," he said, taking the clothes. "But I've got to find my friend."

"Have you given any thought to how you'll find her when you're barely able to walk?" The sarcasm in her voice was heavy.

"I'm going to ask the Sheriff to take me to my car, of course." He turned to her. "By the way, can I use a telephone?"

"And how do you think you're going to drive in that condition?"

He cast a look at her designed to suggest it was a silly question. "Carefully. I'll drive very carefully."

She stood with her arms crossed. "Do you want crutches?"

He stopped undoing the bundle of clothing and smile gratefully. "You'd do that for me?"

"Get changed and I'll bring them to you. The release paperwork and your pain medication will be waiting for you at the nurses' station. You can use the phone there." She turned and left the room, closing the door behind her.

* * * * *

Adam had to wait half an hour before the deputies brought his car and parked it at the curb outside the main entrance. He was managing the concrete steps out front poorly when the nurse hurried out and took his elbow.

"If you're bent on driving that fool car, at least let me help you get to it."

She steadied him as he made the final steps.

"Thanks, really." He said when he was on the walkway. "I can get in the car by myself."

"Of course you can," she said, still gripping his elbow. "But I'm sure you won't mind if I make sure you actually get in the car without killing yourself." He grinned and kept silent.

The struggle into the car was worse than he imagined, but he managed with her help.

"Drive carefully," she said once he sat fully on the seat. "I don't want to see you coming back in here again. Do you hear me?"

He stopped trying to contort his leg inside and extended his hand. "I will."

She shook his hand and turned back to the building.

"Thank you," he said. She waved over her shoulder and hurried away.

Adam slid in as far as he could. As he had figured, he had to sit just right of the steering wheel in order to get his left leg extended near the door and give him room to use his right foot for every pedal. He had figured clutching with his right foot would be a real challenge, but if necessary, he might be able to use a crutch to press the gas pedal while releasing the clutch with his good foot. What he might do if he had to stop and re-accelerate on a hill, he had no idea.

Once he was situated, he cranked the car in neutral and practiced pressing the accelerator with the crutch, revving the engine inordinately high at first. Finally, he said a quick prayer and, pressing the clutch, dropped the lever into first gear, then grabbing the crutch, pressed the gas pedal gradually as he let out the clutch. The car jerked a couple of times until he regulated the gas and drove away, praying out loud as he navigated onto the street. By slowing to a virtual crawl he timed his approach to traffic lights so he would not have to stop. Finally, he turned onto a state road and accelerated.

The day was sunny and warm, though clouds loomed on the southern horizon. He thanked God for dry weather. Rain would have complicated things beyond possibility. He planned his route from there to Maisie's farm taking the least travelled roads, which increased the distance he had to drive, but it was better to take longer than to take the chance of encountering traffic problems.

* * * * *

Riley woke to the sound of singing. He raised his head and ran his hand over his face to wipe away sweat. His soaked shirt stuck to his belly and the texture of the seat cover made ridges in his cheek and forehead. The barn was sweltering. He suddenly felt as if he might be suffocating. His first thought was that Esther or Ray Lee had set the barn afire, but he smelled no smoke and saw no flames, only blackness perforated by bright spaces between the boards of the barn's exterior. His head ached and his stomach growled. The thought of food was almost nauseating, but he felt weak. Whether he liked the idea or not, he would have to eat something.

As he gained more clarity of mind, he realized the singing was not one of the voices he had been hearing. This one was actually pleasant, and it was not very near. He pushed his torso up to see where the sound was coming from. Seeing nothing, he pulled himself out of the car and stood unsteadily as his eyes adjusted to the odd contrast of blackness and brightness about him. He felt for the pistol but it was not there. Studying the interior of the car, he saw it lying on the floor, picked it up and replaced it under his belt. Touching the car fender for balance, he made his way to the barn door and looked outside. He was startled.

A woman was washing the old dusty truck sitting in front

of the old farmhouse. Riley cursed. Slatt had told him the place was abandoned. He had expected to finish painting the car and drive away after sundown. Now, he had this to contend with. Simply waiting for her to go inside was not an option because he would have to drive directly past the farmhouse around the truck, and it would be impossible to do that quietly or without notice. She would call the cops before he could get onto the county road. And he could not assume she would drive away after washing the truck. He would just have to kill the woman.

But first, he would make sure she had food he could eat.

Riley moved the pistol to the small of his back, under his belt, and pushed the barn door open wide enough to step out. The daylight blinded him temporarily, so he shaded his eyes as he walked cautiously across the grassy expanse toward her.

CHAPTER THIRTY-SIX

Maisie looked skyward and saw heavy clouds rolling in from the southwest. "I should have known," she said. "I start washing my truck and rain sneaks up."

At the trailing edge of the dark mass, sheets of grey rain followed like a veil. She dropped her rag in the bucket of water at her feet.

"Okay, a little rain won't hurt."

Turn around.

The voice was the Lord's. She turned to see an old, heavy-set man walking from the direction of her barn. He was walking unsteadily and was sweating profusely. Her first thought was that he was sick and needed help. She wiped her hands on a drying towel slung over her shoulder.

"Hello," she said cautiously. "Are you okay?"

The man seemed to grow angry at her. He quickened his steps and reached behind himself, fumbling for something.

"What were you doing in my barn?" she asked, noticing the door was open.

The man pulled a gun and aimed it at her. Maisie gasped.

"What do you want here?" she demanded.

The old man stopped a few feet away; he was near enough that his body odor drifted downwind to her. He smelled unclean, and sour with whiskey.

"I want some food," he demanded, waving the pistol toward the house. "Let's go."

"I'll feed you, but you'll have to put that away," she said as she moved toward the house.

"You'll feed me anyway, or them two black eyes of yours

will seem like nothing compared to a pistol-whipping."

Maisie began praying silently and stepped onto the porch, the man directly behind her.

"Lord, will these trials never end? I thought things would be fine once I got home."

God seemed to be silent.

* * * * *

A voice came to Riley as he followed the woman onto the porch. *You've done it now, you fool.*

"What did you say?" Riley muttered.

"I didn't say anything," Maisie replied. She opened the screen door and held it for the man.

"I have cold beans and cornbread in the fridge," she offered.

"Heat 'em," he grumbled, following her inside. "And turn on a fan! It's too _____ hot in here."

"I don't have a fan. It feels fine to me."

"This place is stifling. Open some windows."

Maisie shrugged and raised the window in the living room.

"It'll take me a few minutes to heat the food." She opened the refrigerator and fished the dishes out and uncovered them.

"Keep your hands where I can see 'em!" he barked.

"I don't have anything to hurt you with," she said, lighting the gas oven. "You don't have to be afraid here." She turned. "Why don't you put that away?" She nodded toward the pistol.

"Shut up and sit down." She set the food inside the oven and closed it, then moved to the table, pulled out a chair and sat with her hands in her lap.

You're a dead man, a voice said to him.

Riley jerked around, scanning the living room behind him. "Who else is here?"

"No one," she said, but then added, "No other human, at least."

He snapped his head back toward her, his eyes wide. He tried to refocus on her, but her shape went blurry. With his free hand he rubbed his eyes.

"What do you mean by that?"

"God is watching you. The Holy Spirit is here. There might be angels behind you." He snuck a furtive glance behind him. "And the heavenly hosts are looking down, thousands or millions - God only knows how many."

Riley's eyes widened again. He took several steps backward until he could feel the wall behind him with his free hand. Perspiration was visible now on his forehead and temples.

"But you need not worry," she said, "unless you do something to hurt me."

"What about the person that blacked your eyes?"

"He's in jail."

At that moment, the house creaked, startling Riley. He whirled toward the living room with his pistol aimed in the direction of the front door. His shaky hand and jittering movements seemed to become exaggerated. His countenance shifted from fear to terror.

A voice spoke to him once more: *Murderer!*

Riley jerked to his right, thrusting the pistol in that direction.

Suddenly, the roar of a car engine resonated through the open front window. Riley ran to the front door, Maisie hurrying close behind. A car appeared at the top of the drive, bouncing and bounding down the incline toward the house, traveling far too fast for the unpaved driveway.

Riley shoved the screen door open and stepped onto the porch, just as rain began to pelt the tin roof above.

* * * * *

"Adam," whispered Maisie, brightening at the sight, but quickly becoming alert to the danger. Riley opened the screen door to the porch, and she hurried back to the kitchen. Stopping only to switch off the oven, Maisie darted to the back door. She ran out, jumped off the porch as the first heavy raindrops fell and raced around the corner of the house nearest the driveway. She ran to the front corner of the house and moved into the open area where she would be visible to Adam as he reached the bottom of the hill. She waved her arms and thrust them toward the barn in the hope he would understand she meant for him not to stop but turn quickly to his left.

A gunshot rang out and a circular fracture appeared in Adam's windshield.

* * * * *

Adam had lost all control of the car and careened down the steep drive, bouncing wildly, pain shooting through his hip with every jolt. He tried desperately to get a grip on the jerking steering wheel while maintaining his balance in his awkward position on the seat. Huge raindrops splashed against the hood and spattered the windshield. He saw Maisie appear from around the side of the house. She was waving him away - not exactly away, but she was motioning for him to turn to cross in front of the house. Suddenly, his windshield shattered in concentric circles with a clean hole in the middle. It was a gunshot.

Adam's focus shifted instantly from near panic in survival mode to alert anger in protection mode; Maisie was in trouble.

Around the frosted circle of fractured glass, he saw the shape of a man on the front porch. He was aiming a pistol his way. Though the man's features were vague through the increasing rain, Adam knew he had seen that shape before, aiming a shotgun at him. It had to be Potter Riley.

The car hit a rut and the steering wheel spun out of his hands and when the front end hit ground again the car veered to the left, which happened to be the direction Maisie was motioning him to go. He steered even sharper that direction and, without his touching the accelerator, the car sped into a slide that brought the back end of the car too far around. Rain came in a sheet now, affecting the tires' grip on the grassy ground. Still, he found himself unable to control the acceleration. Nevertheless, the car shot forward, sliding and slipping.

He steered away from Maisie's truck and narrowly missed the front fender as the car continued to have a mind of its own, spinning its tires. As he passed the truck, he decided instantly to veer around the back of the house to try reaching Maisie.

As he passed the porch, he heard Riley yelling something, and saw him run off the end of the porch to follow him. A second gunshot burst the vent window on the passenger side of the car.

On level ground, Adam regained control of his seating and pressed the gas pedal with his right foot, despite the pain of moving. He whipped the car around the back corner of the house. With the engine still racing and tires spinning, he bounded toward the opposite corner and slid around it. Maisie appeared as a shape in the rain running in his direction. He jammed his right foot on the brake and slid to a stop.

"Get in!" he yelled. She appeared to be near panic as she jerked the car door open and dived in, soaking wet.

The car jerked to a stop and died as he was unable to get his foot back to the accelerator in time.

"He's coming!" Maisie yelled, looking out the back window.

"Press the gas pedal for me!" he shouted. She seemed not to understand as he pressed the clutch and jammed shift lever in first gear. "Get down and press the gas."

Maisie obeyed, jamming her open hand against the pedal. Adam turned the key and the engine roared louder than ever. He popped the clutch and the car spun tires with little movement. Another gunshot sounded, with the simultaneous clunk of metal somewhere in back.

Adam, clutched again, and the back tires caught. The car raced along the side of the house and up the driveway, bouncing as wildly as it had in descending moments before.

With Maisie kneeling in the floor, and Adam trying desperately to maintain control of the jerking steering wheel, the car gained speed as it ascended. Near the top of the hill, a patrol car appeared, slowly turning into their path from the paved road. Adam swerved to the right, bounded between a pair of pine trees and ground to a halt as Adam jammed on the brake. Rain drummed hard against the hood and roof.

The patrol car stopped as Adam opened the door and nearly fell onto the ground.

Recognizing Sheriff Mobley's deputy behind the wheel, Adam pointed down the hill and shouted, "He's shooting at us. It's Riley!"

Instantly, a bullet hit the grill of the patrol car and, immediately, steam spewed from underneath the hood. Both doors opened and the officers jumped out with pistols drawn, Mobley exiting much more slowly on the other side.

Using the car doors for cover they scanned the area of the house for the shooter. He was nowhere in sight. Their uniforms were quickly drenched, but they held fast to their positions.

Lowe reached inside the car and grabbed the radio microphone.

"Willoughby! This is Lowe!"

"Ten-four, Captain."

"We're taking gunfire at the Slaughter farm on County Line Road. Get a backup unit out here!"

"Gunfire? Roger that, Captain."

The radio came alive with commands from Willoughby and responses.

* * * * *

The moment he fired at the patrol car, Riley cursed. His only route of escape was now cut off. Also, realizing through his alcoholic fog that he had only two bullets left in the revolver, he pushed his heavy body into a run. A box of cartridges sat on the front seat of the car. He had to get to the barn.

As he left the porch, the rain intensified and he seemed to hear footsteps splashing behind him. Looking over his shoulder, he saw no one, only glimpses through the rain-shrouded trees of one of the cars near the top of the drive.

Now you will die!

The voice screamed nearer than was possible for any human who might be trying to follow. It had to be Ray Lee. Riley's breath was coming with difficulty as he reached the barn. He ducked between the open doors and into the darkness and deafening clatter of rain on the tin roof. He turned his head first one way, then the other in search of Colbert. In his madness, he stepped on the wet paint brush lying on the ground and slipped, tumbling to the ground. He screamed in rage and scrambled to his feet.

"No! No! Get away from me!"

At the car, he jerked open the door and grabbed the cartridge box, his eyes darting here and there in terror. With wet, trembling hands, he loaded the pistol with difficulty and shoved the rest of the cartridges into his pocket. Then he rushed to the barn doors again. His heart pounded as he scanned the grassy expanse and the woods between himself and the patrol car. He saw no movement except the heavy downfall. Maybe he hit one of the cops, he thought.

They're coming for you.

The voice was loud. He swung around. Ray Lee was not there. Riley cursed again, He had to get a hold of himself, stop the accusing voices. He had to think rationally about what to do. He could not drive away. The only exit for a vehicle was blocked.

Live by the sword, die by the sword!

"Shut up! Shut up!" he screamed.

You're trapped like a rat!

"Liar! I'm not trapped!"

You are as good as dead!

Rage rose in his chest. He whorled about and thrust the pistol at the darkness and fired three times.

"Shut up!"

Having staved off his tormenters momentarily, he swung back to search the trees for movement. He thought he saw a shape dart behind a tree. Even though it had to be nearly a hundred yards away, he pointed the gun and fired rapidly until the hammer fell on a spent round.

Dumping the casings, he reloaded the pistol and kept his eye on the woods.

Step outside and get it over with.

Riley shouted a curse at the voice, which now sounded like Esther.

"Oh, you'd like that, wouldn't you?"

You've got no place to go. Go outside and they'll make quick work of you, the way you did the rats running from your barn.

He turned about, desperately searching all the walls. Then he saw something he had not seen before - a horizontal line of light that might be the top of a door at the very back of the barn.

"Yes!" he shouted.

There's no way out!

"Liar! I see a way!"

You must die!

"To hell with you!" he screamed, and ran to the shaft of light. It was a door. He pulled at a hole where a latch might once have been. It was wired shut. He jerked at it.

You deserve to die!

Filled with rage once more, he jerked insanely at the door, shaking it and pulling with his weight.

Now you're trapped!

He stuck the pistol in his belt and took hold of the door with both hands and threw his weight backwards. The door cracked like a shot and broke free as Riley fell on the ground.

"Ha!" he shouted, seeing large spaces of rain-filled light where numerous boards were missing. He saw that it was some kind of shed attached to the back of the barn, opening to the outside where lay a clear path into the woods.

No escape! No escape!

He struggled to his feet and charged through the open doorway. Two steps into the shed's space, he stumbled and fell headlong against a wooden pole. The breaking pole cracked like a rifle shot. The roof of the shed rumbled like thunder and collapsed.

* * * * *

A backup patrol car arrived and two deputies bailed out, running in a crouch toward the two officers positioned behind large trees. Lowe gave them details of the shooting. The rain began to slake off, and Lowe, with the two other deputies moved out through the woods. Mobley objected to remaining behind, but Lowe convinced him his limited mobility might make him a liability to capturing Riley.

Adam and Maisie sat huddled inside his car, praying together.

Minutes before, several gunshots rang out from the direction of the barn, as though Riley had been shooting at someone, but no rounds even came close to either car on the hill. No other sounds had been detected since then.

The three officers made their way carefully under cover of the dense trees and soon disappeared from view.

After fifteen minutes of relative silence, a single deputy came jogging back toward the cars.

"Sheriff?" he called form thirty yards away. "Captain Lowe asked if you could come down here."

Adam opened his door and leaned out.

"Stay here, Woods," Mobley said. "It might not be safe."

Adam closed the door and Mobley hobbled off with the deputy.

In the barn, the deputy led the way to a shattered door hanging from its hinge. In the dark space beyond, Lowe was backlit by illumination filling spaces in the outer wall. With a flashlight he studied the interior of the shed. The deputy stepped aside to allow Mobley near the door. When the Sheriff was inside the shed, Lowe trained his flashlight on the ground.

A soaked body lay face down, motionless. Mobley's mouth opened and a gasp slipped out. A jagged pole was impaled in Riley's back, leaving a depression that had filled with water.

The shock to Mobley was not so much that Riley lay there. He expected to see the man deceased. What he had not expected, however, was a scene instantly replayed in his mind that, as a new Sheriff, more than eighteen years prior, he had witnessed in the back of Potter Riley's own barn.

Life could be strange, he thought, very strange.

CHAPTER THIRTY-SEVEN

The process took two months, but Sarah Joella Cotton left Mid-State Hospital in the summer of 1951 and was allowed by the court to be placed in the home of Lorene Mills, since Sarah had no other relatives capable of her care. Through working with Maisie to have Sarah certified as sane and suitable for release, Lorene got to know and love Sarah like a sister. The idea was hers to bring Sarah into her home, once it became clear no one else could care for her and that she would need assistance for a period to help her adjust to normal life.

Maisie and Lorene insisted to the judge that Sarah could be nursed back to health in mere months, and with prayer and close companionship in a home environment, would then require only minimal supervision as she conquered the challenge of re-socialization after years in isolation.

Maisie was shocked to learn Sarah was only twenty-eight years old and had lived in the asylum from the age of thirteen, having been committed by an aunt who could not care for her after the death of Sarah's mother and the disappearance of her father.

Helen Caldwell made good on her promise to bring Blanchard up on charges to the state. He was tried and convicted of fraud and three counts of practicing medicine without a license. As the only victim able to testify in the trial, Maisie declined to do so. Had she done so, District Attorney Warren Staples stated the man would have received a sentence of fifteen to twenty years, rather than twelve.

Ott Mobley resigned as Sheriff. Warren Staples declined to pursue a case against him.

Adam had hitched a ride with a friend to the auto body shop where he picked up his nearly new 1950 Ford - the car Potter Riley had begun painting by hand. He had bought it at auction after the tax commissioner's office took possession of it for non-payment of taxes on Riley's property. When the body shop owner finished buffing the house paint off of it and waxed the car, it looked brand new. Adam had given his 1936 Chevy to his mother; it was still in the same body shop awaiting delivery of a replacement windshield and repainting of the areas damaged on the day of Riley's death.

Now Adam was en route to the District Attorney's office, where Sheriff Lowe had requested he meet him. He had said something about signing a few papers.

Adam pulled to the curb in front of the county courthouse and got out. He could not help admiring the shiny new car as he walked around its front toward the courthouse steps. Winning the bid on the car had either been an act of God or possible manipulation of events by outgoing Sheriff Ott Mobley. Either way, God got the glory for it. Adam would never have been able to buy a new car, otherwise, at the price he paid at auction.

With his hip functioning almost normally, slowed only somewhat by minor discomfort, he hurried up to the second floor. In the hall, he measured his pace and entered the DA's office calmly. Sheriff Lowe stood talking with the DA's receptionist, and turned as Adam came in.

"Well, it's about time you got here, Woods." A stern look came to Lowe's face as he turned to him. He seemed perturbed. "Let's get inside. The DA's waiting."

Adam caught up with him at the closed door to Warren Staple's office, wondering what was eating Lowe. He had thought he was on time, in fact, maybe a couple of minutes early. The Sheriff knocked, but opened the door without waiting for response.

Staples was in a meeting with another man, but stood as

the two entered.

"Mr. Woods," Staples said to Adam immediately, "I want you to meet someone."

The other man, who had his back to Adam and Lowe, rose with the assistance of a cane. He turned and found Adam's face.

The man flushed as his smile contorted with emotion and his eyes glistened instantly.

Adam paused. He stared in wonder at the strange familiarity of the man's features.

"Meet your father," Staples announced.

Adam blinked.

The man moved in his direction, stumbled slightly on the leg of the chair, but caught himself with the cane.

Adam struggled to understand what was happening. The man was walking toward him, reaching for him.

Father? Did he say, father?

He felt as though the room moved under his feet. Who? His father? The face looked like his own, the hair, near the same coloring as his, but with gray intermixed. But his father was...

"Adam!" said the man placing a hand on his shoulder cautiously. "I'm so sorry." The man was now halting through his words, his eyes instantly red and brimming over with tears. His face was rough as it came against Adam's cheek. His body was frail.

Adam pulled back in confusion, staring at the face, inches from his own. Something was making his own eyes tear up, something he resisted but could not control. He broke eye contact with the man to find Staples and Lowe. Both men were smiling broadly as though this were some great joke.

Suddenly, Sonny Ingles was standing in his line of vision.

"Adam, I wanted to tell you before, but I couldn't. I'll explain it all later, but your father's life was at stake, and I had to keep my mouth shut."

Adam looked back at the man purporting to be his father.

"Are you --?"

Bonder Woods was trembling with uncontrolled emotion; tears streamed freely down his face and wet his collar.

He nodded.

"I figure you must hate me, Adam. I loved you in my own way, which is hard to believe, I know."

Adam wiped his face of his own involuntary tears, now.

"Loved me?" he asked. "*Loved* me!"

He jerked the glove off his right hand.

"Then why did you do this to me?"

He held his right palm to Bonder Woods' face.

"I...I wanted..." Bonder shook his head, looking down in what appeared to be shame.

He switched the cane to his left hand, and while his wet, bleary eyes still looked downward, he raised his right palm to Adam.

Adam flinched. The same tattoo was on his father's palm as had cursed his own life from his first moments of awareness.

* * * * *

Maisie and Adam sat in rocking chairs on her front porch. Adam had not felt pain in weeks. Maisie's eye and face injuries were no longer noticeable.

She lifted her glass of iced tea and sipped. She had a mischievous smile on her face as she observed Adam over the rim of the glass. He pretended to be oblivious of her presence.

"When are you going to take that silly glove off your hand?" she asked with mock seriousness.

"Glove? Oh, I almost forgot I was wearing that," said Adam, holding his gloved hand up as though to admire it.

"Hasn't God delivered you from the stigma of that mysterious tattoo?"

"Mysterious? What's mysterious about it?"

"You know exactly what I mean. You've never let me see it."

"Oh," he smiled. "Actually, He did deliver me from the stigma."

"Well, why are you still wearing that thing?"

"I guess I've just become so accustomed to it." He appeared to be completely serious.

Maisie frowned. "You're joking!"

"No," he said with a straight face. "In fact, I was looking for the other glove just this morning." He stopped the rocker and looked toward his car, parked in front of the farmhouse.

"I know!" he exclaimed as though suddenly remembering. "It's in my glove compartment."

"Adam," Maisie said with mock gravity, "What's the point of wearing a glove if you've been delivered?"

"You're right," he said with resignation. "Actually, I was thinking about getting a tattoo on my left hand to match it."

Maisie snatched a pillow from behind her back and threw it at him. He ducked, laughing wildly.

When he stopped laughing, he drew a folded note from his pocket. Now he spoke softly. "I told you my Dad is alive, didn't I?"

"Yes, and that he's getting a retrial."

"Let me read this to you. He gave it to me at the DA's office the day I met him. Basically, he couldn't talk and neither could I."

Adam flattened the page and scanned over it before beginning.

"'Dear Adam, I want you to know first of all – '" Adam stopped and wiped his eyes. He glanced at Maisie. "I can get through this, just give me a minute."

He took a sip of tea and began again, "'- that I love you, and always have. I've not felt worthy to write you, and your mother felt it best not to bring you to visit me. I don't blame her at all. I realized my actions on the night I was arrested, especially my actions toward you, were inexcusable. My explanation is not an excuse: I was drunk and did not know God. Plain and simple.

"'My intention in having your hand tattooed was not as bad as you have thought. In my warped way of thinking at the time, even though I knew I had been a poor excuse for a father, and realizing I was about to be arrested and would probably never see you again, I wanted to leave you with something that would communicate that I wanted better for you.

"'I know it was crazy, but the only way I could express it at the time was with the tattoo. It was my feeble attempt at directing you away from the kind of life I lived. Once, when I was a better person, I had heard a preacher say, 'Don't you know you have been bought with a price? Don't you know He paid a high price for you?'

"'Even though I did not give my life to Jesus Christ until I had been in prison a long time, I never forgot those words. And I wanted that for you. Do you understand, Adam? Can you understand what I was thinking?

"'My prayer and hope is that you will forgive me. Forgive me for everything I did, and for everything I was not there to do for you.'"

Maisie had stopped rocking. She took a napkin from around the base of her tea glass and dabbed her eyes with it.

Adam wiped his eyes again and carefully re-folded the paper.

"Thank you for reading that, Adam," she said softly.

"It makes sense now, though it never did while I hated him," said Adam. "He was, in his way, committing me to God."

Maisie nodded. "You've forgiven him, haven't you?"

"Yeah. It was not that hard, especially after I read that letter. Mama doesn't buy it, though."

"She will," whispered Maisie. "Just keep loving them both."

Slipping the glove off, Adam held up his hand and smiled at the message.

"'You belong to God,'" he read aloud. "And you know what? He had the same thing tattooed on his own hand in prison. I guess he just didn't know how else to dedicate me to God in the brief time he had before he was to be arrested."

"Do you want me to tell you what God spoke to my heart that day you first came out to the farm to help me plant?"

Adam sat forward. "Of course."

"He didn't tell me exactly what was tattooed on your hand, but He reminded me of a scripture in Isaiah 49. Can I read it to you?"

"Sure."

Maisie rose and stepped inside. She came back out, sat

down and flipped through the worn book until she found the place.

"Hold onto your chair, Adam."

She smiled at him before turning her attention to the scripture.

"'Sing, O heavens; and be joyful, O earth; and break forth into singing, O mountains: for the LORD hath comforted his people, and will have mercy upon his afflicted. But Zion said, 'The LORD hath forsaken me, and my Lord hath forgotten me.' Can a woman forget her sucking child, that she should not have compassion on the son of her womb? Yea, they may forget, yet will I not forget thee. Behold, I have graven thee upon the palms of my hands.'"

Adam's eyes opened wide in surprise. "'Graven?'" he said. "Like a tattoo!"

"Like a tattoo."

"That's in the Bible?"

She nodded. "Maybe somewhere in his life, your father heard that passage and it stuck in his mind as God's way of saying no matter how things appeared, whether it looked as though He had abandoned His people, Israel, God would never forget or truly forsake them. He couldn't because He had them written on His hands."

"But – it was on *my* hand."

"Your father thought you would never see him again."

Adam wadded the glove in both hands and tossed it over the back of the chair.

"I was pulling your leg," he said. "I don't really want that."

"I was hoping you'd say that," Maisie smiled.

"Maisie?"

"Yes, Adam?"

"Do you remember me asking you if ever thought you'd get married?"

Maisie stopped rocking, her face blushing. "I remember," she said.

"Don't worry. I'm not going to ask you to marry me," he grinned.

She smiled broadly.

"I just wanted to know if you still thought you might not."

"Well, I uh." She thought for a moment. "Wow, Adam. I guess I'm not prepared to answer that question. But if the time came when it seemed to be what God wanted – " She pursed her lips and blushed again.

"Yeah?"

"I would hope it would be to somebody like you."

Adam grinned. "Hey, that's good enough for me." He looked into her eyes with unabashed directness. "For now, at least."

Eager to change the subject, Maisie stood. "Well, do you remember what else we talked about that day you helped me do some planting?"

"What?"

"I said that when you give your life to Jesus, you're welcome to come out here and worship Him with me."

"Oh yeah."

"Well? Do you want to?"

"I guess – like you said – I'm not really prepared to answer that question."

"All right. I understand."

"See, I don't know how to worship."

"There is no wrong way when you're trying to tell Him you love Him."

"Still. You dance, And well, I, uh – "

"I totally understand, Adam."

"I don't even know how to dance."

"Really, I understand. I would never insist that you have to worship the way I do."

"You wouldn't?"

"Why? Do you want to come out?"

"I mean, I wouldn't want to cramp your style, do you know what I mean?"

"Adam, I know. And you wouldn't. I can worship Him sitting in a chair or standing or whatever. But I don't want to convince you. If you ever want to, you're welcome."

She strolled toward the steps. "I think I'll go rake the barn; get ready for that new calf I've been wanting to buy."

"What time? I mean, if I were to come out here and –"

"Oh, so you're interested?" She turned, smiling.

"I mean, if I were to come out to worship, about what time would be a good time?"

"Adam, come on out and help me rake the barn." She walked ahead, down the steps and across the yard. Adam was just getting out of the rocker.

"No, I need to go. But, really, what time?" he called after her.

She called back to him over her shoulder. "Supper's at six. We'll have peas, squash, tomatoes and cornbread. See you about a quarter till."

Adam stepped off the porch toward his car.

"How did you come up with somebody like her, Lord?" He spoke softly so she would not hear. "You named her perfectly. She is an amazing gal."

###

ABOUT THE AUTHOR

Patrick McWhorter is a former advertising copywriter and account executive. He began writing Christian fiction in the 1980s, after waiting seven years from the time of his commitment to Jesus Christ as Savior and Lord. The hiatus was the result of a further commitment to the Lord to begin writing only after a period of maturing in the Word of God under the tutelage of the Holy Spirit. The author lives in Flowery Branch, Georgia, with his wife, Laurie. The couple has two adult sons.

Discover other titles by the author:

FICTION
Holy Joe
At First Sight
Reward of the Wicked

NON-FICTION
Faith is a Three-Legged Stool

Thank you so much!
I greatly appreciate your taking the time to read my book. If you enjoyed it, please take a few moments to review it at your favorite online retailer.

Sincerely,
Pat McWhorter